DEMETER–VALENCIA LOPEZ

THE
UNREALITY
OF
BEING
FORGOTTEN

DVA With a Handgun Publishing

Copyright © 2023 by Miguel A. Lopez-Bonilla
ISBN **979-8-218-95504-5**

*To Whom It May Concern,

I've blamed you for so long
Cursed your existence in mine
I placed the burden of me upon you
Even as I've let go, it still resides in me
The pain and fear, the desolation

What's become of me since then
The ever present darkness I ignore
I'd once laid at your faults
For what was done, what wasn't
But now I think of my role
In this Lifetime¯ drama life

Was it me all along?
I'd let myself become isolated
Let myself get used and discarded
There's something broken in me
That feels so disconnected from
From everything
As if I don't belong
Anywhere at all

Everywhere I go, I'm outside
With anyone at all, I'm no one
As if I'm a window to look through
Catching a reflection or two
But still depthless and overlooked
Easily forgotten

And the image is often the only focus
Food for the eyes, and nothing else
Another fault I've wrought
For putting it on display so much
Not asking enough for a deeper inspection

So I'm writing you to apologise
For making me your problem
For putting it all on you blindly
When my decisions led me here
From the cradle to the grave
As they say…
I'm sorry,
No Longer Your Concern."

Chapter 0 - Restlessness Consumes Fading Memories

Roni had written with the express desire to disappear. Unironically, and completely on purpose, Roni had been listening to *'How To Disappear Completely'* by Radiohead, a band whose music would be a go to for them when having caught The Mood™.

"They fuel my creativity while simultaneously allowing me to feel my feelings and raw dog reality." They had said, usually, about the subject.

Often, Roni's letters aren't taken seriously or confused for their poems as Roni writes poems frequently and their letters are always written in the structure of poetry. One could see where the confusion comes from. Unfortunately for their family, though, Roni was incredibly serious this time, and would, in fact, disappear.

A fact no one would come to notice... at all.

On the third day of the tenth month in the seventh year of the second millennium, Roni ceased to exist.

"I never wanted to just die, you know. I feel like, as much of a burden as my life is, my death would be worse. And then someone would have to find me and see my lifeless corpse. That's traumatic! I'd rather have just not existed at all. Just like, *bloop!* Gone." Roni explained, "That way, no one would have to deal with my disposal and no one would fakely cry over me and my 'lost potential' that they never believed in anyway and say shit like, 'oh, heaven gained another angel; RIP Roni. Gone too soon.' boo-hoo bullshit."

Roni had found a way to live between planes; the place of The Forgotten. They'd caught glimpses of this *unreality* before, while in dissociative fugue states. You see, along with depression and anxiety, their trauma came with a kind of psychosis that, in extreme distress, would come on and cause breaks in their reality. In these breaks, Roni could see, well, here.

Here, in case you're wondering, is The Plane of The Forgotten, as I've said. A place reserved for those who can see it, for those who need it, and for those who just don't fit in with reality.

Nosey, aren't we? Want to know what it looks like, and all that, yes? Well, think of the wildest, weirdest, *you*-est place you can think of. Did you do it? Right, not even close. Because, as it turns out, humans aren't able to truly tap into their truest selves; stripped of all of societal expectations and cultural norms and whatnot. At least, what's called the *normal* human can't.

Sad really, the few that can see the *unreality* of this place are usually driven mad or to a deep depression and try desperately to replicate what they see and feel here for the world to experience. Artists, whom we all know, sing, write, paint, and even make movies of what they think they saw and felt but none comes close. Although, the product of these endeavours are usually brilliant and held up to the highest forms of what art should be.

Whether a gift or a curse, those that make it here, while they don't necessarily die, their art, their essence is forgotten.

Now you know why it's called The Plane of The Forgotten.

Brilliant as they are, like Roni, they end up here where no one outside can experience their brilliance. But if you ask Roni, they would tell you,

"It's worth it. The pressure and the dream of making it big just doesn't exist here."

Roni isn't alone either. In fact, everyone that's made it to The Plane of The Forgotten has felt exactly how Roni felt in the *reality* and they're all still here, and will remain here for, well, forever.

Here, Roni can find what they've most felt lacking: community.

Though... Not all is as it seems in this *unreality*. As Roni will soon find out.

The magenta shaded sky above—or is it fuchsia?—quickly is enveloped in cotton candy shaped azure clouds spreading wide and far and visibly swelling. Roni looks up and cocks their head at a precise 67° angle—I measured it, of course. Oh, don't look at me that way; fine, I eyeballed it.—inquisitively and expectantly and says something to the effect of,

"Here comes the rain again, by the Eurythmics." and smiles softly.

Is it 'The' Eurythmics, or just Eurythmics?

Semantic pedantry aside, it did indeed begin to rain; geometric droplets that change colour depending on the level of altitude and perception. Their splashes on the spongy black grass happen in 8-bit rendering. And this splash on the black blades below create a sort of bioluminescent colour effect on the grass that brings it to life, illuminating whatever path one sets their mind to.

Roni, absolutely pleased with the aesthetic of it all, starts off with a skip and trods ahead to nowhere in particular. Each step highlighted briefly in hues of the ultraviolet spectrum before fading into nothingness. So, quite literally, there's no going back.

Determined only to see what's before them, Roni pays no mind to the disintegrating path behind. Think of it like one of those forward-moving stages in MegaMan, where the camera pans ahead ever so slowly and does *not* retreat, no matter what you left back there.

You see, another aspect of The Plane of The Forgotten is that it only forms in forward motion. Your world 'exists' in your immediate surroundings and only there, making it impossible to see too far ahead as well as what had immediately happened before. That is until you reach The Stranding.

You'll just have to wait and see what that is. It's not as insidious as it sounds, I promise.

Ahead of them, on the horizon through some trees that politely moved out of the way so that Roni could see, The Stranding—a town that changes with every addition to The Plane of The Forgotten and is a creative amalgam of every mind that inhabits it—can be seen, complete with floating text over it that reads: THE STRANDING.

Roni smirks, "Well that's a little ominous. But I'm into it." and continues on.

"You must be new here!" A voice calls from the rather large mediaeval style gate that closes off the town from the nothingness around it. Of course, there's a tall wall around town that the gate connects to, but just in case you thought it was a standalone gate connected to nothing at all that anyone can just walk around to get into The Stranding, I thought I'd mention the wall.

And yes, it matches the mediaeval theme.

Roni looks around trying to find where it came from, not noticing the tetrahedron-shaped hole in the gate with a round, sweet-looking face inexplicably spinning at a 37° axis that calls out again, "psst, over here! Yeah! Hi!"

"Oh, shi—hi! I'm—yeah, what gave it away besides the fact that I came through, uhh..." Roni looks behind them, "the void there?"

"That's fair." The cinnamon roll face states before beckoning, "Come on in! You'll love it here. We have anything you can imagine."

Which, of course, is true. This is, in fact, a creative's paradise. Not without caveats though, but we'll get to that. Roni walks up to the floating geometrically imprisoned dumpling and leans forward, inspecting it for a while.

"Do you have a body? And do all of you just let strangers into your," they look up, "'The Stranding'?" The lovely sphere face starts to answer just to get cut off again by Roni, "and why is it called that anyway? It's a little off putting."

After a pause, gauging whether Roni will interrupt again, the sweet bao responds, "It's behind the door, silly. And yes. Anyone here is here because of the same reasons—give or take—which means we all can relate to each other and aren't really strangers. For long at least. And it's not what it sounds like."

I told you. Now stop worrying so much.

Worry an appropriate amount.

Inside the walls, a charming modernised Gothic village— and by modernised, I mean it had the aesthetic of a Gothic steampunk village, but the technological advances of the 21st century—with slick cobblestone roads and any shoppe you can think of within walking distance of the centre and, one would imagine, anyone's home, 'gas' light lamp posts, a giant fountain in the centre with a sculpture that is different for everyone—which is often a big conversation piece—and a leisure park over there—Yes, just over there. Go ahead, take a look. Oh, just use your imagination, would you?—is being toured by Roni, whomst is led by,

"Kia."

"What, like the car?" Roni presses.

"The what?"

"Nevermind. Anyway," Roni non sequiturs, "here's Wonderwall."

Kia purses her full, oval lips and cocks her head, "You're funny."

"Thanks, I try. But only on Thursdays." Roni quips.

"Is it Thursday? I don't remember. Honestly I don't even know what year it is." Kia adds.

They continue on, trodding through the lovely town cast in a perpetual twilight.

"Edward would like it here. I think they all would. I mean, it's not like there's any sun." Roni thinks out loud to themself.

"Oh, like from the movies?" Kia inquires.

"Movies? Like plural? I never got to see the first one, it's coming out next year." Roni retorts.

Keep in mind, this plane exists outside of time and space and in Roni's time, it's 2007.

"We *are* talking about Twilight, right?" Kia asks with an investigative tone.

"Yeah, so far there's two books with one coming out this summer." Roni replies suspiciously.

Kia stops and turns to Roni, looking them over and examining their clothes. Roni is wearing an AFI Decemberunderground tee with fishnets underneath, seven different bracelets of metal and PU leather, one with spikes, a spiked choker, Tripp pants that are black with white stitching to match the AFI tee, Demonia boots and heavy black eyeliner and lipstick. Their hair is coiffed over one eye and quite fried by a flattening iron, choppy-cut and voluminous.

"O-Em-Gee!" Kia exclaims, "you're so totally retro!"

A statement that both annoyed and confused Roni. *What did she mean by retro?* Roni thought, *and when is she from?*

Roni's eyes became sharp and narrow with noted frustration, and they pursed their thick, cupid's bow lips tightly. Kia, having noticed this reaction quickly grew concerned.

"I mean, no offence. I just mean, I don't think I was born yet in your time. I only know 'Twilight' from the memes that brought it back to popularity like two years ago." Kia explained hastily, "The Twilight Renaissance!"

"*Twilight Renaissance*? Memes?" Now Roni was even more confused.

"Yeah, memes. You know, like your *Wonderwall* reference? That's a meme. It was all over the internet a few years back. After 'Rick-rolling'." Kia chuckled.

In 2007, memes weren't really *in* the zeitgeist yet. In fact, they were just emerging, without the title. Having remembered this little slice of trivia, Kia took it upon herself to explain what memes are to Roni on the way to the block of flats that had just appeared atop a new coffee and energy drink café that had Roni's name all over it.

"Oh! Yeah, no, I totally get it. It's like the *NewGrounds* stuff, and like *Salad Fingers; The End of the World—*" Roni stops.

"Yeah, like those, I guess. Anyway, here's home." Kia presents Roni with their new flat.

"Whoa..."

"Yass, Keanu, you're breathtaking!" Kia couldn't help herself.

Roni glares at her, "That hurts me in ways."

Kia shrugs apologetically, "Sorry, I just love him. And it's a thing he said. In case you were wondering."

"I wasn't. But this is where—what if I don't want to stay?" Roni probed cautiously.

Kia responded with, "Then it just vanishes and no one would remember it existed. At least, I think. I don't remember if it's ever happened before."

It has.

"Huh," Roni thought out loud, getting lost in their gaze that is transfixed upon the dark stone edifice, "I guess I can check it out."

Without missing a single beat, Kia exploded with, "GREAT!! I'll show you in!"

Chapter 1 - Gaze Into Her Killing Jar

To Kia, the loft-style flat was a blank slate with a bed and some furniture. To Roni, this same loft had everything they'd ever wanted in a home. From posters of what looked like their favourite bands—My Chemical Romance, AFI, Radiohead, The Offspring, Slipknot, Cradle of Filth, Linkin Park, and so on—, to dark velvet curtains draped dramatically over the large, entire-wall-spanning window, a king-sized canopy bed with satin sheets in magenta and black with lovely swirly embroidery on the top floor, to a fully stocked kitchen with the best cast iron pots and pans, old-timey toaster and a gas stove with a grill. It had it all. The stereo system had speakers everywhere and two subwoofers. It even had a studio booth for recording music with everything one might need for just that.

"Holy diver. This place is amazing." Roni gasps in awe.

"I bet! I can't see. I mean, not unless you let me." Kia says, with a sing-songy inflection right at the end.

Roni turns and looks at her, "What? I mean, how? Do I?"

Kia grabs Roni's hands excitedly, "I'm so glad you asked, omaigawd. So, what you do is..." Kia takes Roni's left hand in hers and entwines their fingers, she then pulls out a red thread, "take this strand at the opposite side and wrap it around my hand and I'll do the same."

Roni blushes, wide eyed and staring into Kia's face.

"What's wrong?" Kia asks.

"N-nothing, I—so I wrap it around your hand? And you wrap it around mine?"

"Yes!"

"Isn't that a little awkward, like, to execute?" Roni asks, unsure of how to coordinate.

"For most people. But if there's a strong connection, The Stranding will be seamless." Kia reassures.

"A strong connection?" Roni stutters a bit, nervously, "We just met, how could you know we have that."

"I don't, silly," Kia replies, "I just wanted to let you know, in case it *is* seamless, we do have a natural strong connection. If not, then we can work on it, okay?"

Roni nods.

"Besides, I like you. So I'm hoping we do." Kia adds.

Roni blushes again, and Kia giggles.

They start The Stranding, eyes locked on each other, and like two serpents elegantly dancing their hands move fluidly, wrapping the thread around each other's hands at either end.

"I knew it!" Kia squeaked.

Roni is stunned, holding on to some thread that was left over, "What do I do with this?"

Kia holds her piece and instructs, "move your pinky so that it's standing straight up against mine," she pauses, "like that. Now we tie either end around them."

Roni does just as Kia instructs, and just like that Kia's eyes become like glistening saucers beholding the Gothic-punk wonder that is Roni's loft.

"Your place is so fire!" Kia squeaks again, "Oh-Em-GEE! Look at all of this stuff! And a recording studio!? Are you kidding me!? You are so bomb, Roni!"

Roni smiles softly, loving Kia's reactions as well as her soft, caramel tinted palm against theirs.

The red thread dissipates and frees them, but they hold on for just a few seconds longer before letting go and exploring the loft some more.

Kia, a lovely, dark olive skinned Caribbean islander with thick, curly green hair in a long bob with eyebrow length bangs that lay evenly across her forehead right above her black, angled eyebrows, with her sweet, round, but structured face housing big down-turned, puppy dog, hazel-green eyes, a small, round-tipped nose with perfectly circular nostrils that are visible even from front-view and whose sills are perfectly aligned with the columellar base at the centre of the septum, and a straight, drawn down ridge, those heavy oval lips set above a dimpled chin. Speaking of dimples, she has those too when she smiles, like perfect little crannies.

As Roni watches her admire all that their imagination can conjure, they admire Kia's everything. A woman built strong and small, with shoulders a bit broad, a waist that tapers in but quickly curves out ever enough to form the top curve, then slightly in again and out again, bowing at the thighs. The technical term is hip dips, but I was having fun describing how Roni's eyes raced down Kia's sides like Dom Toretto and Brian at the end of Fast and Furious 6. Roni's eyes glimpsed the robust rump that is Kia's backside, blushed and looked away as Kia turned to face them and walked toward them. Roni tried to keep their eyes from fixing on Kia's smaller bust and smooth, exposed belly that curves out in a cute 'pooch'—what Kia calls it—, instead, their eyes shut tight and open suddenly to Kia's face just a few inches from theirs.

"What? Do I have a stain?" Kia inquires innocently.

Roni struggles to speak, flustered and stammering, "N-no. Uh, no. You just—I didn't notice before."

"Notice what?" Kia probes, poking Roni's round-tipped nose.

"You, honestly." Roni confesses, "All of you."

"Oh! You mean," Kia motions to her body, "yeah. It's hard to avoid, tee-bee-aych. But I-dee-kay, I don't mind you noticing."

Roni sighs in relief, "Oh, okay. I don't want to make you feel uncomfortable or anything. I know how that can be."

"Tee-hee, you're cute. And sweet." Kia giggles, "you don't have to worry. Like I said, I like you."

Roni would have to change their name to 'Tom A. Tow' with how red they've been this entire time. They scratch their head and breathe deeply, exhaling, "Ah, so. Um, maybe it's because when we did the strand-thing—"

"—The Stranding."

"The Stranding, sorry."

"It's okay, go on." Kia encourages.

"When we did... that... it went like, seamless? So, I guess we have a natural strong connection?" Roni's voice reached heights in inflection more unnatural than anything the Dark Side of the Force had access to.

Kia chuckles lightly, "Maybe, baby." Kia stops, "Oh, shi— sorry, is that okay?"

Roni raspberries, "Psh-yeah, no it's cool. It's, uh, cool. I—I like? It?" That inflection again.

Kia smiles and takes their hand, "Hey, how come there isn't a mirror in your flat?" She pulls Roni over to the violet victorian sofa in the living area, sitting and beckoning them to sit.

Roni sits, silent for a long time, swallowing discomfort and a tinge of sorrow before finally expressing, "I—I'm not a big fan" they pause, "of how I look."

Kia's brows arch up and her lips cock to the side, creating a single dimple, "I see. I understand."

"No, I—" Roni cuts softly, "I don't think you do, I mean, you seem to look exactly how you want to, you present how you want to. I'm... stuck in a body, a-a prison that I never wanted. Never felt good in... never was comfortable in."

Kia sucks in sharply, "That's got to be—I can't imagine. But Roni, we're not bound by reality here. The person I see when I look at you is probably not the person you're talking about. I have a good feeling about that." Kia pauses, watching Roni hold back tears, "Give it a chance, Roni. Take a look in a mirror. Tell me what you see. I promise, you're going to feel as good as you look."

A mirror appears across the way. An image catches Roni's eye as they bring their sight up to it, a familiar yet different image. They stand up and walk slowly toward the mirror, afraid of what they'll see.

Roni gasps loudly, alarming Kia who reacts and begins to stand. They have their hands over their mouth, wide-eyed and in awe; utterly in shock. Kia moves over to Roni and places her hands gently on Roni's shoulders, caressing softly, comfortingly. Roni's eyes dart up and down and all around their own body and fixate on their face.

Their face, softly angular with a strong jaw, yet elegant and understated, blending with their neck. A nose with a round tip, ever-so-slightly wide, straight out but short with a small bump on the top of the bridge and a rounded, low-set septum. Below the nose are a pair of full, bow shaped lips dipped in the blackest lipstick. Above their adorable nose, are a couple of dreamy, dark, almond shaped eyes that point upward at the outside, outlined in thick, sharp eyeliner. The irises are dark, yes, but not brown or black; instead, they are a deep crimson. And above those still, are eyebrows that are that, if one were so inclined, one could trace a perfect, wide 'M' shape and are exactly 0.89cm in thickness, with a dual slit cut over the left eye.

As if the loveliness, softness, and androgyny of their face wasn't enough of a wonderful surprise, below the neck is a body they could not have recognized in the best way. Their hands pat and trace slowly around their chest and belly, their hips, feeling drastic changes to what their body felt like out in the *reality*.

Everything was different, but just enough.

"I don't look like me" Roni started, "But" they paused, "I look like... *me*." A single, sparkling teal teardrop ran down Roni's not-too-recessed-but-also-not-pronounced cheekbone, reaching the jawline and seemingly jumping off and glittering away.

They were entranced by their own visage, not believing what they saw was real, forgetting that *real* doesn't *really* apply here and what's *real* is what you want it to be. And without even speaking it into the ether, what they wanted most deeply in their heart, from the moment their body started changing in the *reality*, was to resemble this, this image, this Roni. They didn't have to actively will it so here in the *unreality*, The Plane of the Forgotten plucked that want, that absolute *need* Roni held so passionately—which was another factor to their utter unhappiness in the *reality*—from their subconscious and made it so.

They turn to Kia, finally, and bury their face in her chest, weeping glittering tears of varying brilliance of teal. They didn't stain, of course, but you could see them dissipating. Kia was surprised by this reaction, not knowing what it meant, but then instantly understanding, and immediately embracing Roni and playing with their dark, choppy, big hair.

"You're beautiful, Roni. And I think this might be the first time you finally see that." Kia states softly.

Roni looks up from Kia's bosom with wet, glimmering eyes, a shining shade of crimson now, and sucks in their lower lip into a small bite, then steps slowly away and fixes their face. They're still quite speechless, honestly, absolutely no idea how to feel or what to think. But then, everyone that finds their way into the *unreality* has a similar reaction.

"I had a similar reaction," Kia steals *my* line, "I didn't look like this either in the other plane. And I've been here so long I can't remember what I did look like. And I don't have anything with me from there to remind me anyway."

No one did. Such things are filtered out from the *unreality*, as they must be forgotten.

"No one does," again, Kia echoes, "it's like this plane filters all of that stuff out." Kia stops and paces a bit, "As if we're supposed to have forgotten it."

Kia really needs to stop doing that, I don't quite like being mimicked. Either way, yes, that. The Plane of The Forgotten keeps out everything you want forgotten as well, even if you didn't know you wanted to forget those things, eventually you will as they will be out of sight and out of mind.

With that, there are other things that this *unreality* of ours does not allow for, certain things not forgotten in the parallel *unforgotten reality.*

"Well," Roni starts, "however *this* works, I don't care," They chuckle, "I feel so comfortable, so light, so **me**. I finally feel..."

"Like you belong somewhere?" Kia interjects.

"Yes! Yes. Somewhere I belong... by..." Roni trails off. Their mind fogs up in that moment, as if *forgetting* something.

Kia cocks her head in confusion, waiting for a conclusion to the sentence that will never come. Roni, determined to force themself to remember exactly where they were going with that line, paces around and taps their nose, as if that's going to beckon the thought to appear. Kia watches them, admiring the apparent adorability of Roni's restless remembering as they walk toward the posters as if they'll offer a clue.

Roni had always obsessed over things, as if they'd die if they couldn't remember, or finish, or do the thing. There would be no respite until they had achieved the thing and it was done. This was one such instance, and you could literally see the cogs turning in their oddly wired brain, the smoke billowing from their thrice pierced ears.

Kia's giggling takes a shift toward concern, watching how frustrated Roni is getting as they inspect the posters.

Roni's feet become glued to one spot, their eyes narrowing, "Something's not right."

"What? What do you mean?" Kia walks over to them to inspect the askew poster above the chaise lounge and stuck to the brick wall with black duct tape.

"I mean, I think I know this band, but I don't at the same time? Like they're not *exactly* what I..." They trail off again, this time because of a small realisation, "**remember**. I don't remember. I don't—like, this is familiar, right? But like, *Linked and Parked*? It's like, it's almost something I remember, but I don't remember if I'm remembering it at all."

Kia sucks in a breath and exhales through her nose, pouting a bit, hands on her hips and squinting heavily with her tongue just waiting to explode in response, the words just burning to fly loose from her lips, the words being, "Mc'scuse me, but huh?"

Ah, yes, the words of the deepest philosophical thinkers of any age, they echo generations of the most passionate questions ever asked. Truly, Kia is among these deities of thought, a mind only meant for such a place as The Plane of The Forgotten.

In any case, Roni's mind had been distracted from their original obsession and thrown into a new hole from which there may be no escape. Suddenly, the posters vanish and are replaced with still photographs of dead and naked trees in high contrast and greyscale. These changes went unnoticed, as Roni's mind attempted to fill gaps with familiar themes from a now forgotten favourite album.

"I'm sorry, I was rambling. I'm just—I need to get used to this place I guess, and all the changes from what I'm used to." Roni drops their gaze toward their scuffed *not-Converse* then back up toward Kia who was smiling softly.

"You don't have to apologise for the way you are, especially not here." She extends her lovely, doll-like fingers toward them and takes their small, squared chin, bringing their face up to meet hers, "Although, I should apologise for being so bold and forward with you. I don't mean to be so handsy, you know."

"I—" Roni stammers all flustered, "no it's okay, I'm okay. I mean, I'm stranded with you. I chose to—to, uh, sort of open myself to you. That, to me, goes for everything."

"Okay," Kia takes their hands, "that's true, but that doesn't mean you consent to me touching you, or—"

"Hey, you don't bother me. And I do, okay, I consent. To—to everything." Roni closes their eyes and turns away, leaving Kia reaching for them, "I never really had any friends, Kia. I never even had anyone close to hold me, run their fingers through my hair, take my hands and comfort me. I didn't have—People didn't like me, not really. They pretended, but when I needed them, they would vanish."

Kia places her hand over her mouth as Roni continues, "My siblings were my first bullies, and my parents never protected me, never showed affection. So, um, when I find someone that seems to care, like, really care, I give as much as I receive. And you've shown me nothing but kindness and care since I arrived. And I thought—I thought that maybe, like, this was just how you were with newcomers, or maybe you were just super friendly or something. But then we *Stranded* and I felt your... I mean like, I think I could feel your heart, Kia."

Roni turns back to Kia, tears in their eyes, "I've never felt anything like what you make me feel. And I don't know if this is romantic or platonic—or transcendent; I don't know. But I know it's something in a lifetime of absolutely nothing."

Kia is rendered speechless. She sits on the three-seat Victorian and it poofs out violet sparks out from under the cushion from the force of Kia's emotional *kerplunk*. Roni's jaw trembles as it closes and they take the seat right next to her, also poofing sparks, but theirs were hot pink. Roni plops their head on Kia's shoulder, and in response, Kia lifts her hand up to their head and plays with their hair, "I'm sorry. I didn't mean to pull that out of you. I—I can relate, so, if you ever want to—"

"I don't. I don't want to get into it. But I don't want to forget either, honestly. It shaped me, made me the person I am. I'm afraid that if I forget, I'll lose the parts of me that keep me honest and from hurting anyone like I've been hurt." Roni had cut her off. Kia remains silent, understanding their reasoning and not wanting to continue making Roni upset.

They sat there for a very long time, such a long time that not even time itself knew how long it'd been and became a little impatient until finally darkness came over both of their eyes and time had the chance to skip to an undetermined date.

Time: a sentient, let's say, *being*, of slightly irrelevant, mostly omnipotent, and 92.77% omnipresent—it needs to rest sometime, you know. It's exhausting being everywhere with everyone all the time; you try it, it's not easy— proportions, is a fickle and fragile psyche'd *inmortal Force*— that is, not mortal, not immortal—with an attitude and exists to bring everyone from anywhere and any*when* into the unreality, where it can watch how so many different generations get on with each other.

Imagine, if you would, the Forces of the "Universe" sitting around a cosmic table at the ends of the universe, contemplating how best to make life more bearable for those that share a similar cosmic psychic, erm, *'genetic'* make as them while simultaneously giving them a near infinite form of entertainment that rivals whatever Maker made them and what's referred to as *reality*. This counsel of sorts got tired of being at the mercy of *The Universe* and its *reality* that they banded together inside of what could have been a tear through a black hole that connects into Andromeda, who could absolutely not care an iota less what—let's call them Milky for now—'Milky's' creations were up to and therefore didn't tattle to 'Milky' or The Universe themself, and created a pocket dimension they called *The Unreality*.

This pocket dimension was a proverbial playground for them and an intended paradise for their cosmic psychic siblings that all seemed to reside on Earth, which was odd to them, but then realised that the most unhappy of beings inhabited this planet for, goodness knows why, but they did. But they had, for aeons, watched humans and felt the immense sorrow that certain ones—their ilk—were made to endure for the simple fact that they were *other*. A design which they hoped would help bring humanity together in empathy and love and bring near-infinite lifetimes of synergistic bliss that would not only save every individual human from Darkness, anger, and hate, but also bring them to harmony with the planet itself as well as all the other beings on it which would foster growth that would span lightyears and bring them to the other persons on other worlds across the galaxy that had already achieved this and stranded together. Instead, though, the Earthlings had stranded themselves away from the rest of the galaxy and even from themselves, stranding the siblings of the Forces and effectively isolating them from the rest of the populace.

This is where The Plane of The Forgotten comes in. Those left stranded find themselves in The Stranding to then *strand* together and create a more harmonious and cohesive community where no one is left feeling stranded and isolated.

Chapter 2 - He Tastes Like You, Only Sweeter

Are you still with me? Do you follow? That was a bit much, I know. Good, you're still with me.

We should get back to Roni and Kia, Time's probably gone too far.

Ah, here we are, Kia and Roni are waking up after living together a few blissful—well, erm, we don't really have time measurement here, so let's just go with

While—while. The perpetual beautiful twilight sky is tinted green with feathery clouds of that greyish blue colour— slate? Slate. It's slate.

"The sky's always so pretty." Roni comments.

"Yeah, what colour do you see it? I see it as, like, a greenish tint, the clouds are like that greyish blue." Kia adds.

"Slate?" Roni asks.

"Is it slate?" Kia inquires.

"It's slate. Yeah. I see it that way too. It's almost as if we've become one mind!" Roni teases.

"We are one, one are we!" Kia chuckles.

"What time is it?" Roni asks, after having been giggling along with Kia.

"What do you mean? Like how long have we been sleeping?" Kia sits up a bit, propped up on her hands set behind her, Roni's legs draped over hers, the canopy bed closed on three sides, the fourth, of course, open and toward the window-wall.

"I dunno, maybe that? It feels like we've napped a thousand times and yet it also feels like it's only been a few moments since I got here but I know we've been together for a long while, maybe? Or..." Roni trails off for the nth time in their unreality.

"I know what you mean," Kia starts, "but measuring moments doesn't matter here. I figured you'd have gotten used to it by now."

Time is *funny* here. Because Time itself likes to have fun in this plane, it tends to forget to let things flow, and when that happens and Time remembers, it tends to play 'catch-up' without affecting the 'physical' bodies of the inhabitants. And even with time-telling devices—which are not allowed anyway—you wouldn't be able to measure time. They'd stand still, wobble around, go back and forth, and possibly even poof themselves out of unexistence. A day could feel like a minute which could feel like a year all at once without much thought or notice and fledgling Strandies are left confused as to whether they just arrived ten minutes ago or ten years, or even months. Either way, the motto here is—

"Be presently here and never over there." Kia states, rudely cutting me off.

"Huh?" Roni's mouth slightly agape.

"It's just a thing we say here to remind ourselves to pay no mind to how long it's been since 'x' thing, or how long it'll be til 'y' thing. And just stay in the moment because the moment is all that matters." Kia explains confidently, as if she were a PSA on a local Public Broadcast.

Roni nods slowly, with a mild squint and furrowed brows saying, "Ahuh." and swivelling their legs off of Kia's and rolling everso *gracefully* off the large, soft bed.

"Smooth, babe." Kia comments, having watched Roni crash to the floor.

Before you can finish a blink, Roni is on their feet swiping the hair off from their face, "I know, right?"

"Where are you going?" Kia whines, dragging out the vowels.

"Going to get us coffee down at the shoppe. What do you want?" Roni probed playfully, walking away and putting on clothes, fixing their hair, all with a thought.

Yes, the clothes just kind of appear, as if you were on the outside of those 'magical-girl anime outfit change' scenes. Rather unremarkable, really, clothes just kind of pops on like in video games when you're cycling through your inventory of weapons.

The coffee shoppe was a mildly busy, quaint little cafe with dim, green mood lighting hanging from rustic lamplights and pleasant images of The Black Cliffs of Oblivion, The Voidheart Chasm, and The Forbidden Forest of Forgotten Figments and Figures painted on wood-carved canvasses. The tables and barstools were black iron wrought and angular with copper filigree flourishes and oaken tops for the tables and faux-leather seats for the stools of the comfiest cushioning. It's an open layout, with the coffee bar in the very centre and shaped like a coffee bean, with pastries, pies, and the like, in glass cases on either side and a rather monstrous coffee concocting apparatus in the centre of the centre.

The patrons are all minding their own creativenesses, weaving stories, creating melodies, and bringing two-dimensional characters and landscapes to life. Others are reading the emotional etchings of their comrades' souls and offering positive feedback and much needed praise. One patron in particular began to sketch as soon as Roni walked in. Noticing they're being stared at, albeit intermittently, Roni looks over and catches their gaze; steel-blue eyes fixed upon their countenance and every detail therein. Roni completes their order and stands at the bar, leaning against the counter and trying to avoid paying attention to the random gawker, even if they are quite—

"*Dreamy...*" Roni catches themself saying out loud, even if it is softly, and shakes it off.

They look again, the sketcher's long raven-black hair framing their pale, sculpted face, swept over their left side and draping over their shoulder, layered just enough that the bangs hover mere centimetres over the table. This mystery figure is dressed in a black PU leather jacket decorated with patches and spikes, a grey tank top underneath, you could see their knees through the rips in their skinny light-wash blue jeans, and what look like black Doc Martens. On their fervently moving fingers are rings of steel in various designs that Roni can't quite make out but are mesmerising in the light. This person is intriguing at first sight, and the rate at which they are moving their grey graphite pencil over their 22.9 x 30.5cm sketchbook page is a sight to behold. It is beautiful and aggressive, like the lyrics of Roni's favourite song in motion.

"Two for Roni!" The barista calls out.

Roni snaps out of it and nods, extending their hand out with their first and second finger up as if in a peace sign. They thank the barista and grab the coffees, "Oof, they're hot."

"They never get cold." The barista boasts.

Roni smiles, "That's so awesome."

On the way out, the secretive sketcher shouts to Roni, "Hey!"

Roni stops in their tracks and grimaces, straightens out their face and slowly turns to them pointing at their own nose, still holding the coffee.

The illustrator smirks and brushes their bangs behind their heavily pierced ear with their left hand and says, "Yeah, I want to show you something, come here."

Roni reluctantly makes their way over to the table and takes a seat. They set the coffees down and take a deep breath, holding it a second, then releasing it through their nose and tapping the table rhythmically. They gaze at each other; Roni breaking the gaze and looks down at their hands and then at the lovely long fingers stained with graphite smudging and shapely hands of their table host. Roni has a thing for hands; therefore, I am forced to always mention them when they notice.

"They're always like this when I'm here."

"Huh?" Roni tries to play off the fact that they were admiring those stained hands.

"My hands, you were looking at them; I was tracing your gaze. I sketch often when I'm here and I tend to get my hands covered, obsessing over my need to add depth and contouring." They laugh softly, explaining and motioning their hands around.

"Oh. Heh, yeah. I bet." Roni nervously responds.

"I'm Toni, by the way." Toni introduces themself.

"Roni." They state simply.

Toni smiles again, their perfectly white teeth gleaming, "Nice to meet you, Roni."

"Whoa, you have fangs! —erm, I mean, likewise." Roni expands and retracts.

Toni laughs a rather loud and adorable, stuttery laugh, "Yeah! I'm a vampire, 'let me suck your blood'!"

Roni blushes and giggles, "I just might." They pause and circle back, "Ah, so, what did you want to show me?"

Toni bites their lower lip and sucks in air through their teeth, eyes still locked on Roni, "You caught my eye when you came in and inspired me. So, naturally I had to start sketching you. And when you were standing at the bar, the painting of The Forbidden Forest of Forgotten Figment and Figures was in frame with you in my gaze and the contrast of your brilliance with the foreboding darkness of the Forest was so fucking stunning that I had to combine the two in what's now my favorite piece of art that I've ever done."

Roni is flabbergasted, mouth agape with the shock of Toni's words. A reaction that Toni was quite amused with to which they were even more excited to hold up their self-proclaimed masterpiece. Toni took Roni's shocked silence as a cue to hold up the illustration and present it to Roni's glimmering eyes. *Holy shit*, Roni's expression said, scanning every detail of the work of visual art; from the Trees of Towering Torment to the Vector Light Tunnel Moon-Like Sky Structure—a long-winded name, but it's more of a concept than a structure—to the dreamlike expression of intrigue on Roni's face and their figure, which Roni is thrilled to see in a form outside of a reflection that showcases them in the way they've always wished to be seen.

"The real work of art, though, is you, Roni." Toni states boldly.

Holy shit, Roni's expression says again, though their mouth did as well, followed by, "That was smooth. I-I'm, wow, I don't know what to say. This is beautiful."

Toni sets their picture aside and reaches across the table, taking Roni's hands in theirs, "Say you'll take it home with you. Say you'll see me again. I want to see you again; I want to make art with you—"

"You want to make out with me?" Roni interrupts.

"What? I said *art*, not *out*, but now that you—" Toni explains.

"Oh, shit, sorry, your accent, I guess we hear what we wa—" Roni stops and blushes harder.

Toni smirks, "You're funny. Sassy, too."

Forgive me, I forgot to mention, Toni has a New York accent— it isn't too heavy, but it's there. A tidbit that Roni finds quite amusing.

"You're so interesting, and so creative and talented and beautiful, like wow," Roni rambles while Toni admires, "I don't know. It's so, so tempting. I—"

"Listen, Roni, it's not like I'm asking you to **strand** with me, or anything. I just want to spend time with you. Just being here with you right now is inspiring a million new pieces I could create, whole charcoal works—You're like, my muse, Roni." Toni extols.

Roni grips Toni's hands firmly and cannot help but to rub their thumbs up and down the back of Toni's hands, "Shit, I can't say 'no', can I?"

"You absolutely can, but you absolutely won't, will you?" Toni's eyes piercing through Roni's soul.

"It's literally been like four song's lengths since I sat here and met you for the first time and yet you are so enthralling that you're inexplicably right. You really are a vampire." Roni sighs pleasantly defeated.

Toni chortles, "I never denied it, in fact I admitted to it. Now let me in."

"You're in." Roni concedes.

Time had once again moved things forward, having been engaged in the endeavours of Newcomer, Roni. Time takes special interest in people every so often, and it seems it has become enamoured by Roni and their exploits.

An increasingly interesting subject, Time says to itself, watching and moving things on between Roni and Toni, while keeping Kia out of the loop so that when or if Roni gets back to the flat, it will seem as if they'd just left.

There is something impactful about this human, it's almost hard to fathom how forgettable they've been outside of this space. Time states again, this time twirling its forefinger in infinite motion and floating in the beyond, where no one can see its intangible image made up of light and shadow and golden lines with no visible beginning or end that shifts and flows.

Time yet again speaks, with a hint of mischief in its tone, *I wonder what it's like being in their presence....*

To peer into this moment being experienced between two newfound apparent lovers in a flat which exists in two separate forms still to the eyes of the pair, is to witness unbound passion the likes of which would make even Attraction herself blush. I, of course, couldn't be deterred.

Flesh on flesh, sweat and saliva, an exchange of reckless lust and the beauty of attentive affection.

Unafraid and beckoned to love with nothing held back, Roni traces their tongue and lips down Toni's legs with their underwear in tow, tangled within Roni's fingers. Their lips reach the tips of Toni's toes, parting slightly to welcome them in, their tongue curling to pull each toe inside, sucking them, cradling Toni's foot firmly in their hands and occasionally rubbing with their thumbs along the sole. Toni lets out soft moans intermittently, responding to Roni's oral stimulation, the warmth and pull of their mouth.

An ultraviolet spectral sort of aura in the form of what looks like flames, transparently enveloping Roni's silhouette, spreading up Toni's leg leading Roni's fingers and lips along the path. Toni's free leg spreads in anticipation, with the other slowly wrapping around Roni's head. Toni's hand reaches down to find Roni's head, grasping a handful of hair while arching their back to the shock of pleasure that shot through from their—let's call it; pelvic region, as unsexy as that sounds.

We can't give all the good bits away. Again, use your imagination! Go on, get yourself there, light some candles if you must. Let your mind wander and you may not even still grasp the extent these two went to with each other.

"Would you believe me if I told you this was my first time?" Roni throws their head back on what they perceive as a brilliantly white, thick pillow.

"Ah, heck nah. You're lyin' to me. How dare you?" Toni teases.

Roni rolls to their side and gazes into Toni's eyes, which were already fixed on them, "You're a bitch," they laugh and lightly push Toni's shoulder, "it's true! I've never been with anyone. Ever. No one I've been with has gotten that far. They strung me along but were never interested. No one was really interested in me, in any meaningful way..." they trail off, we can sense a theme here.

Toni waits, anticipating the conclusion to Roni's statement. Finally, Roni gasps in and slaps their forehead, "...until Kia—shit!"

Toni licks their teeth and sucks in sharply, "Kia!? Her!? I know her. She's great."

"You do!?" Roni exclaims, surprised by this revelation.

"Hell yeah, I do. Too clingy though. She wanted to *strand* with me—within moments! I wasn't into it, you know. I'm very private with my—self, if you know what I'm talking about. We're simpatico though." Toni explains.

Roni scans Toni's face and purses their lips, "Ah, okay. Well, I was supposed to bring her coffee. And I'm late... so late," Roni gets up, scrambling to throw on all their clothes, "I gotta go. I gotta get back—"

"What do you have with her anyway? Not that I care or anything. Not looking for commitment..." Toni tries incredibly hard to seem aloof and unattached, waiting for an answer.

Roni stops and drops their boot, "Uhh... I don't—" they slip their boot on and zip it up, "I don't really know, honestly. She stays with me a lot. We're very attached, sweet... but we haven't—you know. Just kissing stuff."

Toni's eyes light up and they sit on their full-size bed on a wireframe, red satin sheets that cover the mattress, "Shit. She's got you in a *QPR*."

Roni grabs the coffees from the adjacent plain-white countertop, "*QPR*? What's that?"

Toni smiles, biting their lip and stands up, pacing toward Roni seductively, "Queer. Platonic. Relationship. Bring it up, she'll explain it." Toni softly places their hands on Roni's chest and caresses up to their neck and closes in the gap between them.

"I—I'll do that." Roni says softly, eyes on Toni's lips.

Toni kisses Roni's nose, "Good." and then kisses their lips sensually.

How curious and absolutely delightful. Time had spoken in an amused ethereal tone. Time is essentially dancing and wiggling incomprehensibly in and out of space having witnessed the initiation of drama to be unfolding. The anticipation of what could happen with Kia when Roni arrives back at their flat is killing Time, whomst can totally cheat and skip ahead but is biding itself for the buildup of it all.

Meanwhile, Attraction scoffs and says sharply, *nothing's going to happen, Time. I've brought those two together knowing all the points between them were completely magnetic. Honestly, you're a child.*

Time retorts with, *Okay, but Toni and Roni absolutely have something between them. The attraction there is so natural, you had nothing to do with it! Let me have my fun, Atty. Roni is increasingly intriguing.*

Attraction sighs, *I'm only sitting in for Kia. Poor girl's had it rough since she got here. It's almost as if nothing's changed...*

I know, Atty, you have a special interest in that one... Time responds, ending the exchange and focusing now on Kia.

Chapter 3 - Fake Plastic Love, It Wears Her Out

Time, if you would bring us back...

Picture, if you will, a couple in the early oos, madly in love through MySpace and sending each other *Blingee* animatics and cute messages every day after high school on their very own Dell computers in their rooms that were plastered with early emo band paraphernalia and the odd Linkin Park poster.

This couple were Kia's parents.

One night, they rendevouz'ed, absconded from their respective bedrooms and met up under the bleachers at the stadium attached to their high school grounds where they let their passion take hold and did the thing. You know the thing.

Yes, that thing.

Exactly 282 days, 4 hours, and 22 minutes later, Kia was born.

Kia's mother was promptly kicked out of her home and banished from her family, where her father's family took her and baby Kia in. This was not without complications, though, with Kia's grandparents being much too involved with the child rearing, being overtly passive aggressive with Kia's mother, and just plain aggressive with her father.

Kia grew up in a hostile environment where everyone felt trapped. Eventually, she, too, would feel trapped.

With glimpses of violence and the echoes of shouting and blows landing ringing in her young ears, Kia silently cried herself to sleep for years. Soon she discovered that music with loud, grating instruments and screamed vocals were a good way to escape from all of that unpleasantness, so she drifted away into forgetting.

But not into The Forgotten. Not yet.

"Kia!" Her mother screamed, "Kia!" again and again. There wasn't an answer. This was because Kia had drifted away, blasting music into her eardrums at exactly 90 decibels with extra bass inside some very stylish noise cancelling headphones that she had previously lifted at a five-finger discount from her local *'Tar-gét'*. They were bright blue in colour, with metallic embellishments over the earphone parts and along the headband. *Blue like my heart...* she'd think to herself whenever choosing anything that had a blue option.

"Kia!!" Her door swung open, crashing into the wall and sending her Funko Pops tumbling to the floor. Her mother had had enough, having just fought with her once beloved and coming out bruised and bloodied.

Kia springs up on her wireframe twin sized bed that has at least 17 blankets, 3 pillows, and 23 stuffies, and pulls back her headphones so that they sit around her neck, "Mom? Que pasó? What—?"

Her mother storms over to her and grabs her by her arm tightly, pulling her up and out of her room, "Ma, you're hurting me, *suéltame!*"

"*Nos vamos*, we're getting the fuck out of here, *mija.*" Her mother declared.

"I don't want to go!" Kia defiantly shouted.

Her mother shot her the meanest glare imaginable, honestly, even I shook a little. She stopped at the top of the stairs, "Kia, *por favor*, right now is not the time to fight me, I'm too tired of fighting."
She pleaded, still fuming.

"Mami, I have my whole life here, all my things, where would we go?" Kia reasoned with her mother to no avail.

"Are your things more important than me, *tu madre, quien te parió?*" The woman's emotions were everywhere.

"*No, mamá, pero,* I can't just go with you without a place to stay, without security!" Kia explained.

Kia's mother's eyes became small and almost lifeless, as if she had become possessed, "If you won't come with me, *pues jódete, entonces.*" And with that, she did what Kia could have never seen coming.

She threw her down the stairs.

And as she came tumbling down, much like her Funko's before her, she thought to herself with tears and a look of betrayal in her eyes, *This was my fault*, before losing consciousness.

When she came to, she was at a hospital with her grandparents vigilantly watching her and a loud argument in the hall outside the door, things she was used to. She pretended to still be out, so as not to alert her grandparents who would no doubt give her hell after, maybe, 30 seconds of comforting words. In that time, she heard the police come and take her mother away with her mother shouting what sounded like, "but he's the abuser! *Abusador!* Tell them, tell them how you love to beat me!" And, "Look at my face! That was all him! He did this!" Her voice cracked in the distance, "He did this!"

Kia tightly shut her eyes, holding back tears and trying to keep from sobbing. Her grandparents whisper to each other indistinctly, trying to let Kia rest and stay out of the mess outside the door. After the screaming fades, she hears her father talking with a police officer who is indeed questioning him about the state of Kia's mother's face. While she can't exactly make out what is being said, he is absolutely denying ever putting hands on Kia's mother, while the grandparents murmur to each other as to whether or not to tell the police the truth.

Kia, feeling hurt and betrayed, and also feeling responsible for everything, decides to promptly get up off the hospital bed and pull open the room door in a fit of rage akin to her mother's and exclaim, "He's lying! He always hit mom! Almost every night, I hear it, dad, even when you think I can't, I hear it. And now that mom's gone, I'm scared you'll start hitting me next."

Her father's eyes widen and then immediately sharpen, glaring intensely at his daughter in shock and a deep disdain. The police officer, studying the father's face and body language, interjects, "Did he do this to you too? Or was that actually your mom?"

Kia shrinks into herself, "She did, and it was my fault. I should have listened; I should have gone with her. I should have—"

The officer stops her, "Perhaps, but her doing this to you isn't *your* fault." The officer, with soft green eyes framed by thick brown eyebrows and layered bangs that lay atop their sharp cheekbones, steps toward Kia's father, "Sir, I'm going to need you to turn around and put your hands behind your back."

Kia's father scoffs and becomes indignant, "What!? You can't be serious. Kia, tell them. Tell them!" He grabs Kia and shakes her.

Kia starts sobbing from fear, "Dad stop!" her voice cracks as she's sent crashing against the door by her father.

The officer immediately springs into action, grabbing Kia's father and shoving him against the adjacent wall, "Sir you are under arrest! Do not resist or make this more difficult." and reads him his Miranda rights struggling to handcuff him.

Kia continues sobbing heavily, with the door partially open, she can see her grandparents just glaring at her with the same disdain her father did, completely silent. Kia looks up at them, "Why didn't you stop him? What's wrong with you!?" She chokes up, "What's wrong with me!?"

If the grandparents seemed cold, distant, and mannequin-like, it's because that is exactly how they are.

That day, Kia lost both of her parents and was forced to live with her grandparents whomst, instead of letting her go into foster care, decided to take her as their own as if it were a 'favour' to her. "Who knows with whom you'd end up?" Her grandmother would say.

"That's right, you could have it *worse* with some random family." Her grandfather would agree.

A worse family, Kia thought, *I'd take my chances. But I deserve this...*

'**I deserve this**' was like a mantra to Kia, she'd recite it often, especially when things would escalate in animosity toward her. While they never struck her, they hurt her even deeper with snide remarks and downright abusive language. Although, it was nothing she wasn't used to. While her mother did have a temper, and she remembers being yelled at unnecessarily throughout her formative years for touching *this* or grabbing at *that*, and even for daring to speak when her mother was in the company of friends or on the phone, she had never laid a hand on her for anything other than comfort. She remembers her mother singing her to sleep after a particularly rough day or a long and loud fight; songs like One More Light by Linkin Park, or Time After Time by Cyndi Lauper. She remembers her mother's fingers gently twirling and combing through her curls. She remembers, curled up in her room, crying silently into her narwhal **Squishmallow**; she remembers.

Days, weeks, months pass by. Kia is consumed by grief and sorrow, by regret, and barely leaving her room save for the need to use the facilities. Her grandparents don't even try to comfort her, to talk to her, to even acknowledge her, which isn't the worst thing they could do—or rather, not do. The blue string lights stapled to the tops of her walls have started to flicker, soon dying out and leaving Kia in complete darkness with blackout curtains having been duct taped to the windows to keep the sun out. Her room is in absolute disarray with figurines toppled over and clothes thrown all willy-nilly, the plethora of scattered blankets to every corner. She had been remembering everything.

Her mother never came back, never called or texted—nothing. Kia had imagined that her mother was infinitely upset with her for choosing to resist rather than obey and disappear together. She thought it over and over, that her mother hated her, that she wished Kia had never been born, wished she'd never met the bastard that trapped her; trapped them both. Kia imagined all of these and more, agreeing with those imagined scenarios and reciting that mantra—*it was my fault.*

Kia's mind also wondered back to her father and how he's now imprisoned for assault and battery, for assault on a minor. Her mind envisioned a million scenarios where the other prisoners would beat him how he had beat her mother. Then she would feel terrible about relishing those thoughts and again blame herself for a predicament of her father's own doing and cry more, whispering, "It's all my fault."

After months of dwelling and remembering, she figures she'll try to forget. The only light in the room, a 6.1 inch amoled screen, displaying Kia's go to **'Sad Girl'** playlist now playing 'sTraNgeRs' by Bring Me the Horizon with lyrics for Kia to focus on so that she can drown her attention with multiple sources of stimulation. She plays the song on repeat for hours, hoping somehow, it'll cure her sadness knowing someone feels as desperate as her.

See, Time? The girl is a perfect companion for Roni. Attraction insists, *they have compatible taste in art, artists, and can relate to each other emotionally.*

Time scoffs, *Don't be ridiculous, there's got to be more between them than that! Atty, Toni has the passion, the intensity that Roni needs without that unhealthy attachment issue.*

Of course, Attraction guffaws, *Toni is a commitment-phobe!*

Time rolls its eyes, *oh, please, I wouldn't say 'phobic'. Maybe slightly **adverse**.*

Understatement of the infinite. Attraction mocks.

Kia's eyes opened after having them shut tightly for a while in the darkness under the blankets in the cave she called a room, she opened her eyes to a watercolour sky of cobalt and pale sage swirls moving ever so slowly across the horizon. She gazes in wonderment and quickly wipes the tears from her eyes to see clearly. Hanging above, as if directly above, is a large source of light—no, not the sun, there is no sun here—surrounded by the swirly sage clouds but peeking through just enough to beam a ray right in front of Kia's bare feet. She notices the light and looks up, squints, then follows the ray of violet light to just beyond her cerulean painted toes. Kia inspects the cold ground below her, feeling the blackness beneath like satin ribbons while watching the area illuminated start to glow in assorted neons and sparkles like a quest trail in an RPG. She spreads her legs quickly apart to get a better look and exclaims, "Wow!"

Kia springs up to her feet, feeling the soft, satiny grass on her soles, and walks towards the glow. Every step she takes, the ray of light moves that much further forward—forward being towards The Stranding.

"So weird," Kia says to herself, "I'm being led somewhere, I know it."

The young woman shuffles on following the neon glow and sparkles further and further, crossing through The Still River of Stagnant Woes, and leaving behind all of her feelings of desolation and despair that plagued her within the plane of *Reality* as she delved deeper into *Unreality*. She crossed over and through into The Plane of The Forgotten, a place where she could start new, where she could shed the darkness and replace it with an overwhelming positivity.

Yadda, yadda, yadda... Time sighs.

"Oh, god, Kia," Toni scoffs, "honestly it wasn't like that!" The white room echoes Toni's voice like an amphitheatre.

"I don't want to fight, Toni, come on." Kia pleads with a knot in her throat, pacing back and forth in her clean bright blue kitchen with granite countertops and a stainless-steel refrigerator.

"So then drop it. Let's just go to bed, I'll rub your feet." Toni implores sweetly.

Kia crosses her arms and exhales heavily, "I just want the truth, baby, please. Just tell me, does he mean anything to you? Is he just a friend, or..." She stops, leaning against the slate-grey wall that divides the kitchen from the living area.

"Kia, come on," Toni follows their hands through their hair and drops them dramatically to their sides, "of course he doesn't mean anything. He's a man, Kia, you know how I feel about men. Friends only, and barely that."

"Are you sure?" Kia pouts, "I just..."

"I won't abandon you, Kia. No matter what happens." Toni reassures her.

After three dozen stolen moments, Kia wakes to an empty full-sized bed—empty, except for the 17 different colour and pattern blankets and 42 stuffies of various kinds and sizes. She shuffles the various blankets around as if Toni would be hiding underneath at least one of the layers. Toni was gone.

"Toni?" Kia called out, "Toni, are you in the bathroom?" She gets up from the bed to investigate her own flat.

Kia crosses her room to the attached bathroom and checks it for signs of Toni to find it empty. She then takes to the stairs, surveying the living area; the simple, gunmetal grey faux leather loveseat, the matching recliner, the royal blue and silver fleur de lis patterned accent chair—vacant. Her eyes begin to glisten, slowly swelling with tears as she makes her way to the kitchen from the mahogany hardwood to the granite tile. Kia's wet eyes search desperately, knowing the truth—she'd been left.

Again.

Kia drops to her knees and lets out a mournful, heartbreaking cry, the floodgates having been burst open by the emotion that was building from the moment she awoke alone. She pounds the floor with her hands balled up then slaps her thighs before collapsing onto her side and clutching her arms tightly.

She forgave Toni, didn't she? Attraction inquires.

Eventually, sort of, said Time, *but it was always awkward between them each time, and Toni never did explain why they left.*

And you think that they won't do the same thing to Roni? Attraction probes.

There's a possibility for it, but I'm telling you that there is something utterly different about Roni, something special, even in this plane where technically everyone is special. Time insists.

We're not supposed to play favourites or interfere, we all said so when we made this little pocket. Attraction remarks.

I know, but I can feel it. I know you can, too. Time retorts.

Attraction pauses for a moment before stating, *I can, and that's how I feel about Kia, also. It's not just that I feel for her, you know, even though—well, look at her. That's just sad.*

I know. Terrible, honestly. I've never seen anyone here get like this. Time responds.

Anyway, Toni never did mention why they haven't **stranded** *with anyone.* Attraction says bluntly.

Time sucks in and blows out a bit of—well, it's not quite breath nor air, but you understand—, *That's—yeah, no, they haven't, have they? That's quite odd, they're the only one that hasn't.*

They both turn to each other, then turn their gaze to Toni and simultaneously let out a rather short, *huh.*

Which brings us back. We *would* get further into what made Kia who she is, but the horrid highlights are sad enough, imagine if we detailed everything that happened in between; we'd all need tissues.

Kia sits up in Roni's bed, feet together and knees bent, and she starts bouncing her legs up and down, doing that butterfly thing, eagerly awaiting Roni's return. The promise of delicious coffee is just a plus on top of knowing for a fact that Roni is returning; it is her flat after all.

Chapter 4 - These Foolish Games

"Hi!" Kia pops her head out from the half wall on the top floor of the loft having heard Roni crash into the flat halfway dead from running while trying to balance two coffees.

"Hey, yeah, hi! I, uh, I'm sorry I got hel—" Roni stammers before getting cut off.

"That was quick! They're good down there. Why are you out of breath?" Kia interjects.

What the hell, quick? I literally just... Roni thought to themself, shifty eyed and furrowed.

Time snickers to itself, deviously.

"Oh? Ah, yeah, they're amazing. The coffee stays hot no matter how long anyone takes getting to their destination..." Roni yet again trails off, slightly suspiciously.

Kia cocks her head like an adorable baby husky, "Weird flex, but okay." She says before blinking an outfit into existence and jumping down to the living room, ignoring the stairs completely, and walks up to Roni and boops their nose, "You're cute. Thank you."

Roni smiles and hands her the stark matte black cup with red lettering in script that reads: CAFÉ LUDENS. The cup doesn't need a sleeve as it's not hot enough to burn, but just so to be comfy enough for whom it is intended; Roni was just caught off guard the first time they picked up the coffees. They both sip from the cup, the sip elicits a unified, "mmm".

"Raspberry mocha, I love it." Kia declares.

"Mine is hazelnut mocha, light on the mocha—how'd they know? I didn't even order..." Roni states a little puzzled.

"You're such a noob!" Kia chuckles, "This place, and everything in it just **KNOWS**; you're a part of it now."

Roni, still feeling from Toni, still echoing their words about Kia, still confused as to why Kia didn't realise how long they were gone from, even here where time moves in ways, tries to gather up how they're going to bring up Toni and if they're going to detail the encounter. Roni, leaning against the kitchen island, is still unsure about what Kia is to them, if they're romantically linked, platonically linked, or anything in between. The battle in their brain had become obvious outside of their brain and Kia does the head thing again, watching Roni fight with themself in their own bubble.

"Hey, is something up?" Kia asks sweetly.

Roni snaps back in, "Ah, no. I—" Roni hesitates, "I met someone at the café."

Kia's eyes light up, "That's great! Yay! Who did you meet? Do I know them? I probably know them. Do I know them?"

Roni scratches their head and sinks slightly into their shoulders, "Yeah, you do."

"Oh! I'm excited now." Kia responds.

Roni is suddenly overcome with the fear that they'll hurt Kia if they say everything that happened, so instead, Roni just says, "It was Toni. They called me over to their table."

Kia freezes a moment, their heart dropping to their soles, and the light in their eyes starts to dull, "Oh," her voice trembles slightly, "that's cool. Yeah, Toni's pretty cool." She drops her gaze and shrinks into herself.

Feeling like they'd made a mistake, but unwilling to let it go, Roni sips in some courage and says plainly, "They mentioned you, after asking me about the two coffees. They alluded to you two knowing each other well."

Kia turns away and walks over to the living room, then sitting on the lounge with her hands on her lap, one still clutching the coffee. Roni follows her and sits beside her. Kia keeps her gaze low, "What else did he say?"

They put their cup down on the adjacent cherry wood accent table, "They said you wanted to strand with him on the first day you met them," they pause for precisely seven seconds and thirty-two milliseconds before adding, "like you did with me."

The intonation in those last five words was a defeated sort of implication of not being as special as they had once thought they were to Kia. There was a long silence between them for a moment where neither of them knew what more to say, all the while saying too much inside their own minds. Both spiralling into their personal insecurities. Kia, in her mind, dreads being told to leave and never return, in a sense, being left once again by someone they've come to love. Meanwhile, Roni dwells on feelings of not being truly wanted for the person that they are, rather wanted for how they can make someone else feel and nothing more, a tool to be used and then thrown away for the next 'shiny new toy' that comes along.

"I—" Kia starts before being cut off.

"—I'm so stupid, thinking you really meant all of that."

It's not like that, you ridiculous human! Attraction blurts out with Time being at the figurative edge of its seat.

"It's not like that, Roni—I don't want to fight, please." Kia implores, having crossed her arms, clutching them tightly.

"Then tell me I'm wrong, tell me, Kia, and please tell me what exactly I am to you because I can't stand wondering, being kept at this weird limbo where like we're together but we're not? I don't know." their voice solemn and grey.

Kia inhales deeply then slowly blows out through pursed lips, turning her honey eyes that are glazed with thick blue tears to Roni and softly says, "I'm sorry... but you are wrong," a lump manifests in her throat, "these past— however many moments—everything we've talked about— have all been precious to me, Roni, like... it's felt like a thousand lifetimes with someone I absolutely adore, and yet as if it was just a moment ago that you walked through that gate and saw me as me and not a floating head in a polyhedronic window. I can't tell you what we are because I don't know either," she pauses, eyes locked with Roni's, "All I know is that I love and cherish you. And for some reason, we were brought together. I don't know if I want to be romantically attached to you, to anyone anymore. I tried that here and it didn't work."

"With Toni?" Roni inquired.

Kia nodded, "Yes. We were together for like, a lot of moments, and a lot of them were wonderful and passionate, and some were—" she stops again, "not. And I learned a lot about them, about who he is once you get past that cool, sexy artist facade."

"I—" Roni's left speechless.

"So, if you want to label us, you can call it a—" Cut off again.

"—QPR?" Roni interjects.

Kia sighs, "He told you that too? That floppy dog!"

"Is everything recycled?" They probe.

"No! Fu—you have to believe me, they just know me so well, you have to understand, we talked so much about so many things. Toni—" Kia rubs her face forcefully and exhales heavily, "didn't want me. He left. We started getting serious and they must have freaked out—I think they had a thing with some guy—and we had a sort of fight and he left." She holds back a flood, "Right after promising me they wouldn't abandon me. So, excuse me if I'm scared of it happening again!"

Roni watches as Kia covers her face with her hands and begins sobbing, having just relived a moment that broke her heart for the nth time. They take their hand and hold it tightly, "Kia..." they start and pause for a few seconds before continuing, "I understand, I—" they suck in air and begrudgingly state, "I believe you. I'll take whatever a QPR is, as long as I can be free with whoever I choose, until you decide if you want to give us a shot at some point. And you have to explain to me what that even is in the first place."

Kia looks up at Roni's stoic, but accepting face, the despair in her eyes dissipating as they fill with hope once more, the blue evaporating into golden sparkles, "A—are you sure? You're not leaving? But you were so upset! How can you just turn your feelings around like that? —I mean, I'm not—" she wipes her nose with her wrist and sniffs, "not complaining, but you were just so upset with me..."

Roni caresses her face sweetly, their face softening and eyes warming to Kia, "It's not important. But one day I'll let you in and you'll understand."

I told you, didn't I, Time? Attraction boasts.

In the darkness of their flat, a haunting, moody melody of dark synth and piano fills the air, slowly emanating from the studio. The waves of music alter the negative space within the flat, changing colours to the darkest blacks with tinges of brilliant pink and magenta as a stark contrast, highlighting hope in an otherwise ocean of hopelessness. Roni's rich, deep, soothing vocals can be heard harmonising passionately, sorrowfully before finally crooning the words to complement the melody.

Cycles neverending
Moods like the wind
A typhoon or twister
Triggered by neglect
Or even the feeling of
Confidence, this façade
I falsify a boosted ego
Keeping my shame and hurt
Deep in shadows
So that none could see
But my heart is lonely
And my soul is searching
A kinship that seems denied
Or shallow and plastic
Under a time limited
It all feels limited
These days my arms aren't keeping
But it is I being kept at length
Though I can't tell the reason
Perhaps I'm too much
Perhaps not enough
Whatever the reason, I'm still
Left in dark, shelved behind better

Better others, better times
Easier to digest, uncomplicated
Things that shine and engage
Without a certain intensity
Things that are familiar and clear
Maybe I'm too unclear...

A stone clacks against Roni's window, then another, breaking Roni's concentration and flow. They take off their headphones, wondering how they could hear the stone through noise cancelling headphones. It wasn't the noise rather than the dissonance of the stone's vibrating waves that caused the break; its vibration went against that of Roni's music and cut through directly into their soul.

The stone stood floating at the window, tapping it in a broken rhythm, Roni stood watching it, and below—out of focus—was Toni, whomst is waving both arms back and forth like a wild bird trying to get Roni's attention.

Finally, Roni's focus shifts to Toni and they frown lightly and do that slanty mouth emoji thing. *What does he want,* Roni thought. It starts to rain, as if by the will of someone's making. Someone, or some*thing*. Toni, having taken his coat off, is getting soaked by the apparent *random* rainfall which causes Roni to motion for them to come up.

"Hey." Toni simply says when Roni opens the door to let them in.

Roni's unamused and slightly annoyed, "Why are you here, Toni?"

Toni walks in after a while of leaning against the doorframe and smirks, "The weather out there is some sort of crazy, huh? You got a towel, gorgeous?"

Roni tries not to react and turns away to get a towel from the upstairs bathroom, "Yeah, hold up, I'll be right back. Don't follow me."

He pauses and smiles deviously and says, "Alright," before pulling off their boots and socks and hanging his black PU leather coat on an adjacent stark white chair and indeed following Roni up the clear, glass-like stairs to the top floor of the loft-style flat, looks over to the full-size, all white bed and frame and back to Roni's backside.

They turn sharply to face him, "I told you not to—" Roni is blindsided by the sight of Toni's frame, wet and only slightly obscured by the white tee that is clinging to their chest and torso, showing everything on top with the sheer nature of wet white tee-shirts. Roni catches their breath a half moment after, "—follow me. The towel's in the bathroom, this way."

"Don't mind if I do." Toni says, biting his lip and following Roni into the bathroom.

There's definitely something electric or magnetic about them isn't there? Time suggests.

Absolutely, it's quite annoying, the fact that I'm actively having nothing to do with it and am trying to repel them! Attraction throws a fit.

Time giggles to itself.

A deeper, more powerful voice enters the fray, *You were correct, Time, it is enjoyable to interfere with these two humans—humans in general, but this pair specifically is most entertaining.*

Time wobbles around and makes an inscrutable sound that echoes throughout their private enclosure that is both away from the Plane of The Forgotten and from the *reality*, but with a sort of mirror into wherever they want to look, *Oh, Nature, I'm **so** glad you decided to join in on the fun. I can't believe we never did this before!*

Attraction scoffs and crosses her tentacles, *I can't believe you took Time's side.*

I do not take sides. I am truly ambivalent, Attraction, I only interfere when the mood takes me, without influence of favouritism. Nature states phlegmatically in their stoic— well, not to be redundant, but—nature.

Oh, of course you are, Natty. You're absolutely unbiased and undeterred by emotional ties... Time responds.

Sometimes, I highly dislike you, Time. Attraction sneers.

Time wibbles about the area, pleased with itself, while the Attraction and Nature watch on at the activities of Roni and Toni in the bathroom. Let's just say this—there wasn't much drying going on; in fact, there was a lot more moisture being produced, and it wasn't the rain.

He's brilliant, Roni thinks to themself, *smoking his cigarette—which, normally, I'd hate but here it's just for aesthetics it seems—as he talks about art over coffee.* Roni strums their guitar gently and admires Toni as they ramble on about different forms of art and why portraits are their favourite, kind of like that one song. *They're so damn enthralling; look at him,* Roni continues in their mind, *with his careless hair, so cool and sensitive at the same time.* They're absolutely fawning over Toni, an attraction beyond a crush; limerence, in a sense.

"It's all just so cool, you know?" Toni concludes.

Roni snaps back to *unreality*, "Ah, yeah. Yeah, mad cool."

Toni sways their long black hair off to the right with a quick head jerk and squints a bit, "You know, you're *groovy*, a real cool cat. I dig you, Roni, you just sort of get me, you know? Without trying, without being a wet rag about the way I can be sometimes. I know I can be distant and in my own dome, but that's just the way I am, baby, and you understand that."

Roni smiles a little, "I'm glad you think so, though I'm supposed to be pissed at you; I just can't help but..." Roni trails off, as per usual, but finds their words, "...not be."

Toni laughs heartily, "*Pissed*!? At *me*? And why would that be, dolly?"

Roni sighs, "We had a sort of fight; feelings got raw. All because of that seed you planted in my head."

"What seed?" Toni asks, sitting up at the perceived sterile, white table, "Oh, that little ol' thing I said at the end with a kiss. Did you ask about the QPR thing first or did you mention me first?"

Roni gulps and reluctantly admits, "I mentioned you first. Honestly, the QPR thing didn't come up til we were already in it."

"I never said to mention me. I knew she'd flip her lid. That one's on you, kid." Toni shrugs.

There's a small silence between them as they finish their coffee, a tension, a craving. Roni cannot quite explain why they feel these feels for Toni, or even what those feels were. They knew they wanted more of Toni, they wanted to Strand with them. Coming to that conclusion, though, brought on more anxiety. Roni knew that Toni is *Strandless* by choice and seems averse to the thought, but also knew that Toni was feeling a different way about them than he ever felt about anyone else. How they knew that fact, they could not explain or fathom, but they just did. I will say, this knowledge, as with much of Roni's unexplained abilities, comes from their pure connection to the Plane of the Forgotten and the Forces themselves.

The Forces continue to tune in on this episode of "Roni Unraveled"—working title—as the silence softens and the moods of the pair shift to a more harmonious one. Roni continues composing a song while Toni pulls a sketchbook and pencil from their coat and puts pencil to paper to sketch Roni once more, as they are, with the backdrop of the window and the horizon behind them. The white of the paper perfectly captures the room for Toni so that they could focus on the desired object; Roni.

Chapter 5 - Emptiness Is Heavier

A soft, warm full-size mattress sitting upon a platform bed frame that doubles as storage with the platform being a large wooden thing of cobalt with pine accents, two large drawers on either side of the bed, on top of which sits 37 blankets of varying patterns and colours and precisely 42 stuffed toys scattered throughout, and underneath said blankets, seeking a warmth that seems completely unattainable, Kia lays in the fetal position, clutching three of those 42 stuffed 'babies'. Bereft and despondent with glitter-turned tears staining her under eyes, Kia had demolished herself with obsessive thoughts centralising around Roni leaving her forever and not wanting to ever see her again. She couldn't help it, mostly because she couldn't be alone. To Kia, solitude is akin to torture when there's someone whomst she could spend every waking moment with, it was a hell dimension all her own. She felt this because when they are apart, she can't know what the other is feeling for her, whether they still wanted her or not; she felt herself fading.

"Absence doesn't make the heart grow fonder," she says, "it makes the heart forget." This was her experience, of course, and no one could convince her otherwise.

Soft footsteps upon the dark wooden floor toward the booth once again. Feelings were being felt, many, all at once. Roni's mind wandered in and out of feelings of being wanted, fully, and being needed, wholly. How Toni, with reckless emotion, fills them with what could be love, what's definitely lust, and an infatuation so deep that Captain Zissou could never hope to discover the strangeness within. To Kia, whomst loves Roni so foolishly and earnestly that her life would have a vacuum so endless without Roni that not even a Reaper could exist. *Kia*, Roni thought to themself while smiling.

There was a warmth associated with that name, so many moments were spent with Kia that Roni thought they could spend an eternity recollecting and reminiscing. Kia, whomst saw Roni for who they are and never questioned, whomst flirted so innocently and sweetly. Kia, whomst took to Roni, not out of duty, and certainly not out of desperation, but out of a kindness that felt genuine and selfless. These were the thoughts and feelings circling around Roni's head, quite literally, that was how I was able to recount them to you. They're right there, just look. No, *there*! Just above Roni's big hair. Like a comic book thought bubble, but sparkly and extradimensional.

In these feelings, Roni began to hum, their long, thin fingers caressing the keys of the 61-key MIDI keyboard controller with drum pads and knobs and such for music production as they hummed into the microphone that hovered above it. The caressing turns to slow palpations, manipulation of the keys into notes being gently strung together into something that sounds like heartbreak and hope. Roni's voice starts to mingle with the notes, a harmony of dissonance.

Their lips part to give way to tender, velvety reverberations of the soul.

I see you in shades of blue
Gazing through my windows
Smiling through the pain of
Living being left behind again
Like ghosts, you're haunted
Those memories sting like today
They won't let you go
They won't let you grow
Oh, honey, I'm sorry I can't be
Everything you need is right here
You're running away and I won't chase you
But, darling, I'll leave my door unlocked
You don't need to knock
Somehow you lost your voice
Without ever saying a word
Believe me, though, I can hear
And I'll listen if you try
I know, you're broken hearted
It all still feels so fresh
You won't let it heal, though
You can't, it's too real now
Oh, honey, I'm sorry I can't be
Everything you need is right here
You're running away and I won't chase you
But, darling, I'll leave my door unlocked
You don't need to knock

You don't need to knock...

Kia... They thought again, this time a GIF-like image of her, smiling lovingly, circling their mind; an image not unlike when they'd first met and Kia was just a floating, smiling head in a polyhedron of sorts. They felt regret at the overreaction to the information provided by Toni and blew a half raspberry, shook their head, stood up and said, "Alright." before promptly heading out the door and blinking a new outfit into existence; ripped black skinny-jeans, tight fishnet top underneath a black tank-top and two three-row studded belts crossing each other in an 'X' fashion, big combat boots as an added flourish—if you must know.

It was raining again, but Roni loved the rain. The violet tinted clouds crying white rain drops in a zig-zag torrent over the bustling hamlet. The cobblestone roads shining slick under the faux gaslights whilst the fountain bursts with colours and sparks with every splash from above, some Strandlers rush to their destinations, others enjoy the stroll in the storm. One individual in particular seemed to, as if by some whim or inspiration, springs forth from a door to Roni's left at the very same moment that some magnetic force beckoned Roni to look the opposite way with a ghost of a vision of some obscure interesting thingamabob that floated just outside a full on perception but had been so captivating that now Roni is on that very same slick cobblestone from before, rubbing the side of their head and cursing *en Español*. The Strandler had realised the big thump and subsequent fall and heard the cursing and scrambled down to Roni's side.

"Oh, my goodness, are you okay?" said the Strandler.

Oh, who is this now!? Exclaimed Time, rather annoyed.

Another force chuckled lightly from the void, *Just a new addition to the mix to keep things interesting.*

Ugh, scoffed Attraction, *must you all sabotage what I'm trying to build here? Really, Feelsie, how dare?*

I wanted to join in the fun, and also explore the depths of their emotions. Feeling explained with what could have been construed as a playful shrug in their otherwise incomprehensible corporeality.

Time held on to a thought for a moment, then sighed, *I imagine it's only fair. Of course, I do wonder what kind of effect all of this...* Time seemed to gesture its—you can call them—arms vaguely at the entire situation before them, *play will have on Roni and them.*

The Forces all fell silent in contemplation before simultaneously letting out an indifferent, *Meh,* and continuing with their meddling.

"I'm fine, 'cept for my ass, ah." Roni said getting up and then catching a good look at the beautiful Strandler and being reminded of someone.

The Strandler was a lovely, medium build—from what one can make out in their current fitted track pants and a raincoat outfit—fair skinned—with a slight rosy tint to the cheeks and a quasi-olive tone—brunette, with blue streaks in their just-on-the-shoulder hair, brown irises like black coffee in the Puerto Rican sun set in smallish, liddy, pointed and cat-like eyes, with a not-to-long, slightly curved, but angular and narrowish nose—thrice pierced—round tipped and the loveliest, dainty little rounded nares, below of which laid slightly thin, but full, perfect pink cupid's bow lips. All of these features had been framed by a strong jawline leading to a thin, round chin, high and pronounced cheekbone apples, within an oval head.

All of those little details shone brightly when the beautiful Strandler smiled at Roni's remark, showing their small, white, squared teeth—save for some natural fangs.

"Your poor ass," they giggle, "we must do something to ease its apparent distress."

Roni, lost in the Strandler's smile for a moment, chuckled lightly and retorts with a quick, "Oh, must we? And what would that be?" Their flirtation skills have sharpened.

The Strandler laughed nervously before responding, "We'd have to figure that out..." they hesitate, "over lunch maybe? —I'm Sam, by the way."

"Roni," they grin a bit, "and I would love to. But perhaps another instance—" they stop to admire, "Definitely, another instance, love."

Sam's face fell slightly, then beamed up again, "Oh, of course, how presumptuous of me to believe I could steal you from whatever errand you are on, dear," they soften, "to a moment with me."

"Yes, well, a moment with you is very tempting, and I'd quite love to oblige..." Roni breaks off for the slightest moment and picks back up sweetly, "but it would make the moment much more saccharine to wait a while for it to come. And come it shall."

Sam bites their lip instinctively, without even noticing, "Quite right you are, dear. And I will hold you to it. You can find me here," they motion to the bibliotheca of which they had just sprung out and whacked Roni with the door of, "most of the time."

"Ah, an avid reader, then?" Roni probes.

"And amateur writer. I come searching for inspiration, but it seems inspiration found me." Sam adds.

There was a shared knot between them, a searching, and a mix of emotions. Roni finally spoke, "You flatter me... but I best be off, lest I lose my momentum."

Sam nods, "I'll see you, then." A half question.

"You will, love. Soon." Roni reassured before bowing slightly and quickly and then departing.

Both were left wondering why they'd been interacting with each other as if they were vampires in the 1800s, just naturally riffing off an accidental accent slip somewhere in that conversation that neither could place exactly where it happened. I can though; it was with the words "ease its apparent di**stress**"—emphasis on 'stress'. And another peculiarity was how uncannily familiar they were to each other. As if they'd met before.

No, I will not say if they have. You can speculate on that if you'd like, especially with my unwillingness to shed light on the subject; by all means, infer away.

Melancholy filled the bubble surrounding a blue laden Kia whomst sat atop the outer edge of her building's roof, alone with her thoughts. *It's all my fault,* Kia thought to herself, *I set them off, I didn't tell them about Toni.* Kia dwelled and dwelled, and then dwelled some more. The issue had come and gone, and had been let go by Roni to the point where it was mostly forgotten—even for a place where the forgotten thrives. But Kia could not forget, in fact, she dreamt up *what if* moments and alternate scenarios, things she could have done differently, said differently. None of this was, of course, logical, Kia was too consumed with pure emotion to think logically. Though it was her emotions that kept her from feeling fully alone; empty. She had remembered all the times she had to fake emotion, feign smiles and optimism to seem welcoming, to feel a warmth to others that she so desperately wanted to feel for herself to chase away the cold inside her chest.

Kia, stop, they said everything's okay, she pleaded with herself before turning against her own resolve to pull out of the deep, *but how could it be so quickly? How could they just flip a switch and be okay?* Kia was convincing herself on both fronts, that she should be wary and sad because Roni must have lied to make her feel better and that's why they haven't seen each other in a few countless moments, and that it truly is all okay and that she should let it go because Roni had clearly done so themself and that she was blowing this all out of proportion by letting it get to her head.

She was incensed with her inner voices, with her heart. For the first time since Toni, she was *emoting* again, truly, not that false and unfaltering optimism she was known for. She'd been lying to everyone, to herself, in hopes that she could turn that fake happy into a real one. Then she met Roni and it did; naturally, organically—to her knowledge— it did.

Roni had sensed somehow that Kia was feeling some type of way as they approached Kia's building. And that type of way was in the negative sense. The palpitation in their heart changed its beat and hastened, filling them with adrenaline and fear which they used as nitro ignition to jettison them up four flights of stairs and burst through Kia's door.

"Kia!?" Roni shouted, searching the immediate area with their eyes.

There was no response.

"Kia!? Are you here?" They continued, stepping in cautiously and investigating deeper into the flat.

Still nothing.

Oh, no... they thought to themself, grief and worry washing over them like a rising tide during a moonless night; dark and foreboding.

Roni walked all over the bottom floor of the flat, the blue and grey of it all adding to the gravitas of the moment. Blue and grey, sorrow and grief; a sort of calm despondency saturates the flat's atmosphere, affecting Roni's demeanour *in ways*, as they'd say.

Upstairs, Roni spots a large lump under a pile of blankets of varying patterns and colours and calls out, "Kia?" before patting the lump only to find squish and fluff.

Fuck, they think to themself upon discovering the stuffies.

They're wracked with emotions, desperate and defeated, *where could she be?* they ponder. They sit on the bed, left with their own thoughts, their not-yet-faded memories inside Kia's empty flat.

What are they doing? Nature inquires.
Sulking, remembering. Feeling responds.
 Well, that's not good, they're still pretty fresh, all things considered. Attraction adds.
At this point, though, there's nothing I can do—nothing we can do—to stop it from happening. Time states with a sigh.
Nature sucks their—well, they do that noise one with teeth does when they suck them in sharply and quickly, *Indeed, I cannot will Kia back inside with extreme storms or anything. She wouldn't pay them any mind in this state.*
Kia is also remembering, dwelling on her dark emotions. There's not much we can do to sna either of them out of this and bring them together. Feeling explains.
Time sort of growls, *You're right, I guess we'll just have to see how this works out...*

And so the Forces looked on intently, on the edge of their metaphorical seat. They'd be biting their nails if they had any.

"It's hopeless, she's probably gone; tired of waiting—tired of me." Roni contemplated, "Just like always before. Just like..." they broke off, stopping before allowing those painful memories from resurfacing.

The memories of their parents leaving, disappearing from their life. One disappearing altogether, physically and emotionally checking out, while the other stayed in body only. They wondered if Kia had started to emotionally check out after the fight, if she couldn't believe that they were actually over *it*. The fight, the one that Kia had wanted to avoid and diffuse that Roni had incited and later regretted letting get so tense. It certainly wasn't the biggest fight, of course, it was just that conflict of any kind made Kia spiral, a fact that Roni hadn't previously known but picked up almost immediately in the midst. They understood, their parents fought all the time, also, and it had left scars; emotionally and physically. Emotionally and physically was a theme that recurred in Roni's life, for they couldn't escape being wounded in both respects by family, friends, and lovers alike.

These were the thoughts that now circled Roni's crown. Ugly images of pain and what caused it, tears and darkness, an empty room inside an empty room. Images I care not to see and relay to you any further than I have, though, let's just say that they're becoming darker as more memories resurface.

There's no poison greater to either Kia or Roni than desolation and isolation.

Chapter 6 - Disarming Loneliness

What is it like to have been abandoned by everyone you thought loved you? Roni thought through the darkness of the expanse between the now and then. Their mind has travelled back to the initial moments that wrought this endless lonely feeling and how adverse they are to isolation.

Like a stage play, the image of characters are illuminated by spotlights in the dark room of Roni's memories, acting out moments that were burned forever into their soul. Over there, a man yelling at Roni, who'd just arrived from school very excited to share their day with him, telling them in a growl, "Why are you here?! Go back to your mother, I don't want to see you. You chose her, remember?" The stage light disappears.

On the far side, just there, a plethora of instances where a small Roni tries to get a woman's attention to no avail, only to be shushed, threatened to be hit, and told to go away. Another one, just to the left of those, the same woman lays in bed, despondent, ignoring a tween Roni's attempts to connect long enough and enough times that Roni eventually learns to take care of themself and to live with loneliness in the physical presence of another.

To the right and behind, that same woman is seen telling a 12 year old Roni to call their father to take them to do groceries. That scene is followed by Roni wandering a grocery alone with a cart full of food and then bagging them alone. After, sitting on a curb waiting for their father to arrive.

Way back there, another scene where Roni's brother asks for time on the computer, to which Roni replies, "okay, hold on a bit. Lemme tell my friend I'm getting off." Their brother reacted by grabbing Roni, punching them in the head, and throwing them off the chair.

Too many scenes with Roni's many brothers attacking them physically or emotionally.

Those images disappear, giving way to a young woman obsessed with Roni one moment, the next striking them and humiliating them. That same woman appears again, silent, ignoring Roni as they try to beg for reciprocation of affection, of love, of even any sort of attention.

These scenes were repeated again but with another woman, this one more volatile and violent. We see at the forefront Roni being screamed at in their face, Roni trying not to react, and then being punched in the head several times.

That same woman later appears attempting to overdose, Roni scrambling to stop her and save her from herself. She disappears.

Many other scenes played out. Some were friends that just evaporated from Roni without warning or reason, some were strangers that seemed to just want to harm them.

Roni descended deeper into the darkness. A happenstance so completely unique in a place such as The Plane of the Forgotten. Everyone was supposed to forget their trauma, forget their pain, and just live eternally in creative bliss—so long as they stayed in The Stranding.

They need to snap out of this soon. This is why they're here in the first place! Time says with a harrumph.

A storm is always at its worst before it breaks. Feeling says plainly and softly.

What does that mean, Nature inquires, *they're going to break?*

They can't break, it's impossible to break here. They can't break, right, Time? Attraction says anxiously.

Calm down, Feelsie just meant that they're gonna come out of it. The storm is the darkness they're dealing with, so it's going to be breaking, the storm is, not Roni. Time explains dryly.

The other three Forces let out a collective long '*ah*' of realisation before taking a back seat and letting our lovely Strandlers come to terms with their darkness, their shared despair.

"I probably can't die here anyway..." Kia sighs, correct in her assumption. Death doesn't touch this plane.

Oblivion does.

The doorknob rattles and clicks, the door slowly swings open and Roni perks up with a red exclamation mark appearing over their head accompanied by an alert sound and they rush from Kia's bed to the bannister to see a sluggish Kia walking into the flat.

"Kia!" Roni yelled like Eric Matthews to Mr. Feeny, "Kia!!" again, "Kia!!" The third time extending the 'i' in Kia. They floated down from the top floor after mumbling parkour while flipping over the bannister and rushed Kia who was frozen, surprised that Roni was even there.

Being amply squoze, Kia strains, "Roni, what are you doing here? Not that I'm complaining..."

Roni lets go and plants a sweet kiss on Kia's nose, "I was worried about you. I had this weird feeling that something was wrong, that you were going to..." They trail off yet again, "My arachnid feelies were prickling—" Roni stopped a moment, squinted tightly with their lips pursed and nose scrunched, "that sounds off somehow. Is that—?"

"It does sound wrong—but what? How? Like, you knew?" Kia said, confused.

"I can't explain it, but yeah, I did. I just knew, and I knew I had to come and be here for you."

Kia's eyes welled up with tears that sparkled into the air, "Oh, Roni—I—Thank you." She mushed her nose with the side of her hand and threw her arms around Roni, squishing them against her chest tightly.

Oh, my Creator, they're okay. They made it through their storms and back into each other's arms, how lovely! Attraction blurts out.

Look at them, you could see the negative emotions melt away from them and dissipate into nothingness. It's beautiful. They're blooming and it's filling me with so much... me. Says Feeling with a dreamy whisper.

The curly one seems much happier now. I'm glad I didn't drench them, the progeny would have gotten wet from all of that squeezing they did. Nature adds.

Time zooms around, *Yes, yes. Hopefully this is the last we'll see of that Darkness, lest it expand to The Stranding.*

Mahogany shelves taller than two Shaqs and wider than seven movie theatre screens arranged in the shape of a labyrinth and filled from top to bottom with volumes upon volumes of stories both false and true that no one had ever heard of, along with those written by citizens of The Stranding and are organised in the chaotic fashion of third alphabetic—the third letter of the title—and moment written. Which can be a little tricky since moments happen constantly but also happen to appear in the past, present and future all at once. One book could appear now, but also had been there for a while, whilst another could appear moments later but have happened at whatever present it is. It's all relevant, really; relevant to the author that is. Understandably, one on the outside may be confused, but to one whomst lives to consume books, the moment it arrives doesn't matter; it's the moment spent within that means the most.

One such consumer, the avid reader, Sam, hangs off the 17th shelf of the weastern quadrant—just over there, yes, that's weast; somewhere between east and west but not quite either and not quite centre—having just slipped off the walking ladder, book in hand and reading as if they're not a few metres above the white and gold marble floor, completely unbothered.

"Need help up there?" Roni says with a sly sarcasm.

Sam looks down, moving the book from their eye line, "Oh, hi. Uh," they look around, "nah, I'm just hanging out, you know."

Roni giggles, "Nice, hilarious."

"You like that one, huh?" Sam smirks.

"Drop down, I'll catch you." Roni extends their arms.

"You're cute," Sam states, dropping gracefully, their hair and clothes flowing as they float down, toes touching the marble below, "but I got it."

Roni was mesmerised, they swore they saw sparkles and bubbles surrounding Sam as they descended, "I see. A strong, independent human."

Sam slides their feet into the sandals that had fallen off when they slipped and ended up hanging and states with an exhale, "Indeed, love."

"So the coffee here never gets cold." Roni says, having brought Sam to the Café Ludens underneath their flat.

"That's awesome, the coffee at The Forest of Letters always stays cold." Sam responds.

"Speaking of," Roni starts, "you know, I haven't been hungry the whole time I've been here. It's odd."

"What's odd," Sam says, taking a bite out of a chocolate hazelnut croissant, "is that you thought that was a 'speaking of which'. Like, which part of that relates to The Forest of Letters?"

Roni chuckles, "What do you mean?"

Sam smiles, a flake of croissant on their lower lip, "Me either, by the way. I just like how things taste. Also, the art that goes into the food here is just so beautiful, it feeds my soul more than my belly. I don't even need my belly fed."

"That's interesting. Yeah, a lot goes into cooking and baking, I definitely appreciate it as an artform, especially the moment I put it in my mouth and there's an explosion." Roni adds.

Sam snorts, holding in a guffaw, "Oh, yeah? An explosion?"

"An explosion." Roni parrots, deadpan as all.

"Ahuh," Sam collects themself, "anyway, so take this croissant," they display the hazelnut and chocolate filled flaky French confection, "it's flaky, like, it's got a fun mouthfeel because it both squishes and slightly crunches while giving that 'fall-apart' texture of the flakiness."

"Mhmm." Roni follows, amused.

"Then the creamy insides that both taste and feel like heaven; so smooth and rich."

"Yes, yes."

"It's thick, right? And it takes over the whole of my mouth every time I go in for more."

"Go on."

"Then we have the presentation; this long, slightly curved structure, perfectly browned, drizzled with dark chocolate in a thoughtful and intentful zig-zag, and sprinkled with powdered sugar to contrast the dark colours with a bit of white. It's just enough so that it doesn't cover any of the beautiful details; the creases, the cracks, the flakes. It's beautiful, it's almost a shame to take it in my mouth and ruin it."

"I wouldn't figure your mouth for ruining."

"Only food." Stated with a sultry, inviting tone.

Roni shook a little and slowly, instinctually sucked their lips in, licking them and returning them with a small bite on the left side of the lower lip, "You tease."

"I'm only talking." Sam shrugs.

"It's how you say it, love." Roni leans back in their chair.

"And how is it that I am saying it, darling?" The accent returns to Sam's cadence with a hint of flirtation.

"Like it's not the croissant you're talking about, love." Roni replies.

Sam sucks in air and leans in a little, "Then what, pray tell, am I referencing, my dear?"

Roni sucks their teeth, doing that *'tchk'* sound and pauses a moment, "I will save myself embarrassment by inferring something that isn't there and just say, I'd like to find out."

Sam does a *'psshew'* tail-ended with a short, loose lipped raspberry, "Well, that's no fun."

"It can be..." a dramatic silence, "if we did want to explore 'not-food'."

Sam licks their sharp, right canine tooth in an act of intrigue, leans all the way back and cocks their head at an exact 78 degree angle, "What is it about you that's just so enthralling. I'm way too invested and intrigued by you—I don't know, and I'm sorry I'm blurting this out like this, breaking character, but I'm like,—yes. Yes."

"Yes?" Roni raises The People's Eyebrow.

Sam regains their composure, "Let's abscond, love."

Why are they like this? Attraction disapprovingly states.

Like what? Time says with amusement in their tone.

They're just following the vibes, and perhaps creating them unknowingly. Feeling adds.

It seems that they cannot help or hold back. It is embedded in their soul, and others cannot get enough, getting sucked in. Nature observes, knowing.

Well, I'm glad they and Kia made up and decided that for the moment, at least, remaining platonic lovers—

—Not lovers, then, Atty. Time interrupts Attraction.

Right, not lovers, but still in love—platonically. Attraction clears up.

The purest love, it's so sweet. I cannot get enough of how lovely they are together. They really bring out the best in each other. Feeling extols.

Unfortunately, only when they are together. Nature interjects.

The Forces nod in agreement, Attraction in particular is bothered by that fact, fearing the worst if Roni and Kia do not intertwine often enough to keep the Darkness at bay.

And what exactly is Darkness? The absence of light, yes, but also the absence; completely. In this small, hidden pocket of the universe, Darkness—a sort of entity at the moment in and of itself—is oblivion. Oblivion of all things that came to be within The Stranding, as it had been in The Voidheart Chasm, within The Forbidden Forest of Forgotten Figments and Figures, as well was the first failure—not to mention The Black Cliffs, which exists much beyond. These places exist outside of The Stranding, just beyond sight, yet they threaten to be seen, and paintings serve as a reminder of what could eventually be. Though the paintings are just vague images of an unseeable fate and nothing like the locations they feign to be.

But who exactly could have painted these? There seemed to be dreamers in The Stranding that see without seeing and can explore The Plane of the Forgotten without ever leaving The Stranding. Artists whose vision extends beyond, as it always had even in the *reality* where their vision was seen as too strange or too derivative, too anything and yet, simultaneously not enough, leading the artists to a madness, a sorrow which they could not recover and sought asylum from, landing them in The Plane.

Inflection on your tongue
Meets the infliction of intent

And the chills are running down
Wishing my hands were running up

Your body's feeling warm
Your skin is tingling this sensation
Of elation at the thought of entering

Oh won't you pray for me
Down on your trembling knees
Your sweet idolatry
Keeps me coming back for more
I'm, I'm coming for you, for you
Oh

Tempting fingertips laced
Between and traced across renting
Flesh against flesh, a moment
More and we'll be ripped apart

Your lips expressing "please"
Your eyes' wide open with dilation
Delectation from everything received

Oh won't you pray for me
Down on your trembling knees
Your sweet idolatry
Keeps me coming back for more
I'm, I'm coming for you, for you
Oh

The scent; desire so reckless it hurts
To taste, your fire, I'm drowning in you
Enthralled and coming for me

I won't stop till you're completely
Mine

Oh, baby, you'll prey for me
Down on your trembling knees
Your sweet idolatry
Keeps me coming back for more
I'm, I'm coming for you, for you
Oh, and I'll prey for you
Yes I'll prey for you, too

"That was beautiful, in a sexy way." Sam comments.

Roni half-smiles, looking up at the sheer top of the canopy, laying flat on their back and gazes over at Sam with just their eyes, "Thank you."

"What inspired it, may I ask?" Sam caresses Roni's face, tracing down to their sternum, satin blankets strewn all around them in Roni's bed.

"You, in part. And someone else. Someone I think is using me, until I'm in their grasp and then I think I'm everything." Roni confesses.

Sam scoots closer and pulls Roni's naked torso toward them, "Me? And another mystery manipulator. Should I be offended? Worried?"

"Neither. I don't feel those feelings with you. I can tell you're honest." Roni says softly, rolling onto their side and gently kissing Sam's shoulder and pronounced collar bone repeatedly in a sort of path to and fro.

Sam strokes Roni's hair sweetly, whispering, "Whatever you say, love."

They share a kiss, it deepens, building passion on top of passion, on top of desire. Their hands search each other's bodies patiently, caressing, grasping, and lightly dragging nails. Soft moans, heavy breathing and sharp gasping follow light tugging and teeth gripping bits of flesh with fervour. Their passion had peaked, and their patience had worn thin. Roni climbs atop Sam, a leg between Sam's pressing into and rubbing against them beckoning a louder response. Sam responds in turn by gripping Roni's shoulders tightly and switching positions, slamming Roni onto their back and pinning them down, their lips exploring Roni's body from lips, slowly down their neck and chest, their nipples for a moment, eliciting a deep moan before travelling further down, Sam's hands caressing and clawing down Roni's sides to their hips where they take hold, anchoring Roni in place for Sam to sink their teeth into the area of the femoral artery—the inner thigh, just around the centre of it, but a little lower. Roni's left hand takes hold of Sam's wavy, medium length hair, gathering as much of it up in their hand as they can with a tight grip pulling.

They belong to each other for this moment, forgetting all else and focusing solely on each other's pleasure.

Things went a lot further, and just like before, I'll save you the details hoping you could fill in the gaps with your own imagination instead of me having to get too... into it. I shouldn't have to, honestly, we all know where things lead between two people that are together in this kind of situation.

Chapter 7 - The End of Heartache

Love does seem to heal all things, Feeling says, *and it's at the heart of everything. The reason for everything, even in absence, don't you think?*

Kia takes a stroll around The Stranding, taking in the dusky atmosphere, admiring the hues of blues and purples, and the slight, but pleasant smell of orange and cinnamon. They pass by The Gate, where a Strandler is, at the moment, becoming the Kia to someone's Roni. Or quite possibly—and they hoped it wasn't the case—the Toni to someone's Kia. She smiled warmly, then the smile grew wistful, listlessness in their now 100-yard gaze, the depth of which contained a multitude of emotions that danced around mixing and separating like paints in a spinner or blood in a centrifuge.

They thought, *a film would be nice. I wonder what's playing.* As they shook off the Darkness that started creeping like Facehuggers up their shoulders by shaking their head and trodding toward the Theatre that stood across from the bibliotheca—I'm sorry, **library**.

As she approaches the ***Theatron Philoscaena***, a face catches her periphery as it exits the Forest of Letters; Roni, followed by Sam, as they hold the door open for them. Kia feels a sting, followed by a heat in their cheeks and then a cold washing over her from curls to toes. Mouth agape turning to a giant grin, Kia states contently, "Cuties." and 180's into the theatre.

Whoa, that is... that is unexpected! Time said.

She's growing. Roni's unconditional love is water and sunlight to her. Feeling adds.

*Hm! Well, at least they're together and in **some** sort of love. I am accomplished.* Attraction scoffs.

Time glares, and Feeling sighs dreamily, meanwhile, Nature is happy seeing something grow.

The film was an ambitious visual festival of what nightmares can bring when one unlocks their mind to dreaming in constant even in waking life. A concept and a theory so frightening in an existence where one can simply think up anything they'd like—well, anything without sentience—and most things are possible. What if, the film proposed, one could dream up sentience and make it a reality? Giving birth, essentially to a being of pure creative energy, unbound to any laws of the universe.

Of course, as with all human creations, it goes horribly wrong and infiltrates society in such a way where the Nightmare Creatures—dubbed the Crestfallen—form themselves into a mockery of humanity, of deities, of whole systems, all the while using the bodies of humans as conduits for pure physicality, and the energies of humanity as a means to transcend physicality and become the universe itself.

There is no happy ending, no ***Final Girl***, no hopeful message at the end. The Crestfallen win, undoing centuries of evolution and becoming the owners of the known and unknown. The last scene sees these creatures coexisting in harmony with themselves and animals alike.

This begs the question, are they, the Strandlers, Crestfallen? Or are Crestfallen an inevitability? Or something else entirely that has no deeper bearing on life in The Plane of the Forgotten? Everyone leaving the theatre chooses the third option.

After the film, Kia wanders out of the Theatron Philoscaena and stops to admire the beauty of The Stranding framed by the hazy red sky in its permanent twilight, the rainfall is gentle, kissing every surface it touches upon and emitting magenta glows. The drops themselves are black and thin, like pencil lines on a sketchpad.

Speaking of sketchpad, Toni sits at the fountain, scanning the scenery for inspiration when they catch sight of Kia at the theatre. Kia's eyes slowly lock onto Toni's as she realises who is staring back at her.

The moment seemed to last a thousand lifetimes.

Toni knew there was no escape, no avoiding. Their emotions swirled and sank, a deep heaviness dropping in their chest and the feeling of moths flapping frantically in their stomach evoked a sense of panic that they had not felt since before the *Unreality*. They were always so calm, so cool and collected; a pretence that is held together by actively avoiding deeper emotions and keeping people at arm's length.

This technique was perfected here in The Stranding where Toni met, wooed, and quickly abandoned countless Strandlers in an attempt to fill their soul with inspiration and a sense of being wanted that they never had in their unfortunate *Reality* without the fear of someone getting tired of them. They'd leave that person behind and be everything they wanted to be, be who they idolised when they were young; the coolest, baddest motherfucker in town. Gone were the days of insecurity, dead was the anxious and often overlooked Toni that no one could want because they were so different, they weren't what was traditionally coveted in those times.

But not at this moment. That anxious and insecure Toni was back and they were petrified.

Kia's eyes sharpened, her eyebrows furrowed seriously, and her lips tightened before taking off like a little rocket and marching furiously toward Toni.

Toni's eyes widened into large saucers with oceanic pools at the centre.

"Hey! We have to talk!" Kia envisioned herself like a lioness roaring as she made her way through the theatre-goers.

Toni was frozen, "Uh, I—um," they gulped, "ah, shit."

Kia squared up, standing centimetres from Toni's face which looked a lot like Shocked Pikachu, "You left me." she said, "You left me, and completely destroyed my heart. I was a mess, Toni."

"I—" Toni started before being quickly cut off.

"Don't talk. I don't need you to talk. I need you to listen, okay?" Kia's tone had brought back an accent she thought was gone. She reminded herself of her mother.

Toni nodded and said in barely a whisper, "Okay."

"You told me, you assured me, that you would never abandon me, that you wouldn't leave me. Now, I believe you that whoever you were with aside from me meant nothing to you, *pero*, you played with my feelings. I told you about my past, Toni! I told you about my insecurities, I trusted you. You not only hurt me, but you **betrayed** me. *Carajo*, Toni, I loved you! Wasn't that enough? I wanted you, and I cared about you." Kia started to tear up.

She wiped her eyes and took a breath, "*Pues, con to' y eso*, I forgive you. Toni, I forgive you, not because I think you feel guilty, I don't. *Pero, por que creo que...* I deserve peace. I do. And *sabes que?* So do you, Toni. I hope that you get the peace you deserve and can finally bury all the demons that make you..." Kia cocks her hip and sighs, "like *this.*"

Kia leans in and kisses Toni's nose, smiles sweetly, with a hint of pain that seems to fade into the abyss, and then walks away.

Whoa, like, whoa. Did you see that? That was intense! Time comments.

That's my girl, she's gotten so strong. I'm so proud. Attraction said.

Oh, she's swimming in so many lovely emotions right now! It's flowing through her and giving her even physical sensation. Just watch, do you see? Right there, she's tingling, floating. Feeling adds.

Like a thunderstorm and a flower, a cosmos coming into itself. Beautiful. Nature said plainly.

I still can't believe she just sort of marched up and extolled her feelings like that. Roni is absolutely having an effect on her; she wouldn't have done that pre-Roni. Time said in a gossipy tone.

Oh, I know. She was a regular Xena—I always liked that show. Attraction gushed.

Toni had gone back to their flat, shaken and an incredible mess. They slammed their door shut and fell back into it, sliding down onto the floor. The door—on the inside—is a slick onyx with a golden rectangular door handle and matching hinges. The floor is mosaic tilework of greys and blacks with bright emerald tiles thrown in at random spots for a beautiful embellishment that matches with the walls throughout. The grout was also golden. As mentioned, the walls are a brilliant emerald green, like a forest in the sun. This theme persists throughout the entire flat, with the stairs to the top floor being a transparent green. The kitchen is devoid of counters or appliances, just a small, round glass table in black and green with gold trimming and one lonely chair that pairs with it. The living area has an easel in the centre, just before the one-panel, wall window; nothing else. Upstairs, the bedroom has but a single bed with a patchwork quilt atop it that Toni made themself. The patches are varied in colour and many have images of things that Toni loves; reptiles, coffee, easels, trees, an apple, an octopus, a severed hand bleeding and meant to signify horror, and finally, a platypus wearing a leather jacket and riding a motorcycle at the centre.

This was Toni's home. A home for a solitary person. A home not meant for company, for sharing, for love of any kind.

On the floor, Toni followed their hands through their hair and wacked their head against the door. They laughed, a forced laugh, before descending into a slow building sob. A Darkness begins to creep up around Toni, shadowy hands, fingers crawling towards them as their thoughts manifest into blank canvases and floating paint brushes threatening to ruin the purity.

They begin their work, painting faces stuck in moments of strong emotion, so much to see in the eyes. One face is Toni's, bereft and blue, a story within whispering loss and blood and broken bonds. Another is the face of a loved one, Chino, a man whose face is captured in a moment of rage and disgust, glowering eyes screaming hate and confusion and refusal to understand; ignorance. The next face was an older face, a face with an expression that showed a deep disappointment and a sense of loss, the eyes reflected mourning, though the mourning was self-imposed, therein also lied a severing of ties and the lack of acceptance.

More faces came, more faces went, each telling vignettes of moments that scarred Toni and left them a shell, a vampire, unable to connect in any meaningful way or give any bit of themselves beyond their body to anyone at all.

That is until Roni walked into the Café Ludens and into their life.

Roni's face was the last one to be painted. It was a beautiful likeness of a moment where Roni had given Toni a soft smile. The eyes were warm, they spoke of acceptance and admiration and love that isn't quite *the* love, but it was a love that meant Toni was wanted and seen and not needed or hated. Toni felt the darkness melt away like ink blots running into nothingness as they focused on Roni. Roni understood them, foundationally, and held them in such high esteem that they couldn't believe it's real. Roni praised their art, had let them go on and on about techniques and strokes, pencil types and charcoal, the grain of paper; anything. Every moment spent with Roni was freedom, every moment was bliss. And in moments of passion, Roni was unmatched, every touch was fire, every kiss—their mouth—was heaven. Toni hadn't felt anything like these sensations—or emotions—in or outside of the *Unreality*.

Ever the avoidant one, Toni dwelled on these moments, on the one painting, forgetting all of the painful ones and keeping only the blissful ones. A single tear rolls down Toni's cheek, this time it doesn't dissipate, there are no sparkles, just a wet, light blue trail leading to the corner of their mouth that starts to crack and rise into a smile that says joy and sorrow.

Whoa, I didn't think Toni could cry like that. Time reacts.
I'm incredibly flabbergasted, honestly, Toni isn't a complete and total shit. There's a human in there. Attraction said.
They couldn't deny who they truly are through an empty facade anymore. They, too, are growing. Nature comments.

It's strange, Toni was always hiding from their emotions, always running away and always keeping them from flourishing. Roni walks in one day and unlocks a door in their heart, and since then, things inside them had started to flow and flood and fill them with all of the things they were so afraid of. It's a beautiful tragedy, the sad happiness, the joyful despair. Toni's emotions ripping them every which way, their guilt finally surfacing over what they'd done to Kia. The guilt is something that threatens everything, my siblings. It beckons The Darkness; this time being kept at bay by Roni's image, but for how long? Feeling expresses.

*We shouldn't worry about it. Roni is changing things! You've seen, just thinking about them keeps **It** from fully manifesting.* Time states nervously.

*I don't know, Time, it's looking like it's becoming a problem. It's started manifesting much more and much quicker than the **others**...* Attraction trails off a bit sing-songy.

Yes. I don't want to see another beautiful place full of colour and life be drained and left a monochromatic mess. Nature huffs.

It was true, The Darkness had been much more present than ever before. It's not just with those we've been following either, but with other Strandlers as well. Just a few moments ago, one lovely Strandler was seen crying with gangly partially transparent shaded hands emerging from their shadow and rising up their legs like spiders, stopping at their neck and chest and gripping tightly. The Strandler was then seen dashing through The Gate and disappearing into a fog that surrounded The Stranding, headed for The Forbidden Forest of Forgotten Figments and Figures. They were never seen again.

Within the privacy of their flats, many Strandlers started **remembering**. This instance had indeed coincided with the arrival of one Roni Last-Names-Do-Not-Exist-Here. An odd sort of perceived coincidence that Time had kept hush-hush from the other Forces; even if there was yet another Force that knew. A reluctant Force that was drawn in by the others and coerced to be a part of their little experiment, going against the **Rule** and the wishes of *Them.*

It's going to happen again, Roni can't stop it, if that's what you're hoping for Time. Warns the mysterious Force.

Ugh, who invited Chance to the conversation? Time reacted rather strongly.

Here to prophecise again, Chance? Attraction added, with a sting of attitude.

I'm just saying. It's bound to happen. And for me, personally, Roni is the one to make it happen faster. How long do you think we can keep Darkness from coming? Chance says plainly.

Chance may be right. Darkness—Nature starts before being interrupted

THE Darkness, The. It. Okay? Time chides.

Nature rolls what would be her eyes if she could be perceived as having them, *The Darkness, Time, is not one to be ignored as we have.*

*It feeds the—It. But also can turn **It** against us.* Feeling hesitates.

Time takes a moment to reason things out, *I still believe that this time it's going to work.*

Everyone of the Forces either scoff or sigh or have some sort of disapproving reaction to Time's willful naivete, although a couple of them remain hopeful.

While we're on the subject, Time, why not take a look back at what led Toni to us? Feeling suggests.

Yes, enlighten us, you're the only who can, we're bound to the here and now, you don't have those chains. Nature states.

Fine. But I promise you, it's a lot less pretty than the pictures painted. So brace yourselves. Time obliges.

A twirl of the limb-like structures and some wobbling around, and we're given a tube television shaped window into Toni's moments outside of the Plane of the Forgotten; in the *Reality*.

It was New York City, it was *Greaser* times. Think *West Side Story* mixed with *The Outsiders*. There weren't people breaking out in musical numbers, but you can hear the old island sounds from windows of buildings as well as Sinatra from passing cars and inside mechanics' workshops. It was true, the Italians and the Puerto Ricans weren't exactly on speaking terms. But there was a couple that bridged that gap and fell in love. A short and stocky Puerto Rican man with intense eyes like the clear island waters and hair as black as coal, skin like suede and a moustache thinly over his thick upper lip and his wife, tall and thin, pale skin and brown eyes that her husband equated to fuzzy coconuts because they were so light and he could drink them up forever, her hair was long and thick with loose curls, it was a light brown with natural red highlights, her nose was long and arched while his was short and round, her lips were full and drawn, and she had a black mole just under her left eye, two fingers from the outer corner.

They had met when her father's car had broken down on the block where he and his father worked the shop. He saw her in distress and had to go help her, she was beautiful, he thought, and he had to go to her. He managed to push the car into the shop and convinced her to let him take her to a movie. The night of the movie, he was met by her brothers and ended up in quite the scuffle. The not-yet-wife showed up just as he had one brother in a headlock, the other under his foot, and the third just about to tackle him; she stopped him.

After that night, they kept meeting in secret, going to his parents house since they were much more hospitable, and eventually fell madly in love. They soon moved in together and married secretly, much to her family's chagrin. They were run out of New York by her family and ended up just one state over, in Connecticut, where mechanics were heavily needed.

She had become pregnant, and soon Toni was born.

Toni grew up to an absent father, his job was extremely demanding, and his mother had grown into a deep depression. This persisted throughout, with fights and broken dishes and holes in walls on a weekly basis. Toni's father tried, he did, he wanted to be there, he wanted to understand his wife's depression, but at that time, not much was known about the inner workings of the mind of a depressed individual. Toni's father had decided, after years of not being there because of work and frustration, that Toni needed at least one parent. This led him to bring Toni with him everywhere to keep them out of the house and away from a mother that just couldn't. So Toni grew closer to their father, because at least he was there sometimes, he tried, and he brought them to work with him. They'd work on cars together, they'd go watch movies, they talked.

Soon, Toni became a part of the Beatnik scene, as well as being a part of the still lingering Greaser scene. They loved both things. They loved the smell of oil and the sound of a motor, the leather and the jeans and the toughness. But they had a much deeper sensitivity, an artistic side that was fostered by the kids in museums and poetry bars. They were never a good writer, they tried writing poetry that spoke to their soul but it was never received too well. One moment, they walked up to the microphone in the hazy bar full of black clad patrons in sunglasses, smoking and sipping coffee or liquor, and nervously performed a poem;

It's not enough to say
And often feels as if actions fall short
Of what's deserved, the emotions
Involved, the feelings evolved
My world has come crashing down
In the sweetest destruction
My heart's eruption

A desire changed to necessity
A need's become a part of me
Appendage, organic growth
You're deep within me
And I cannot function without

You'll always be found here
Dissect me and in my chest you'll see
My heart's been replaced with you
Your essence, your all, is my survival

Behind my eyelids, you're all I see
In death, you're all I dream

In dreams, you're all I chase
And in life, you're all I breathe

Incomplete and deformed
Is what I would be without you

The crowd was silent, no one reacted at all. Toni felt humiliated and angry, they had worn their heart on their sleeve, performed a work that they had been struggling with for months that was inspired by the boy they loved that didn't love them because of how he saw them, and was met with nothing. The absence of reaction. Had it been so bad that it didn't even warrant hate? They stormed off the stage, knocking over the microphone and disappearing into the night.

After that instance, they swore to never write their feelings again, instead, taking up paper and canvas as their medium of art. They found that their hand was elegant and passionate and was able to create beautiful things as well as fix cars.

Their father saw their work and marvelled, but reminded them that there's no future in art and they had to focus on something tangible, like fixing cars. Toni's mother had found her heart in the paintings, in the sketches, and was overcome with emotion, breaking down so profoundly that they couldn't function.

Then it happened. One night, Toni had woken up in the middle of the night to use the bathroom when they found the door locked.

"Mom?" They called out.

No one answered, they called again, "Mom? Dad? You in there? I gotta pee."

Again, no one answered. They walked down the hall to their parents' room, to check which parent is missing. They creaked open the door slowly to not disturb the sleeping parent; their father. *It is mom,* they thought to themself, walking back to the bathroom door.

"Mom, come on, hurry up, I'm gonna go on myself!" They danced around and knocked on the door.

They kept knocking lightly to no answer, "Mom!?" Their voice filled with increased concern. It had been a few moments and they'd gone desperate, losing the urge to pee to the growing worry.

They went to their parents' room and woke their father, "Dad! Dad wake up, mom is in the bathroom and won't come out or answer when I call or knock."

"What? *Ay, carajo...*" He said groggily and as if he knew what had happened.

He rushed to the bathroom door, knocking, he shouted, "*Amor! ¡Abreme la puerta!* Open the door, honey, *no hagas esto.* Baby, come on!" He pounded on the door to no avail.

After a few moments, he burst through the door, breaking it from the hinges with Toni's help and saw before him, in the porcelain claw foot bathtub, blood tinged water and the near-lifeless body of his wife. She was alive, but barely, slightly conscious and looking up at her husband.

"I'm sorry," she manages, then looks over at Toni, "I-I lo..." she reaches out.

Toni is stricken with grief, anger, and pain, eyes welling with tears.

"...I love..." her eyes closed, "you..." she passed out from the blood loss.

Toni's mother survived the suicide attempt, but was committed to a mental institution for troubled women. There, she was under constant surveillance and kept drugged so as to keep her from attempting again. She was visited often at first, then after a while, her husband stopped visiting altogether as he couldn't bear to see her like that. Toni never stopped visiting though, and brought her paintings and sketches, and would often sketch her during the visit, adding flourishes and beauty where there was a dull, listless shell of a person. There was nothing in the eyes, they were devoid of all feeling.

Toni tried to move on from the incident, growing into themself more and figuring themself out in ways that would keep them from the death their mother had experienced. They had correlated their birth to their mother's depression and decided that they'd never have children so that they'd never feel that hopelessness their mother felt.

And then they figured out who exactly they were and who they wanted to be. This, of course, didn't go over well with their father, whomst was a traditional man of "God". At first, he was confused, chalking it up to a change in hormones, the grief they'd felt around their mother's situation, and being around all of those *artsy*—F-words, let's say instead. You can infer what that word was that he called them. Toni was heartbroken at the thought of their father not truly accepting them, opting for the old, "I love you, but I don't love *that*. I accept you, *pero no acepto eso.*"

"Then you don't love me or accept me if you don't love or accept everything that I am!" Toni would say in response.

"*¡Mira, no me hables así!* You respect me." He'd say.

"Respect me, first!" Toni would fire back.

To which Toni's father would slap them and say, "*Esta es mi casa,* you are under **my** roof, okay? You are who I say you are, you do what I say you do, and you don't talk back. *Me entiendes, Toni?*"

Holding their face, Toni held back tears and scowled, "Now I know why mom did what she did." They promptly turned away and ran out the door, never looking back to see the shock and pain in their father's face from that final comment.

Toni had taken up residence at their best friend's house, sleeping on the couch all day and spending all night out drinking and painting murals—monuments to their pain under bridges and on the sides of buildings. Toni vandalized their father's shop with an effigy to who they used to be in their father's eyes as a big "fuck-you" to him.

Their father, upon seeing this, threw all of Toni's paintings in the dumpster by the shop after tearing the canvases and breaking the frames apart, and set them on fire. Toni had watched him do it from a distance, crying into their friend's chest.

"Chino, I—" they choked out.

Chino held them, "It's okay, man. You can start new now."

Toni looked up at him and nodded, wiping his tears, "You're right. From now on, I have no more tears to shed."

Chino and Toni had grown close; to Chino, like siblings, to Toni, it was more than that. One night, after a night of drinking and "fucking shit up", Toni and Chino were sitting on top of Chino's car, parked overlooking the Long Island Sound, the smell of salt and smog filling the night air, Toni couldn't help but keep stealing glances at Chino, whomst was completely unaware and drinking from a silver flask wrapped in brown leather that belonged to his father that had served in The War.

Chino was the son of a friend of Toni's father's family. Chino's family had moved to New Haven from Puerto Rico precisely ten years, four months, six days, and thirteen hours and twenty-two minutes from this moment, opting for a smaller, less busy, more industrial city by the water— they couldn't not be by the beach—rather than the bustling, hard streets of New York. Chino had his jet black hair slicked back with a single lock loose over his face—Cry Baby style—, dark, dreamy eyes like pools of chocolate, a small, arrow head nose, and lips like pillows, two shades darker than their caramel skin. He was handsome in a boyish way, not yet rough and sculpted by age, having a velvety smooth face.

Toni had loved looking at him, sketching him many times over as he stared often toward a distance unimaginable, stoic and beautiful. This moment, Toni wished they could sketch him again, but their sketchbook was in the car. He looked like Michaelangelo's David.

"Why are you looking at me like that?" Chino said.

Toni snapped back to the moment, "Oh, uh... you got something on your face."

"*No jodas,* what is it?" He said, searching his face frantically.

"It's right there, stupid. Look," Toni moved in close, "*aquí...*" they brushed his cheek, just by his lips before going in for a kiss.

Their lips met for a brief moment before Chino pulled away and reacted angrily, "What the fuck, man?"

"I'm—I'm sorry!" Toni stammered.

"Fuck! Man, you're like my brother! Isn't that what you wanted, like—?" He said strongly.

"I-I know, I know. I'm sorry, I didn't—" Toni said nervously.

"Didn't what? Come on, man, what kind of freak are you!? I'm getting the fuck out of here. Find your own way home." Chino said, pushing them off of the hood of the car and hopping in. He gave one last hateful glare, threw Toni's bag out of the car, and drove off.

"Chino! Don't leave me!" Toni screamed, feeling their heart break again.

But he had left, and they were alone. This time, Toni was true to their words and didn't cry. They held it all in, all of the pain, all of their sorrow, all of their anger and anguish, and rifled through their bag to grab their sketchbook. With it in hand, they flipped through the pages, tearing all of the pictures of Chino out and breaking them apart.

Toni wandered through New Haven, not knowing it well enough to find their way out to anywhere, since they couldn't go back to Chino's place. They'd found themselves walking towards the train tracks where a group of young men were lurking in the shadows of the alleyways.

"Hey, kid, what're you doing out here?" One of them called out.

"Oh, man, I think the kid's completely out of it." Another laughed, noting the lack of response from Toni.

"Let's teach the kid a lesson, wandering out here in the pitch dark where they shouldn't be." A third spoke out.

"Yeah, the kid should know better than to be on our turf at this time o'night." Said the first one.

Toni was despondent and continued walking until one of the men grabbed them and threw them to the ground. All the others joined in the assault. Toni hadn't fought back or screamed or even cried when the men hurt them, which, after a while, freaked the men out.

"This ain't fun. The kid's like a fish!" One said.

"Fuck it, let's get outta here, boys. Ain't worth the effort." The first one declared.

"What a waste, not even a scream." Another murmured.

Toni was in pain and somehow managed to get up from the concrete and continue toward the train tracks. They'd survived because they didn't show any emotion, they didn't cry, they didn't scream, they weren't there. Toni was completely unattached from the situation, from *reality*.

They made it to the train station, but didn't get on the platform. Instead, they went toward the tracks up from the station and followed them for a while. They were oncoming tracks, and the train would come barrelling down soon, Toni knew this, they counted on it. Toni was convinced this was the only way to stop the pain.

The train came, Toni collapsed to the ground in-between the rails, *I just want to stop hurting*, they thought to themself, *I just wish I didn't exist, then mom wouldn't have hurt herself, then dad wouldn't have hurt me, then Chino wouldn't have left me...*

The train's horn blared, the lights hit Toni as they held their arms open and closed their eyes.

This is it...

And indeed it was. It was the moment they materialised into The Plane of the Forgotten.

Toni's eyes opened slowly, having realised that they hadn't felt an impact, hadn't smelled the salt or the smog, and hadn't heard the rattle and screech of a train headed right for them. They hadn't felt any pain either, though they didn't realise this little fact until after they'd gotten to their feet and checked felt nothing. They twirled in confusion, searching their surroundings for anything familiar. Instead, they saw the black blades of grass, the emerald sky with soft lavender clouds that looked like her mother's thick curls on a Sunday morning; wild and expansive. Then it began to rain, the diamond shaped drops came down in the brightest cyan Toni had ever seen. After a moment of enjoying the rain as it washed them clean, they noticed the grass illuminating a path of amber—not quite orange, not quite brown, but something in-between that shone crystalline despite it being quite overcast—that led Toni through a small cluster of trees that shuffled out of their way to bring them to The Stranding.

"Hey, sweetheart." Toni said, now a floating head in a polyhedron of sorts.

"Uh, hi? Where's your body?" Kia asked.

"Behind the gate, babe, come on in, I'll show you around. And you can see my body all you like." Toni flirted.

Kia blushed, "Sounds like a plan."

Between moments spent with Kia, Toni found themself compensating the rejection and heartbreak they had faced with Chino by flirting with, seducing, and engaging in hollow, shallow physical relations with any Strandler they found attractive. Of course, Kia wasn't too keen on this behaviour, but they hadn't yet become romantically involved, even though Kia had developed an attachment to Toni. After each engagement, Toni aborted the mission and fled the Strandler's flat as if they'd committed a crime. The truth was, they felt dirty and unfulfilled; empty. So they left and ran to their flat to shower and numb themself to keep their emotions from surfacing.

Toni liked Kia, they saw their mother in her, but only when she smiled and when the light hit her hair. Kia had seen Toni for who they are and was happy to always stick by them, to compliment them and to encourage their art. Kia smiled at them often, and looked off into the distance, much like Chino did, and it was in one of these instances that Toni broke out the sketchbook and began to work on a beautiful portrait of Kia; side profile, a soft smile and her hair blowing in the wind, the fountain behind her and her eye fixed on Toni—she had noticed Toni sketching and looked over, holding the pose and keeping her hair from her face with her hand.

Toni later took that sketch and used it as a frame of reference for a painting on a 16x30 canvas, giving it life in colour, adding strings of red into Kia's hair that lit up in the simulated sunlight of the upper left corner of the canvas. Kia never saw the painting, it stayed in Toni's flat, where no one but Toni had been.

"Are you sure?" Kia pouts, "I just…"

"I won't abandon you, Kia. No matter what happens." Toni reassures her, feeling the sting of regret swelling up in their throat, their eyes breaking away from Kia's to the floor.

Toni held Kia in their arms until Kia was fast asleep. It was then that Toni kissed Kia's forehead, shut their eyes tightly and whispered, "I'm sorry, sweetheart. I can't..." and stole into the metaphorical night.

In their flat, Toni fought back tears, fearing they'd break the promise they made to themself to never cry again, their voice shook as they reminded themself, "I have no more tears to shed..."

Since then, Toni had avoided Kia, knowing all of the places she frequented and steering clear of them, often staying home and painting or sketching so that they wouldn't feel so much, a catharsis to stay numb. Then, as if it had always been there, a café appeared; Café Ludens.

Surely she hasn't discovered this joint yet, Toni thought to themself. So they started frequenting the Café, as it had vaguely reminded them of something, until they looked up from their blank sketchbook and saw Roni. Toni's eyes lit up—literally—to neon blue, glowing in the back of the dimly lit café, where Roni had glanced over and they were mesmerised by each other's gaze.

Time, darling, we know the rest. We were there. Attraction remarks.

Sorry, got carried away... Time shrugs sheepishly.

So sad, the poor thing never had a chance in Reality. It was too rough for someone like them. A sensitive soul, though they had allowed their heart to be calloused. Feeling expresses.

Calluses are caused by repeated impact with something abrasive. Life was abrasive and repeatedly impacted their heart. It was bound to happen. Nature explains dryly.

Unfortunately, yes. Absolutely bound. But they've softened, and they'll find themself again. Chance chimes in.

Love, true love, acceptance, forgiveness, that's all they ever needed... Feeling says dreamily.

Chapter 9 - Situations Are Irrelevant

Toni clutches their painting tightly, shifting their feet and fidgeting in the hallway leading to Kia's door.

"It's not a big deal, it's just an apology. She won't freak out on you, Toni, it'll be cool." They reassured themself, pacing back and forth and then hesitating to knock exactly a hundred and twelve instances.

Finally, three tiny, spaced out, shaky taps on Kia's door later, Toni is a pale blue from the wash of anxiety that's taken over them waiting for Kia to have heard whatever those 'knocks' were and open the door. Toni contemplates leaving the painting and disappearing again, or just running away altogether. Before they can make another move, the doorknob rattles, turns, and the door slowly opens. Toni holds their breath.

"What are you doing here?" Kia says, surprised and curious.

Toni exhales, "I—"

"What's that you got?" Kia inquires.

Toni looks down at the painting, then back up at Kia, "It's for you."

"For me?" Kia gasps, taking the painting from Toni and holds it up to give it a good look, "Is this... me? You made this of me?"

Toni nods and turns their gaze to the floor, "I wanted to," they gulp, "apologise. For everything. And I know you said you've moved past it and all of that, but I couldn't forgive myself if I didn't explain myself and say sorry."

"Toni—"

"You didn't deserve that. I was scared, but you didn't deserve that." They confess, "I didn't want to hurt you, I wanted to avoid being hurt."

Kia sighs, eyes softening to Toni's declaration of sentiments, "Come in, Toni. I have time."

Toni's eyes shoot up, not having expected that response and meeting Kia's face to see her smiling warmly at them, nods again, and enters Kia's flat.

They're opening up to Kia?! Attraction flips the metaphorical table, *After the thing they did!?*

Growth, change, just like they're meant to. Nature adds.

It's not unprecedented, I mean, we should have seen it coming after their breakdown. Time chimes in.

Still, I didn't think they had it in them. Attraction remarks snidely.

*The beauty within them had been set free by Roni. Free to emote, to sense, to be the Toni they always **really** wanted to be. No longer bound by fear.* Feeling explained.

...Right. What Feelsie said. Time comments.

Well, I hope this means they'll no longer speak ill of Kia, as they are in the midst of rectifying things. Attraction says, with what would be her nose turned up.

Oh, don't worry, I did bank on this one after all. Time reassures.

That's what I am afraid of... Attraction sighs.

Toni's eyes are stormy whirlpools with bright blue and purple sparks emanating from their eyes like fireworks, "I wish I could just cry real tears." They rub their nose with their wrist, looking rather like a cat.

"I know, lovely. I know." Kia says, taking Toni's hands in hers across her tabletop, "It just doesn't hit the same way."

Toni nods and rubs Kia's hands with their thumbs, "It's just so crazy, you know? I thought I'd forgotten all of that, like, let it go to the point where it existed just outside of my thoughts; a ghost."

"And now you came back haunted." Kia shoots rapidly, as if it were pre-loaded.

"Yeah, something like that." Toni says slightly.

"I know what you mean, though, it's been like that for me. Like, I had some stuff resurface and it's like I'm remembering things I didn't even know I forgot. But it, and Roni, helped me get the courage to go up to you like I did." Kia explains.

Toni sits back in their chair, "Interesting, so then, I got Roni to thank for this whole... thing. Good to know."

Kia smiles and sucks her teeth, "Yeah, our mutual—" she pauses and fixes her gaze on Toni's eyes, "*friend*. They are just a friend right? You haven't—"

"—Kia! Stop," Toni laughs, "we totally did. And you know it. You know me."

"You slut!" Kia exclaims with a chortle, "not that I'm slut shaming. But you're such a man whore."

"I know, shut up. But I'm *your* man whore now, or whatever."

Kia gasps playfully, "*Mine*? Oh, really, bitch? Now you're *my* man whore, okay."

Tony crosses their arms and gives Kia a stoic look, "Ahuh."

A number of moments of silence falls between the pair as they gauge each other and meld energies. Toni had opened himself up to Kia, bleeding and raw emotion, displaying all of the ugly and tragic for Kia to absorb into herself. Kia had been receptive and empathetic, sweet and supportive, and overall, full of unconditional love. It had been an experience that Toni feared but never knew he needed. And they absolutely needed this particular catharsis.

"Toni?" Kia's voice like warm silk.

"Yeah, babe?"

"I had no idea you had hurt so bad. I'm so sorry."

"Ah, don't worry about it. I'm still sorry I hurt you like I did, knowing you had some issues around abandonment."

Kia exhales sharply, "You didn't know everything, I didn't know everything until I remembered it after Roni."

Toni scratches their head, "Roni seems to be at the centre of all of this, huh? Anyway, yeah, we didn't know everything and we made mistakes, but honestly, I fucked up a lot worse. I'm lucky you even gave me the chance to talk."

Kia taps her nose, "You know, Roni *is* at the epicentre of all the things. And, sweetness, I wanted to give you a chance. I was pulling a you when I confronted you, baiting you like you did with me. Except, you know, more aggressive, el-oh-el."

"You're such a bitch!" Toni erupts in a hearty chuckle, "Wow, you fucked me up on purpose? You and me, we're done professionally."

"Professionally, huh? What about, *un*professionally? Also, is that from something? That line sounds familiar."

Toni shrugs, "Not that I'd ever heard before. But yeah, uh, I can dig being unprofessional with you."

Moments later, a heated exchange takes place in Kia's bedroom. They had kissed and ripped off each other's clothes on the way up the stairs, down to their undergarments. Kia breaks the kiss and gives Toni a strong, desire-filled glare that would murder the weakest of men, which sends shivers down Toni's spine and causes them to do that lip biting thing as they scan their eyes up and down Kia's voluptuous, curvy body. Kia smirks and lets out a delighted "*hm*", then shoves Toni down onto her bed. Toni falls, legs kicking up and splaying askew, then backs up on the bed before being stopped by a leaning Kia whomst reaches and grabs a handful of Toni's thick black hair and kisses them hard, bites the lower lip, lets it go, then moves on to Toni's neck. Toni gasps and moans, hands planted firmly behind them, holding themself up for Kia who then pushes them onto their back and kisses down their body, slowly and sensually, flicking her tongue along their nipples and down their soft, but defined abs, navel, and hip. Kia looks up and smiles, her fingers curling around the waistband of Toni's underwear, pulling and she kisses and nibbles Toni's protruding hips. She pulls their underwear off at a steady pace, keeping up with light kisses down their legs to their toes. Kia kisses Toni's long, lovely toes, their slender, shapely feet, their dainty ankles, back up their legs, tracing to the inner thighs and pulling them to the edge of the bed by their hips as she gets down on her knees for leverage and comfort. They catch each other's gaze just before Kia holds her mouth agape, tongue ready, while Toni throws their head back and grips the sheets tightly. A sharp inhale, an audible exhale with a hint of "*ah*".

And by this point you'd guess what happens next. Oh, don't fuss, you should know by now that I don't get fully into it—as Kia just did. Now, as your imagination runs wild, we'll take a moment to unwind, if you will. We've earned a break.

Oh good, you're back. Let's have a look, shall we? Kia and Toni are as we had just been; unwinding. Toni manifests a cigarette, takes a long drag, gazes over at Kia whomst is admiring Toni's all, and smiles. There's something different about Toni's smile, there's an absence of something. There's an absence of sorrow, of doubt, of guilt. It, while a simple and soft, loving smile, was beaming, filled with satisfaction and adoration. It was *filled*. A sensation they'd not felt in ages, it seemed; to be filled, to be full, to lack absence or want or need. It was new, it was exciting. Toni didn't know what to make of it, but they knew that it wasn't something to fear or even make a spectacle of, it was something to accept and live with. It was a sensation unknown to all of the other Strandlers, as the reason for their being in The Stranding was an endless longing and unfathomable emptiness that they could only hope to fill with an eternity and the freedom to create without judgement or discouragement. A fact unbeknownst to all that end up in this plane. The duality of it all.

"So, what's the deal with you and Roni?" Toni asks plainly and cooly.

"Dubya-Y-Em—erm, what you mean?" Kia responds.

"Like, what are you two? Like, lovers? That queer platonic thing?" They trail off.

Kia throws herself back and huffs, "Why does it have to be like that? It goes deeper than that."

"Deeper?" Toni sits up, furrowing his brow.

"Roni's like my mother, a master... Half of me belongs to them." Kia states seriously.

"Do you love them? Like..." Toni pushes.

"Nothing like *that*, does it have to be one or the other?" Kia says slightly annoyed and exasperated.

"I mean, usually. But I know that you ain't like everybody." Toni backs off.

"Roni is the most beautiful, artistic, fully human, eccentric person with such a balanced duality of sorrow and joy that you'd only see beneath the waves of cool and in the glints within their eyes that I'd ever met." Kia's mind wanders nostalgically.

Toni drops down on their stomach and rests their head on their hands, "I know what you mean. There's just something about them that draws you in and changes you. It's so weird, like, you get all confused by the way they love you that you end up thinking it's something else, and they oblige you, until I guess you figure it out and then they accept where you stand with them and love you in that way."

"Yeah, pretty cray—zy. Wait, have you—?" Kia glances over at Toni.

"I'm figuring it out now. Between you and them, Ki, I've realised that I was seeing them all wrong. I was so obsessed with how they gave me space to be me, to be free, to talk and express, that I selfishly turned that into the kinda love that you mix with sex. I made it shallow, when, like you said, it goes deeper..." Toni stops short, falling into a thought.

Kia turns to their side to face Toni and smiles big, "You're getting it. I can see it," her voice sing-songy, "you're glowing, you're connecting!"

"Kia," Toni sits up, struggling awkwardly on what he perceives as a plain white bed, "I, uh," they shift their eyes around, fidgeting with their fingers, "Kia, I wanna **strand** with you."

WHOA!! Who had money on that? I know I didn't. Time throws their limb-like product up in the space around them and wobbles them everywhere.

Shocking! Toni and my Kia? I wish I could have thrown a wrench in that... Attraction shakes what can be mistaken as her head.

I saw it coming. It was a highly probable and innate connection. Nature shrugs.

Honestly, Attraction, it's not fair of you to write Toni off like that. Your distaste for them is kind of unfounded at this point. They were hurt, and hurt people hurt people. Kia forgave them, why can't you? Feeling implores.

It was going to happen, it had to. Whether you like it or not, Attraction, these things are bound to happen. Can't fight it. Chance condescends.

Ugh, well, still. Amends don't erase sins. But whatever. Attraction gives in.

Time, still wobbling around and dancing back and forth, sings, *Can't win them all Atty.*

Vocalisations in smooth alto to falsetto fill the air inside Roni's flat; a voice that is not, in fact, Roni's, but Sam's. Sam steps down the stairs singing ala Christine from ***The Phantom of the Opera***—if it were a robe Christine was wearing, and not a beautiful gown. Roni had been tinkering in their studio and upon hearing Sam's voice, popped their head out in wonderment and awe and the deliciously goosebump inducing saccharine notes that inundated their ears with bliss and infatuation.

"Oh, my gods. Sam, your voice!" Roni exclaims.

Sam snaps out of their singing abruptly, "Huh? Oh, yeah I dabble with singing."

"Dabble? Bitch, you're amazing! You're like opera meets pop-punk! Your range, your tone, you're so smooth and buttery but powerful and chilling." Roni praises Sam scrambling out of their studio and over toward Sam, meeting them in the living area.

"Oh, *shah*, stop. I'm not that good." Sam blushes, having had their hands snatched by Roni.

"I have to record you. I have to write a song just for you. You're the missing ingredient! You're exactly what I need."

"Just for my voice?" Sam cocks an eyebrow.

Roni turns red and stammers, "No, uh, n-no. Of course, not just for your voice. You embody your voice, your voice the—the beautiful spectre that haunts the immaculate palace that is your..." Roni does a weird low growling screech trying to find the right word, "everything."

Sam chuckles lightly, "Nice save."

"Thanks, I sorta winged it." Roni shrugs.

"Oh, yeah? I wouldn't have guessed."

"I know, I'm that good. Sincere, though."

Sam shakes their head with a smirk, "Aha, I'm so sure."

"Stop!" Roni says playfully, "I'm serious! It's true, it is. I mean it. Stop looking at me like that. Sam, please, you're being a bitch, how dare you?"

Sam scoffs with a feigned attitude, "Oh, ho-ho, first I'm immaculate, now I'm a bitch. I see how it is, Roni. What's next?"

Roni's face drops and becomes sullen and solemn, "On the battlefield, you never think about what's next."

Sam's face says amusement mixed with bewilderment, "What's that from? Is that from a book?"

"Fuck if I know," Roni throws their hands up, "it just kind of came to me, like something I might have experienced before. Like, *before*, before."

Sam shifts their stance, favouring their left side, a look of contemplation upon their face, "You've been halfway remembering stuff too?"

"*Halfway remembering* is a good way to put it. Yeah, it's hitting me every so often. And like, names of songs or bands always hit the tip of my tongue but then just get bitten off short. It would be frustrating if I didn't somehow immediately forget and move on. It's strange." Roni explains.

"It definitely *is* strange. Book titles, movie titles, just randomly saying a line that plays off a situation as a reference to something that's weirdly familiar, yet totally escapes me." Sam relates.

"Yes! That too! Oh, my gods, I remember when I first got here and met Kia, we were talking about a book that apparently became movies but I only remember the books and that there was going to be a movie..." Roni adds, "It was a vampire thing. They, uh, don't hunt people and I guess, instead of burning in the sun they—"

"—Sparkle!" Sam interrupts.

"Yeah! You know it too?" Roni asks excitedly.

"I do! I remember reading them and loving them and being excited for the upcoming movie, but I can't remember what *exactly* it is!" Sam crosses their arms in frustration.

You can infer the *Saga* they're referencing; Twilight, which indeed was spoken about and mentioned by name before. But that was *before*. The *fog* of The Plane of the Forgotten hadn't settled into their brains completely yet. Yes, **Brain Fog** is absolutely a thing in the *unreality*; a forgetting of things, a distracting from things, a hyper focusing on things that leads to a neglecting of things.

"Anyway, Sam, I have to bring you into my booth. We gotta record, stat." Roni circles back.

"What booth, I can't see what you see, remember? Your place is just a blank space, baby." Sam responds.

"Right, fuck. Well," Roni hesitates before reluctantly asking with the fear of being rejected, "you, uh, wanna **strand**?"

Sam sucks in a deep breath, eyes fix on Roni's in the Kubrick stare fashion, and then exhale with a short blow.

Chapter 10 - Seen Love Die, Seen You Cry

*Why **is** Roni so desperate for connection?* Attraction inquires sharply.

They never had it, not anything real, at least. Time responds.

Are we taking another trip to the past to observe the memories of another unfortunate Strandler that's had to suffer? The suffering really hurts me, even if it fuels me. Feeling adds.

I'm honestly intrigued to see all of the instances that led Roni here, to this moment, and will lead them to their fate. Chance says with mild excitement.

This is no ordinary Strandler, this is the bringer of Darkness. Nature states.

__The__ Darkness—and we don't know that yet. Time insists.

Chance opens their harbinger of vocality to speak but is quickly interrupted by Attraction, *Shut up, Chance. We don't want to hear it.*

I was just going to say—

—Stop hooting, spoiler nocturnal bird of prey. Nature snaps.

Is that from something? That sounds like it's from something. Feeling says, curiously.

Some angry game channel on the human internet's video tube. Time explains before saying, *Now shush, the show's about to start.*

Time wiggles its bits in the atmosphere and opens a dark rectangle with rounded edges which expands and suddenly turns on with a horizontal flash that opens to a white light with a pleasant, but eerie sound that pauses for a moment, which makes the Forces lean forward in anticipation, and then fades to black with a softer slightly more haunting sound and logo in the centre of the screen that is 'RONI' rearranged to look like a three-dimensional figure.

The logo dissipates to a black screen that fades in a woman in a busy hospital hallway, pregnant, and waving down a nurse from a gurney.

"Hey! I'm giving birth here!" The woman shouted.

A nurse turned and rushed to her, "Are you sure? You don't seem like you're in pain."

"This isn't my first time," she said, irritated, "but I'm telling you, I'm giving birth. Right now. Look!" The woman showed the nurse that the baby was crowning under her gown.

"Oh! You *are* giving birth! Let's get you in a room," she grabbed the woman's gurney and shouted down the hallway, "get the doctor, this woman's baby is about to fall out!"

"Don't make me laugh, he'll fly out!" The woman chortled shortly.

"It's a boy! What's the name?" The nurse said.

"I'll name him after his father..." The woman responded.

"Where *is* the father?" Asked the nurse.

"Away," the woman looked down, disappointed, "working in the states."

"Dad! Look, can I have this?" Young Roni asked.

"What? No. Not today." Their father responded.

They were at a K-Mart, walking by the toy section along with Roni's older brother who saw the Star Wars toy that Roni wanted and grabbed it and showed their father, "Can I have this? It's my favourite. You know I love Star Wars, dad, please?"

"Put it in the cart." The father responded.

Roni stopped walking and watched their brother and father for a moment, having not believed what just happened. Their father agreed to buy their brother the same toy they were denied moments before.

This trend would continue throughout Roni's formative years. Be it toys, musical instruments, or video game consoles, they were told no while their brothers were told yes. Roni had five older brothers, each of them loved differently and seemingly 'more' than Roni.

At many points, Roni's mother would actually let her kids go outside to play in the expansive grounds of the projects, these grounds were mostly green, and there was room for all kinds of play, but Roni's two youngest older brothers would want to go elsewhere.

"You can't come." They'd say sometimes, others they'd just flat out leave Roni behind to chase their whims.

Roni would find things to do alone, not far from the kitchen door; finding pill bugs, attempting pull ups on the metal pole that held the clothesline, or just sitting alone, waiting.

Sitting and waiting while alone would be a recurring event.

"What do you want for your birthday? You're about to turn 11!" Roni's mother said.

"I want a Dreamcast, Bernando doesn't let me play his so I want my own." Roni responded.

The mother nodded.

Later, for their birthday, they're given a Boombox and a Sega Genesis v3—the small one—and was taken to a pawn shop to pick out three 2–5-dollar games.

Why does my brother get a guitar, the other one gets the things I ask for first, and the other two get money for whatever, but I get this? They point to the Sega, price tag still on that reads $19.99. *It doesn't seem fair,* they thought to themself.

Now, one would immediately look at the situation and say something about being grateful for what you're given and not comparing oneself to others around you, but in their lifetime, Roni was constantly compared to their brothers, to family friends, to anyone really. That, and give some regard to the fact that there were clear preferences in Roni's household when it came to the siblings. Roni had five siblings, yes, but only lived with four of them, which were very close in age in pairs—about a year apart. Let's explain; one and two were ten months and seventeen days apart, three and four were twelve months, two weeks and two days apart exactly. One and two are three and four years older than three and four respectively. Brother zero was living in Puerto Rico and was fifteen years older. All of this meaning, Roni was isolated. Their youngest elder brother was five years older, so you can do the maths on the rest. They were each other's best friends and rivals and enemies at certain points, while with Roni, if they were anything, most of the encounters were apathetic or antagonistic.

With their parents—they each had their favourite sons which tiered all the way down to Roni at the bottom of the barrel. That's also when they deigned to show their kids any affection or attention. Roni's father worked two full-time jobs and had a not-so-secret after work life with a mistress. Roni's mother was too busy entertaining her friends, talking on the phone, and later being on internet chat forums to be a functioning parent outside of cooking and cleaning. The only time that Roni's parents brought them anywhere was as a 'family' trip to a department store or those few times where Roni's mother went hunting for their father in the middle of the night, waking them from a deep sleep and throwing them in the car. The *hunting* was to catch Roni's father in the act of adultery. Why she felt an eight-year-old needed to experience that escapes even me, and I know everything.

After their parents' divorce, the gloves that always seemed to be off really came off. The second eldest would be even more unhinged with Roni *and* their mother, with unprovoked insults, microaggressive comments about Roni's appearance and voice, threats toward both of them, and an overall hostility. Roni's father had become more distant, got fired from his jobs on purpose to avoid paying too much in child support, meanwhile working under-the-table jobs. On one occasion, Roni had gone over to their father's flat to visit with him and their brothers and found the fishtank they had had broken with pebbles and ornaments and glass scattered everywhere.

They had heard of an altercation with their father and second eldest brother where their brother had smashed a coffee carafe over their father's head to stop a rampage. Another day, after school, while hauling a baritone saxophone that Roni had played in middle school band— they were quite good, it was how they found joy in music and performing—arriving at the door to their father's flat, their father had opened the door to them and glared with a scowl,

"What are you doing here? You chose your mother. Go home. I don't want to see you again! Go!" He bellowed with scorn.

Roni held their tears in and walked—hauling that saxophone that was about their size—to their third-floor flat with their mother, whomst was preoccupied with the internet, and closed themself up in their room, dropping the saxophone and throwing themself on the mattress that sat on the floor.

They never cried. They just held it in, all of it.

After that, they never went over to their father's flat again. Their mother had tried to make their father come around, he'd promise to come and take Roni out, but would never show up. Roni sat by the window, looking outside to catch their father's car coming, but it never came. For a long while, day in and day out, Roni would sit and wait for someone who never came.

Then their mother had moved them again to another flat further from where their father and brothers lived, and Roni had regained contact with their father, if only for rides to the grocery where he'd drop them off to walk the aisles picking food from a list and some that wasn't on the list, again alone to then pick them up a half hour after they'd called to let him know they were done. And so, Roni sat and waited.

In Roni's teen years, they'd been accustomed to loneliness, to the waiting, to the absence of warmth. They'd begun their obsession with music, video games, and with social media sites in their infancy—their only connection to others.

Roni's social conditioning—or lack thereof—by their family had left them awkward and uncommunicative in person and thus didn't have many friends if at all until high school; two best friends that they'd bonded with over anime and video games, and by proxy, extended friends and acquaintances that they'd been introduced to through those two *bffs*. Outside of that, they thrived online, even flirted. They could be who they wished they could be in *reality*.

Unfortunately, those connections weren't enough to stave off *The Darkness* inside of them that silently festered and metastasized into an insidious depression. It was the kind of depression that masqueraded as a numbness, a *grey* feeling that was easily masked with fake smiles and forced, learned reactive laughter.

A depression that kept them stuck before a screen, living vicariously through virtual characters and feigned interactions with strangers online—a learned behaviour. Roni had always been an observer, learning how to human correctly by watching others, by watching television and movies—sitcoms and romcoms so that they could mimic typical social behaviour—which made them very adept at masking, as well as a complete disregard for themself that was beat into them by their life; they'd rather make sure others are comfortable and taken care of than their own comfort, which they'd learned was what they were made for, or so they'd resigned to.

For a long while, Roni ended up taking on the role of parent, of themself and their mother. They raised themself through consumption of media, mimicry, and trial and error. Meanwhile, their mother's emotional and physical state continued to decline, and they'd had to take care of her, try to comfort her, keep her from falling whenever her body decided to fail, go to the *bodega* and buy her cigarettes—as a young teen, mind you—et cetera, et cetera, I could go on.

School had become irrelevant, to the point where they attended two or three times a week and came up with excuses which their mother never investigated beyond face value. They'd been forced to abandon band since their high school didn't have a saxophone available and their parents refused to buy one, which led to a further decline in grades, attendance, and emotional stability. *The Darkness* was growing, though you'd never see it on their face.

Later, Roni had thought they'd been in love. A girl had stolen her way into their heart by becoming a walking collage of Roni's special interests; the alt scene—goth and punk aesthetics, Roni would hate if you'd call it 'emo'—music of that scene with bands like Killswitch Engage, Slipknot, Korn, HIM, AFI, My Chemical Romance, Linkin Park—artists and bands that helped them through the depression and the grey, their isolation and solitude; she didn't like Radiohead, by the way—, anime, and video games. She feigned interest and knew enough to get by and fool Roni while distracting them with the attention they never had, making them feel as though they were finally loved by someone in a way that was deeper than just a connection of special interests. Someone had wanted to hold their heart and fill it with warmth, or so they were led to believe.

Soon, though, she would show her true self, but it would be too late, for Roni would be much too invested and isolated from anyone that could help them get out from under her to leave. She'd insult them, accuse them of cheating, strike them, belittle them and their identity as queer, saying it was an abomination and that they were greedy for being pansexual.

Thus far, it's worth noting, Roni had lived as their assigned gender at birth, though they always felt an inkling that they weren't that at all.

She eventually left Roni—in pieces. Roni tried reconnecting with friends, but they wouldn't oblige, having been neglected through Roni's systemic isolation by their former partner. Instead, they wandered the city on foot as much as they could with music cranked up to eleven in their ears when they weren't burying their attention in immersive games like Fable, Oblivion, and Metal Gear Solid, even enthralling adventures in Hyrule through The Legend of Zelda.

They met another love interest, this time they'd sought her out on a whim, she'd been attractive and seemed interesting and kind and not someone who would falsify interests to hook someone and manipulate them. And that, and that alone, she was indeed. But she came from a background of financial privilege with parents that didn't much care for Puerto Ricans—Roni had often had a complicated relationship with their identity to begin with, and it was interactions like these that made it worse. This fact caused tension in many of their interactions, interactions that contained microaggressions and passive-aggressive remarks about Roni's heritage. The girl herself partook in these remarks from time to time, admitting that she'd usually hate Roni's *kind*, but that Roni was *different*, and that somehow made it acceptable to say such things.

After a few months of a 'hot and cold' relationship—having essentially been living together—, things began escalating to levels that mirrored Roni's childhood. The arguments, the thrown plates, the screaming and insulting, the hitting began. Again, Roni felt trapped in a situation they didn't know how to get out of. A situation that became increasingly abusive with the added bonus of gaslighting, a technique she was rather adept at.

Things came to a head on a night when Roni's mother was visiting a friend when Roni broke and threw her iniquities in her face, causing her to become violent and strike Roni's head in an attempt to get them to hit back.

"You should just kill yourself!" She screamed.

"Why don't you? Since you're so unhappy with me." Roni said.

That response elicited a glare and a sharp, "Maybe I will, then you'd have my death be your fault."

She then took a bottle of benzodiazepines from her bag— she intended to stay the night—and sat in front of Roni, opened it, and started taking them one by one, while yelling and spitting. When that didn't elicit a reaction, she called her mother on her cell phone and told her that Roni had told her to kill herself, so she was swallowing pills to overdose. Roni sighed and tried to get her to stop, but she wouldn't, and she fought back before locking herself in Roni's bedroom and continuing with the false attempt. Roni managed to get into the room and wrestled the pills from her while she sat unresponsively staring into space until her parents showed up, then she got up and gathered a few of her things and left.

Roni never saw her again.

They had other lovers here and there, but those two had left them numb to the idea of romantic love, seeking only physical sensation and gratification with a shallow connection that was only enough to keep their interests. But they, too, left eventually. Roni couldn't give them what they wanted, and they couldn't fill the hole inside Roni. But still, Roni craved a connection, they just didn't know what kind and how anymore, it's the only reason they kept looking for lovers, for friends, for anyone. But no one would be enough, no one could eradicate the darkness that had been growing inside of them.

Roni had wanted to sing their heart out, to purge through their voice, but their voice had been silenced time and time again by those that claimed to love them and those who were supposed to. They didn't know what they would truly sound like because they hadn't been allowed to explore their voice. Everyone had put so much effort in telling them their voice was worthless, awful, and unwanted, that it wouldn't get them anywhere. One lover, though, was soothed by their voice and sought it out as much as she could, but Roni had a hard time believing her. They used their voice regardless, as it would be what she wanted and that's all that mattered.

The time came that Roni realised who they were, their truth and vied to pursue it. They'd secretly try on their mother's clothes, remembering having done so as a smaller child, they'd put on makeup and style their hair then immediately shower so that their mother wouldn't see. They'd play along with what their mother's image of them was while she was around, but experiment when she wasn't or when she was in a depression nap, which was often.

One day, on the second day of the tenth month in the seventh year of the second millennium, they decided to confide in their mother about their identity.

"*Mami*, I need to talk to you." they said.

"*Que paso, papi?*" she responded.

"You know how I always wanted to keep my hair long—"

"*Si, como los rockeros y tus hermanos.*"

"Yeah, sure. Uh, but not really. So, ever since I was little, I always wanted to dress like—well, like whatever. I used to sneak upstairs and put on your heels and walk around, try on your pantyhose, stuff like that." Roni explained.

"Okay, that's normal, kids do crazy things sometimes."

"I mean, sure. But like, it wasn't because of that though. Lately, I've been doing it again—actually, it's been months! And with your foundation and eyeliner too."

Their mother gawked at them in slight disbelief, anticipating an unpleasant revelation, "Ahuh..."

"So, I've been reading and talking to people online and seeing stuff on TV about it and I think I know why. And it makes sense, and it makes sense why I always hated how I looked and hated picking out clothes and all of that; never felt comfortable."

"*Papi*, you can't go trusting people on the internet, they try to trick you, to confuse you. And the TV is all sorts of crazy things." She tried to keep her cool, her voice getting shaky from adrenaline.

"I know that, but I know this information is true, I looked on official websites, *Mami*. I'm not gullible."

She shifted in her seat uncomfortably, fidgeting with her hands, "Okay..."

"*Mami...*" they hesitated, "I'm transgender. I'm not a boy, Ma. I don't feel like I'm a girl either like a lot of the transgender people online, but I know that I don't feel like a boy, and I never have. Also, please don't call me by the name you gave me, I want to be called Roni." they had managed out nervously.

Now, I wish I could tell you that it was a warm and fuzzy reaction of acceptance and love, but I'd be an unreliable narrator if I did. Instead, Roni's mother's anger bubbled and exploded, she might as well have been a volcano, or even visibly red.

"No. Absolutely not, no. You're my son. You're a boy, you were born a boy, you're going to live as a boy, you're going to die as a boy. *No me hagas esto.*"

Roni's mouth was slightly agape, and their eyes began to glaze with tears that never actually flowed, "Ma, I'm not a boy. I'm telling you. And what do you mean? I'm not doing anything to *you*."

"I didn't raise you to be like this. I didn't raise you to be some-some *thing*! No! *Callate!* I don't want to look at you right now. I don't want to hear you anymore. Don't talk to me!"

"*Mami...* Please, why can't you see me how I am?"

"How you are? You're crazy! You're insane! '*Not a boy*'?! Then you're not my son because I didn't raise you to be whatever you are!"

Roni became angered by her continued refusal to accept them, "You didn't raise me at all! I was alone! *Mami*, I was alone all these years, you were never there for me! You weren't there for me when my brothers would hit me or insult me—hurt me! You weren't there when my exes would do the same! You weren't there when dad would make me feel worthless and unwanted! You were never there, Ma!"

She slapped Roni, "*Tu no me faltas el respeto asi, carajo!* How dare you? I am your mother! You respect your mother!"

Roni held their face, "You're not even here now, when I need you, because you hurt me. You don't respect me, you don't love me, you don't accept me. Why am I here?"

"You're here because I gave birth to you, to a *boy*. I do love you, but I don't love what you think you are; I don't accept it."

"Then it's like I said, you don't love me, you don't accept me. It's okay, I know it's hard to love. You don't have to worry about it though, Ma. It'll be okay, like I never said anything..." they said, before thinking to themself, *like I never even existed...*

The thoughts and voices they had managed to keep silent and locked away in the back of their mind and in the deepest dungeon within their heart had started surfacing all at once. *I want to die; I have to die.* They repeated over and over in their thoughts in a plethora of variations all meaning the same thing; the end of everything. They obsessed over the notion of not only dying but disappearing from existence altogether—never having been born at all. They had watched the film, **The Butterfly Effect**, a few dozen times—the director's cut, mind you—and wished they could be able to do what the main character had managed to do. Not only that, but erase the conception completely, thus not having ever caused anyone any inconvenience, themself pain, even before having been brought into living.

It had been the string that broke Link's back, the cheese wheel that caused an over-encumbrance, their mother's reaction and venomous words. I use silly idioms as comparisons to diffuse the and lighten the gravitas of the moment. The truth of the matter, ugly and solemn as it is, is that Roni had held in so much and held together through all of the adversity, agony, and sorrow of their life for what seemed like an eternity, often feeling as though they'd been born for the sole purpose of carrying the burdens and pains of others and absorbing them—as well as their abuse—to absolve them of it. To Roni, everyone that had shattered and destroyed them, left them in desolation, used them until they felt better about themselves and moved on, had come out of their parasitic relationship with Roni better than they entered it. The ex-lovers had found significant others that they actually cared for and loved, the ex-friends lived full and fun lives with other friends that they had actually wanted to spend time with their brothers were doing fine without a care in the world. Even their parents always seemed to be in higher spirits after having had a volatile interaction with them.

But it was this interaction that broke Roni beyond repair, it cracked the mask and left them unable to find any other to replace it. They'd become desperate, trying to recover, trying to stop the bleeding through, the flood that was behind them had finally caught up and put out the fire inside them and there was nothing Roni could do to stop the downward spiral.

The Darkness had begun its consumption.

It took exactly twenty-eight hours, forty-two minutes and thirty-seven seconds for Roni to decide what they were going to do. Their existence had been denied, their identity invalidated and hated, their feelings subverted, and in response, they'd give into that denial and subversion of their self. It had to end. *I have to die,* they resigned. So, they threw on Radiohead's *'Fake Plastic Trees'* on their Sansa Sandisk MP3 player as they wrote The Letter—the one that would look like a poem as all the others that came before that either went unread and tossed out, or dismissed as bad *'emo'* poetry—, earbuds in, with an ominous calm that radiated death.

"I've seen a place," they started, "in my dreams, my daydreams..." Roni trailed off for a moment, then continued, "in between here and there. It feels like freedom. It feels and looks like, I don't know, I guess, heaven?

"It's strange because I only see it when I'm not actually seeing, through the periphery and, like," they groan in frustration, "I want to go there. I want to disappear completely."

Just then, *'How to Disappear Completely'* faded into their ears, as if beckoned by Roni's words. *I want to go there,* they thought again and again.

They stripped in front of the bathroom mirror, looked themself over with disdain and discomfort, the song still playing while the tub filled with hot water, and then slowly stepped into the bathtub. It was scalding, the water, a normal person wouldn't be able to steep like a bag of tea in this boiling human-sized cup. Roni had what they needed laid out on the side of the bathtub, they reached for their instrument and reasoned with it, admired it, hated it and loved it for what it meant at this moment. It was a release for them, a cure for the neverending pain of being. It meant never having to hurt again.

Exit Music (For A Film) faded into their ears as they faded out of consciousness.

On the third day of the tenth month in the seventh year of the second millennium, Roni ceased to exist. But not the way they had intended.

Roni faded into The Plane of the Forgotten, noticing their music gone, being clothed and unwet, laying on the black grass below, they opened their eyes to see the magenta—or perhaps, fuschia—sky above. They smiled as they got up on their feet and watched the azure, wispy cotton candy clouds cover the ultraviolet twilight.

"Here comes the rain again..."

I couldn't just let them die. Time states apologetically.
   Of course not, then Dar—The Darkness would have consumed them and— Feeling stops themself.
   Which would not end well for anyone involved, considering... Attraction adds.
   The screen goes dark and disapparates.

Chapter 11 - Rather Waste Some Time With Blue, And Yellow, Too: Part One

I'm so sorry you had to cry to be heard
And I'm sorrowed that you suffered so
That you could never hold a candle to others
And everyone just seemed so much better
I'm so sorry you were abandoned, time and time again
That they all just left you behind and forgot to care
You were screamed at, thrown things at, belittled
And you wondered why you were even kept around
I wish I could tell you it gets better with time
I wish I could lie to you and tell you people change
The only thing that's true is that it's you that rises
It's and always you that deserved so much better
You watched from so far away, everything unfold without you
You watched from the shadows as the fires destroyed it all
And then you were pulled away and isolated just to be left again
No one was ever there to hold you close and comfort you
I'm so sorry you had to learn to soothe yourself
And I'm sorry you had to fight for anyone to care
You were made to be so grown while still so very young
Acting like the husband lost you never wanted to be
I wish I could tell you it gets better with time
I wish I could lie to you and tell you people change
The only thing that's true is that it's you that rises
It's and always you that deserved so much better

You threw yourself into people recklessly
In hopes of finding someone that could bring any warmth
You cared too much, you gave too much
In the end they took from you and left like they always do
I'm so fucking sorry you had to learn to be lonely
Craving any form of love you could find
Like a starving dog given scraps to be kept along
You stayed, abused, hurting inside out of fear
Afraid to lose what little bit of affection
The kind you never had before
I'm sorry, I'm so goddamn sorry
I'm so fucking sorry it was me

Sam's haunting vocals fill the recording booth, a sombre and sour piano with sparse percussive synths accompanying the backtrack. Roni wipes away a tear as the last note fades and claps, praising Sam's perfect performance. Sam clasps their hands together and crinkles their nose with excitement and pride and takes off the headphones and hangs them on the microphone before them.

Sam hurries over to Roni and asks, "So? How'd I do? I can't believe that was all one take!"

A smile grows slowly on Roni's face, "It was perfect, love. You were immaculate. I damn near sobbed."

Sam throws their arms around Roni and squeals happily, "That's amazing. I'm so glad. And I had you to work with! So don't count yourself out of the perfection 'cause I couldn't have done it without you."

"I only added the music and the words. You gave it all life and soul." Roni says bashfully.

Sam playfully shoves Roni's shoulder, "Stop, you're amazing. Your words already had life. And the music! Oh, my god, the music is so good."

There's a silence between them for a while as they stand in the studio admiring each other but also feeling the sting of the subject matter.

Finally, Sam says softly while grabbing Roni's hands, "I'm so sorry all of that happened to you *out there*. No one should have to go through what you went through."

They hug and Roni tries to downplay with a shrug, "It's what brought me here and inspired me to make music. So, it's more a blessing than a curse."

Sam frowns and shakes their head, "No, Roni. You had that inside you always. It may have brought you here, but you were always brilliant. I'm just sad it took you disappearing for anyone to see it."

"Yeah, well. I mean," Roni scratches their head, "that's how we all got here, isn't it? That seems to be the theme. Being unseen, being unheard, left behind and *forgotten*."

Well, they seem to be catching on... Attraction comments.

Yes, that could be a problem at some point. Why don't we— Nature starts.

We cannot meddle more than we already have, especially that invasively. It wouldn't be right. Says Feeling.

I could tell you what this brings— Chance teases.

Enough! Time exclaims sharply with a hint of fury before returning to its usual, jovial demeanour, *We can't erase whole thoughts and experiences, only ones tied to things not forgotten. It's a thin line, but we don't cross it. Erasing whole trains of thought and manipulating experiences is forbidden for a reason, it would betray what we're trying to build; it would strip them of freedom.*

Okay, I understand, Time. But it's troublesome, can't you see? We've never had anyone have so much clarity or insight into The Plane like Roni does. Attraction pleads her case.

Time replies curtly, but calmly, *Atty, I will not have you question me, we will not discuss this further. Whatever may come, my dear siblings, is what is meant to in the end. Everything ends, even you, even I...*

"Your apartment is beautiful!" Kia says of Toni's flat as she twirls around the open, empty living area with her arms out like wings.

Toni's cheeks become flush, and they stroke the length of their hair, "Thank you. That... Well, it means a lot. My apartment is my soul if my soul was a home, y'know?"

Kia turns to face Toni, dropping her arms to her sides and grinning so widely that her eyes close joyfully, "Aw, Toni. Your soul *is* a home. To me, at least."

Toni smirks a little, just enough that a crease forms on their left cheek and sucks their teeth before saying flirtatiously, "You're sweet on me, ain't ya?"

"Oh, stop. You know I am." Kia scoffs lightly.

Toni closes the gap between them and Kia, "Well, babe, I'm sweet on you, too."

Kia turns her face down a moment, then her eyes, large and glistening, change into a bright violet, up to meet Toni's neon cerulean, "I know that too, bae."

"You're beautiful..." Toni whispers breathily as he takes her chin with their forefinger and thumb, his lips drawing closer to Kia's.

"Yeah, but..." She says quietly, brushing her lips on his, "you are too."

Their lips meet delicately, pressing and caressing; dancing perfectly in tune with one another.

I think we made a mistake, initially. Time admits.

With what, exactly? Attraction inquires sarcastically.

With trying to set either of these two with Roni instead of realising how perfect they are with each other. Time explains.

Yes, well— Attraction starts.

You weren't using your sentiments, your hearts. You were thinking too much. Feeling interjects.

Either way, they wouldn't have been "perfect" without Roni's interference. Attraction states with her usual cutting attitude.

After those sweet and lovely moments between the two pairs, a sort of *invisible* pull that seemed to compel them, as if someone or some*thing* had tied their strands together and tugged at the knot until finally, they'd come together at the centre of The Stranding; the theatre entrance, to be exact. It felt natural, of course, the *Force* that beckoned their union. An idea, a passive nudge, the image of cinema, a passing comment; all of those happening across their individual paths like a serendipitous circumstance. Though one knows not a thing happens here by coincidence.

The neverending twilight above had been shadowed by ink blotted clouds highlighted with chartreuse lightning that clung to them with the ferocity of a screaming baby in its mother's chest. Screaming, it would seem, was what the thunder sounded like. A sort of deep bellow more than a scream, though it did have a higher pitch as it broke through the silence.

The rain, this time, had a dull ring as it pitter-pattered across the stone and concrete, droplets falling much too rapidly to notice their shape—prismic parallelogram, in case you had been wondering—and the hue had contrasted with the lightning in neon orchid. Strandlers had been huddling in front of the *Theatron Philoscaena* in anticipation of a brand-new film that had been premiering that moment.

Part Two: Sharp Objects

A Tragic Winter's Tale

And I saw her lying there, the white stained crimson from the sin committed against her. I arrived too late, he had gotten to her and there was nothing I could do. I walked slowly toward her lifeless body, wide-eyed and mouth half open. The other stood there knowing what he'd done and diverted his attention to the thick blanket of white brilliance which covered the ground, holding the bloodied instrument that allowed him to commit such a crime, sorrowful and filled with regret. I stand over the shell that once was filled with beauty and love, Anne. I lost her to jealousy and greed, at the hands of Richter who wanted her for himself and did not see fit for one such as I to take her from him.

They were both nobility, and I was a common man. Common if that is what you wish to call it. The snow shone in the moonlight that bathed it in its glorious splendour, the blood darkened and tinted the white that surrounded her. I kneel onto the ground and caress her cold pale skin and stroke her raven-black hair. I kissed her lips for one last time and pick her up, her arms and head limp. Richter looks up at me and I turn away and walk, leaving him in desolation. Heaven begins to fall upon us as I walk across the field and up onto the edge of the cliff. Tears run down my face and the sun begins to rise. The rays of light begin to burn our skin. I close my eyes and hold her in sombre resplendence. A zephyr forms and carries our ashes away with the falling snow.

Three months earlier, the tale of Winter begins.

It's 12/21, the Winter solstice, the longest night of the year, Spain 1637. The Queen had sent out invitations to a ball on this night to every person of "noble" blood. To my surprise, I received one. I wondered what she meant by "noble". I'm not a noble, but my blood is different from many. I have a condition that the medics call Porphyria Cutanea Tarda, but the locals and the town witch say it's not that, they say I'm a vampire. I think it's nonsense, but it would explain a few things. I can never leave the house during the day, and there are no windows or cracks where sunlight can peer through. My little shabby stone home. Cold and empty with the exception of a bed, a table, and two chairs. The floor is uneven and paved concrete. I essentially modelled it as if it was a cave, and all the colours turn to grey. When I found the letter on my floor at dusk, I was worried as to what I had done to merit the attention of the Nobles. The envelope was white with the royal emblem on the red wax seal.

I took the envelope and walked to the table in the middle of my cave and had a seat. I inspected it by candlelight, careful not to burn it. Reluctantly I broke the seal and opened the letter. It was exactly that which I mentioned before. It read: "David H. De La Miseria, you are cordially invited to the Queen's Death of Seasons ball." Death of Seasons ball, it definitely sounds inviting. I only had an hour to get to the Queen's castle at the edge of town, so I quickly put on my best black and red garments and set off on my black steed. My long black jacket with red lining on the inside flapped behind me from the stallion's velocity. I make it a point to arrive at such events earlier than expected. The castle was seen up ahead, growing closer and more massive. It was a magnificent sight to behold, such a marvellous structure. Ebony stones make the castle walls and gargoyles watch the surroundings from the tops of towers, ever so frightful and still as the very stone they are crafted from. I arrive at the massive black iron gate held by thick rusted chains. The black fully armoured knights at the front stop me and ask for evidence of invitation. I reach into my pocket and pull out the invitation. One of them snatches it from me and reads, "'David... cordially invited... Seasons ball.' Alright, let him in. We'll stable your horse here." He hands the letter back to me and I dismount.

I enter the castle and look around at the spectacular decor as I make my way to the ballroom. Extravagant chandeliers and candelabra, the elegant draperies of deep reds and purples and shadowed blacks, the lovely carpeting that seems to go on forever and into every corridor. The furniture crafted from the finest woods and by the best carpenters of the land. I found my way to the ball room and was overwhelmed by the crowd of pale-faced men and women from all over Spain. One of the women caught my eye, she was tall and beautiful beyond comprehension, she wore a black and red corset dress, her hair as black as the shadows, her eyes as fierce and beautiful as that of a feline but pleading for salvation, her countenance was a beautiful pale, soft snow-white skin. She looked as if she didn't belong amongst the other Nobles, so alone. I fear that I alone see those who finally ceased to feel that they're alone inside this place. We are the misplaced, her and I. Then another girl appeared by her side, her very mirror image. This one was dressed in black and white. I didn't get the same odd feeling toward her. I stood by a wall across from them and watched her subtly. Her sister must have noticed me since she pointed me out from the large crowd in between us and I quickly diverted my attention to the Queen as she motioned for the ball to begin. I saw the Queen look over at the two girls and then at me. I again diverted my attention, this time to a woman who had noticed me standing alone and asked for a dance.

"No, thank you, señorita." I said politely.

I got my wits about me and decided to make my way to the dark angel of my desire on the other side of the room, pushing my way through the crowd. Finally, I made it to her, and there I stood, half frozen. She looked at me with those pleading eyes which sang the sorrow of a million years and bathed me in her radiance.

I melted and finally said, "I couldn't help but notice you, you seem different from the other Nobles. More beautiful as well."

She saw sincerity in my eyes and smiled, "Thank you, Señor..."

"De La Miseria, David De La Miseria... A gloomy name, I know."

She giggled and said, "Well, Señor De La Miseria, pleased to make your acquaintance. I am Anne Le Cantare."

"Please call me David, and the pleasure is all mine, Señorita Le Cantare."

"Only if you call me Anne."

We exchanged smiles and I inquired, "Le Cantare... isn't the—"

"Yes," she cut in, "the Queen is my mother."

"Not just a Noble, but a princess. I guess my hopes of romancing you are shot down seeing as I am neither royalty nor Nobility."

"Don't count yourself out just yet, I despise the fact that I am royalty. I get treated differently just because of my mother. Yet I get treated badly by everyone in this room! So unbearable. What do you mean not Nobility? How did you get an invitation then?"

"That is what I'd like to find out. But, my darling Anne, I would not dream of mistreating you."

She smiled big and said, "Strangely, I believe you."

"I'm glad. Now, would you join me in this dance of misery?"
I extend my hand to her and she takes it, "Of course."

And we danced on, and they never stopped playing our
song. It felt as if we were the only ones there, moving to the
romantic verses, looking deeply into each other's eyes. Her
eyes. They began to show a glimmer of joy. Everything melted
away around us: the crowd, the furniture, the walls, the
castle itself, everything. In our minds, we were dancing in the
endless field of grass with the moon shining high above and
the Winter's snow falling down over us, covering the dark
green with brilliant white. And we dance on as the insects
sing the coldest sound. As we dance, the Queen and Anne's
sister watch us closely.

"Who is that man, mother?"

"A man who knows not his Noble origins. Lost and alone.
His family was killed by the English when he was an infant.
They were part of our counsel back before you two were
born."

She smiled slightly, "Now, Emily, go cut in."

Emily just nodded and went off to dance with the
mysterious David.

"I beg, may I cut in?" asked Emily.

Reality came back to us in an instant and our surroundings
became small and enclosed once more. Back in the castle's
ballroom with all of the Nobles. I neglected to glance at her,
but agreed and took her hand in a dance. It'd have been rude
to refuse. As Emily and I danced Anne made her way back to
her mother and began to converse, looking over at me. I had
not the slightest clue as to what they were saying, but I could
tell it was nothing negative.

"You know I'm just meant to keep you busy while Mother
talks to Anne about you." Emily said, "Mother says you're of
Noble blood. You do look it. The appearance is uncanny."

"I'm sorry, what? Noble blood?"

"Yes, your parents were on the counsel before they were murdered by the English."

"I had no idea... That explains a few things."

The song soon ended, and we parted, "I'll see you around Señor De La Miseria."

As she walked away, I went over to the table and grabbed a glass of red wine. I sipped it, and noticed that it tasted different, more metallic and thicker.

Moments later, Anne had returned to me, "Mother said she approves of our courtship. I said I had wanted to be with you, that I felt a strong bond towards you."

"I see. That's good. But would it be rude if I were to ask to depart from these festivities with you?"

"No, not at all. Mother said we can do as we please."

I smiled at her and took her hand, "Well, let's get some fresh air."

She smiled at me, and I led her out of the castle. I glanced back at her occasionally and we caught each other's eyes. That radiant smile, those eyes, I'd seen them before but couldn't remember where, or when. We arrived at the stable where my ebony steed was taken and stopped. I looked into her eyes deeply; they shone brightly in the moon's light. They were honey brown with a hint of yellow, like that of a wild cat of the Southern continent. They told me everything I needed to know, everything she was thinking.

I gently caressed her soft pale face and held it as if I were holding the most precious gemstone. Suddenly I felt her crashing into my arms, I wanted her. I felt a strange urge overtake me and I pulled her face up and kissed her, holding her in a firm embrace. She didn't agree, but didn't refuse, I knew her. Then she softened and warmed. She parted her lips a bit more so I could swallow her fear. Then I kissed down to her neck and bit it. She flinched, then moaned softly in pleasure. All the bite marks impressed a need to be there, and a need to see.

As I pulled away from her neck and met her eyes, she blushed and said she would stay with me forever. The time we had was so tangible, and I'll never let it go.

"I must be back in the castle before the dawn." she said, "Mother says I must keep out of direct sunlight. I have a condition."

I nodded and said, "I know, I'm the same. I was born with it."

"As was I. It seems only those of Noble blood suffer from it."

I ran my fingers through her silky black hair and kissed her forehead, "I'll have you back before then, we do have enough time. 'Tis only but midnight, and there is no sun at this time."

I took my dark rider and mounted him, I then helped Anne up onto him. We rode to a place I'd been to many times before, a large field that leads to a cliff where only one tree stands, withered and alone as I was.

"Yo he estado aquí muchas veces antes, y regreso a comenzar." I said, "This is my home away from home, I come here every time I want to start again."

She just listens. I dismounted and helped her down. She landed as lightly as the new snow.

"I was born here many times. I'd stand here on this narrow ledge and stare up at the moon. I always knew I was meant for much more than what I was given. I always knew I'd find the one that would complete me and save me from my hell. As I stared up at this moon, I saw it all. That's where I saw you," I pointed at the moon and stared intently, *"there.* **She** *showed you to me, your eyes, your smile. Everything. This is sacred ground. It's infused with spiritual energy of my people. Well, my mother's people. My father was not of this land. I was told he came from Nobility and settled with a woman from this area. There used to be a village here."* I turned to her and held her hands, *"I know I'm not human, I know I'm not like the people in my town."*

She stared into my eyes, *"David, your eyes. They've turned yellow."*

I shut my eyes and looked away. *"Anne, you say I'm of Noble blood. Well, I guess my father is to blame for that. But my eyes are a gift from my mother. The one I was raised by told me she was of Wolves' blood."*

She gasped, *"Wolves' blood?"*

"Half Wolf, half Noble. I shouldn't be alive. The Nobles had always shunned me. That is, 'til now." I turned and faced the moon again.

Anne stared at the back of me and placed her arms around me, resting her head on my back, *"I don't care what your past is or where you come from. I feel a connection to you. I can't just ignore that."*

I turned my head and looked back at her, *"I feel it too, darling."* I turned to her and kissed her softly, *"I will refrain from hiding all of me from you. But I must take you back; it will be almost dawn by the time we get there."*

She nodded in agreement, and we mounted my horse.
"What's your carrier's name?" she asked.

"Hunter, this black steed is called Hunter." We rode off into the darkness lit only by the moon and the stars above, burning bright.

That night I had taken her back to her castle and we parted ways. We wrote letters to each other every night until the next time we'd see each other. Her letters always smelled of her, and her perfume. They told of what she'd be doing and how much she'd miss me and little things about her I wouldn't have known unless she told me. Mine were just about the same. The night before I was to see her again, her letter was drenched with excitement:

"Oh, my darling David! I cannot wait 'til tomorrow's moon! I get to see you again. Oh, I've missed you terribly, my heart aches and longs for you. Why can't it be tomorrow already? I must get ready, make the servants clean the castle more hastily and thoroughly. I need to look my best! Sorry if I seem stressed, I'm just excited. David, there's one more thing... I think I've fallen in love with you. Now, you don't have to reply to this letter, just show up tomorrow. 'Til then, my love.

Yours eternally,
Anne Le Cantare"

The next night I wore my third best garments and rode off on Hunter to the castle to see my Anne. On the way I got a strange feeling, as if there were someone in that castle that intended to harm me and keep Anne and me apart. As to who it was remained a mystery to me. This night was cold and still, no clouds in the sky and no wind, only stars. The moon was absent that night, which explained why I felt weaker than usual. I got to the castle gates, and it was the same routine as last time. I then made my way inside and was met by servants which escorted me to the indoor garden. That was where I was to meet Anne. It was a magnificent sight. The garden was dominated by violets and black roses, whose deep purples and shadowed blacks complemented each other. There were blood roses as well as white oleanders, chrysanthemums of white and orchids. Vines of beauty stretched all around the garden walls, dark green thickets all around with small bursts of red and purple covered the grounds at the base of the walls and around the tree in the centre of the garden. The tree had a familiar feel to it and resembled the one in my place of rebirth, tall and twisted, dark and gloomy, bare branches reaching out in all directions like long bony fingers. It exuded spiritual energy, but different than mine. It was dead. The tree's spiritual energy kept those other plants alive. Death for life. The floors of this place were the same ebony stone as the castle walls, and there was no roof to the garden. Those plants were the only living things in the castle that could bathe in the sunlight.

I felt it again, this time I'd felt it stronger. It was a man, and he was near. I looked back and no one was there. The feeling subsided and Anne had entered through her quarters and snuck up behind me.

"Hello, my darling."

I turned to her and wrapped my arms around her, "Good evening, mi amor." I kissed her sweetly and held her still. Her eyes radiated joy.

She smiled, "I'm so glad you showed up and weren't scared away by my last letter."

"Why would I be?"

She looked away slightly then back into my eyes, "Because of something I had said. I thought maybe you didn't feel the same."

I held her soft face, "Look into my eyes as I say this," I stare intently into her eyes and her into mine, "I would be a fool to not love you. You are everything I'd ever wished for and more. Darling, of course I love you, it'd be hard not to."

Her eyes welled up with tears of joy, and she smiled sincerely, "Oh, David, I love you too." She said as she buried her head in my chest, and I held her close and tight.

She then looked up at me and I caressed her lovely pale countenance, and I kissed her nose, she giggled and smiled. Then I kissed her with all of the love in the world, and we escaped into our little world where the insects sang again. I sent for the gods' grace that night, and I think it was found. And what followed had led us to that place where we belong with all erased.

Our world was made to crumble by the dreadful feeling and the words that accompanied it, "You should not be here, Half-breed. You disgrace this castle with your presence."

I heard a voice then say, "Take your hands off the princess or die!"

I looked over to the shadow by the wall where he hid. Anne and I parted but held hands, I felt her fear, "I know you're there; I can sense you."

Anne remained silent.

The voice spoke with arrogance, "Ah, yes. I can't hide from the nose of a Wolf. How silly of me." He stepped out of the shadows and revealed himself, "Now you can see me. I am—"

"Richter! How dare you spy on me!" Anne said, cutting him off, "You have no right."

"My dear Anne, I have every right to keep my eye on you. I wouldn't want you falling into the arms of a dirty mongrel, after all." He said, glancing at me with a sneer.

I grit my teeth and growl a bit.

"Oh my, the mutt is getting angry! Be careful, he might maul you, Anne."

"It's not me who should be careful, Richter, it's you."

"Me? Ha! I'm not frightened by a dirty, half-witted, Half-breed. Especially one of his lineage. Wolf loving father of his, Disgusting."

I growled louder, "Don't talk down to me you pretentious, high-class, snake!"

Richter scowled and sneered, "How dare you say such atrocities to one such as myself! Someone needs to teach you a lesson in manners."

"Oh, and who will that be? You? I doubt a weakling like you can. Go on, try and hurt me."

I gave Anne a look to stand back and motioned to Richter to take a shot.

"More insults! The nerve. I'll show you who the weakling really is!"

Richter unsheathed his sabre and lunged at me full force, clouded by anger. He had no chance. I dodged all of his attacks effortlessly, lunge after lunge, slash after slash. He couldn't land a hit and grew ever more frustrated. No feign nor trick worked, but then he looked over at Anne and vanished. I looked around and sensed him near Anne.

"Anne! Behind you!"

Richter appeared behind her and placed the blade to her throat, "Surrender or I'll slit her pretty throat. Walk out of this castle never to return."

I glared intently at him and watched as Anne stood helpless and afraid. I thought of what I could do to stop him, "You wouldn't. I could see it in your eyes. You've never even killed a man." I walked slowly towards them, "Ah, and I sense that you secretly love Anne. Well, I'm sorry she chose me over you, but you must realise that if you really loved her, you'd let her go." I was close enough to make a move. Richter trembled in fear. "So, let her go." I reached for his blade, "Let her go."

"NO! I'll never let you have her! She's mine!!" He slashed my hand and stabbed through my heart. Anne screamed in despair and broke free of Richter.

"No! David!" I fell back in shock and half dead.

There were no flowers that time, no angels gracing the lines. I felt myself slipping into oblivion. I waited in despair for the ecstasy, for the tragedy, for the point of my ascension. Anne held my hand, kneeling over me, her tears falling on to my face, like light kisses gracing me. Richter stood in shock of his action, then ran.

With the little life I had left in me, and my last breath I said to Anne, "I don't want to die tonight; I don't want to fall into the light, will you wish upon me? I don't want to die tonight... Will you believe in me tonight? Anne, am I your anything?"

She looked upon me with such sorrow and despair and said, "No... David, you're my everything." And she lay upon me what seemed to be the last kiss.

I wasted away hearing her cries, hearing her begging me to stay.

"David."

I heard a woman calling for me, "David. Come here, David."

Everything was black; it was all one big dark room.

"Yes, David, come." A man called out to me.

Their voices echoed in the dark. I walked without a light to guide me, just hearing the calls of the lonely ones, "How did I ever end up here?"

They were familiar voices, like those I heard long ago, back before I could remember. Their voices were serene and comforting. As I walked, I saw soft creatures draped in white. Their shape changed as I drew nearer, from nothings, to a Wolf and a Bat. Then I stopped just a few feet away and they walked to me, changing. The Wolf into a woman of the Wolfine tribe and the bat into a man of Nobility.

"David." They said, "David, welcome David."

"Where am I? Who are you?" I asked, knowing the answers already.

"David, you're in the spirit realm, David." The woman said.

"Yes, David. You died, but only temporarily." The man said, "You see, David, your lineage, your blood, won't allow you to ever fully die. The Nobles are of vampiric bloodlines, and vampires never truly die. As long as there is a vessel for their soul to reside in, they will never die. Your body has not been destroyed, only wounded."

"Yes, David," said the woman, "And the Wolfine tribe are of Wolf bloodlines, though we can be killed, it is hard to dispatch us, for we are reborn with every death. Those of the Wolfine tribe gain strength through wounding, so when your rebirth takes place, you will be stronger than any Wolf or Noble."

"You would have ascended." They said in unison.

"David, it's time for you to awaken and be reborn, your Anne has taken you to your place of rebirth. She buried you so the sun would not harm you. It is time." said the woman.

"Yes, David, go forth and keep out of the sun, it can destroy your vessel still."

I looked at them both, and they placed their hands on my shoulders, "GO!"

I awoke in the land of the living and pushed my way out of the ground. It had been two moons since I had died. It's the last month of Winter. I rose from the ground and let out a loud whistle for my horse.

Moments later Hunter arrived, "Come on Hunter, we've got unfinished business at Castle Le Cantare." I mounted him and rode off to the castle.

The guards stood at the gates, "We can't let you pass without authorization. No authorization, no castle. Have a good night."

I dismounted and said, "I need to pass."

"Sorry sir, can't let you do that."

"I'm going in one way or another."

I ran towards them and jumped, kicking them both in their faces. I then jumped on top of the raised castle bridge and slid down. The gate was closed so I grasped the lower bars and forced it open, making my way down the corridors to the main room where everyone, including Richter and Anne, was.

"ANNE!!" I yelled with ferocity. Everyone in the room looked back at the entrance door which I had kicked open.

"David!" Anne screamed in ecstasy.

"You! I thought I killed you!" Richter exclaimed angrily.

"You did. Look what you've done to me, you've made me perfect." I smiled.

"I killed you once, I can do it again!" He unsheathed his sword and lunged at me.

I caught his blade and said, "You'll have your chance to try in a week, on the night the moon hides. On the field of my rebirth, the old Wolfine village."

I gripped his blade and snapped it in two, "And you'll need a stronger blade. 'Til then, I bid you all farewell.

Come Anne, escape with me." I extended my hand to her, and she ran to me and took my hand. We ran out of the castle together, hand in hand.

We rode off into the forest by the old Wolfine village and took shelter in a cave where no one would find us. For days we stayed there, laying in each other's arms, wrapped in cold. We kept out of the sunlight, bathing in the water underground, the spring in the cave. We ran into the fields and kissed under the trees, and in our cancer of passion, we made love under the stars. The snow fell over our soft pale bodies and camouflaged us with the scenery. Our passion could be heard for miles.

"I love you, Anne, with all my heart."

She smiled, "I love you, too, David."

The time had come. The night with no moon was at hand. Before I left Anne in the cave I asked, "Will you wait for me?"

"Endlessly." She said.

I rode off into the field where I'd meet Richter and duel him to the death.

There he stood arrogantly, "I have come to dispatch you and take Anne for my own."

"Ha, lie and smirk in time, your arrogance will suit you well, 'til fashion is dispelled."

"No more words, mongrel. We settle this with steel."

He pulls his blade from his sheath and readies himself.

"As you wish." I say taking mine from the side of Hunter's red and black saddle.

There we stand ready, the air still and silent, no snow falling and no moonlight. And we charge toward each other with the intent to kill.

That battle began. We exchanged blow for blow, slashing and stabbing at one another, parrying each other's attacks. He seemed to have gotten stronger and more focused, thus having gained some skill. But I was stronger, faster and more agile. He was on the defensive and I was on heavy offence. He parried one of my attacks and struck me on my left side, leaving a large gash that bled profusely. I countered with a stab to his gut, going through and charging forward to pin him to a tree. I pinned him to a large oak and struck his face with my fist repeatedly. He blocked a hit and kicked me in the gut, then kicked me with both legs, sending me reeling backward and on to the snow. I recovered quickly but he had broken free of the tree and charged at me. I dodged his lunge, grabbed his hand and tossed him several yards away, taking his sword. I then appeared in front of him holding the blade to his neck.

"This battle is over, surrender. I'll not kill you."

"No mercy, you dirty Half-breed, kill me!"

Just before I stabbed through Richter's throat, Anne screamed, "David, don't!"

I stopped myself and Richter appeared behind her as I looked in her direction. He held a knife to her neck and said, "I told you to kill me. Now if she can't be mine, she won't be yours either!"

I ran to stop him and save her, but I was too late...

And I saw her lying there, the white stained crimson from the sin committed against her. I walked slowly toward her lifeless body, wide-eyed and mouth half open. Richter stood there knowing what he'd done and diverted his attention to the thick blanket of white brilliance which covered the ground, holding the bloodied instrument that allowed him to commit such a crime, sorrowful and filled with regret. I stand over the shell that once was filled with beauty and love, Anne. I lost her to jealousy and greed, at the hands of Richter who wanted her for himself and did not see fit for one such as I to take her from him. The blood darkened and tinted the white that surrounded her. I kneel onto the ground and caress her cold pale skin and stroke her raven-black hair. I kissed her lips for one last time and pick her up, her arms and head limp. Richter looks up at me and I turn away and walk, leaving him in desolation. Heaven begins to fall upon us as I walk across the field and up onto the edge of the cliff. Tears run down my face and the sun begins to rise. The rays of light begin to burn our skin. I close my eyes and hold her in sombre resplendence. A zephyr forms and carries our ashes away with the falling snow.

Richter stood in the sun and let himself be destroyed by the light. The Nobles covered up this incident never to be spoken of again.

Centuries Later—

Spain, 2037, The 400th Death of Seasons ball at Le Cantare Mansion.

"Excuse me Señorita Le Cantare; will you join me in this dance?"

"How do you know me Señor...?"

"De La Miseria, David De La Miseria. And I met you before I was born, mi amor."

The credits roll, the audience cheers, and everyone rises from their seats elated and with mixed emotions; none were negative, really. Many Strandlers found the film a tad cheesy and heavy on the romance, but overall, it was fun. Apparently, it had been an old project that had never come to fruition; a relic of the filmmaker's teenage years inspired by conversations with their former lover. They hadn't thought about the idea at all since arriving in The Plane of The Forgotten, but recently, it had surfaced, along with fond memories of a long-lost love.

"It's like a fog lifted..." they commented.

Part Three: Smothered, Warm and Alive

They had exited the *Theatron*—Sam and Roni separate from Kia and Toni—, laughing and commenting on the film and what it had meant and as both Sam and Roni began to come to a familiar, simultaneous conclusion, Kia and Toni had spotted them.

"Hey! Oh-em-gee! What are you two doing here!?" Kia shouts

The couple the question had been directed at turns slightly to their left and Roni says, "We just got out of *A Tragic Winter's Tale*. You?"

"Ditto." Toni says shortly and coolly, walking up with their hands in their pockets and Kia's arm linked through their right elbow.

Sam smiles, "Well look at you two, all linked up."

"Wait, you know each other?" Roni asks curiously, eyes darting back and forth from Toni to Sam to Kia and back around.

"Yeah, we're familiar..." Toni exhales, eyes wandering around avoiding Sam.

"Who doesn't know the infamous Toni in The Stranding?" Sam comments, then adds, "No hard feelings, dude. It was just sex for me too."

Roni's jaw drops and they gawk surprisedly at the two, "Wait!"

"Yes, Roni, we're all butt buddies apparently." Sam laughs.

Kia giggles, "That's one way to put it."

Everyone sort of laughs shortly at Sam's comment as they stand about outside of the theatre with the crowds around them thin to emptiness; the Strandlers all shuffling to their own errands and habits, routines and all of that. An awkward silence falls among them for a moment until Roni sucks in air and prepares to break it.

"So, Sam and I were talking about how familiar a lot of the lines and themes in that movie were. Like we've heard them before somewhere else; like, I don't know, probably from music. There was something dramatically musical about it all."

Sam adds, "Yeah, like the whole thing was like," they throw their hands up and gesture a scene, "'DRAMA'. You know, like it was so hammy, but it was so good, and I felt like I'd been there before, in that content."

Kia ponders a bit, stroking her chin, "You know? It's true. I think I'd heard a lot of that too, but like, maybe in passing. Somehow it reminds me of you, Roni, from when I first saw you."

"Well, it's new to me." Toni interjects, shrugging, then adds, "It was cool stuff, vampires and werewolf stuff but sexy. I remember seeing, uh, Dra—uh, shoot. I don't remember the name, but there were movies I seen flicks with a vampire guy going after some girl or something, and there was also a flick about a guy that turns into a wolf while sitting down I think."

"Why are we suddenly remembering this stuff? I hadn't thought about vampires in a long time; I was obsessed with them..." Sam breaks off, "*out there.*"

"And those lines, the names; *Death of Seasons*? I know that from somewhere, like it—it's on the tip of my tongue." Roni says, slightly frustrated.

"Yeah, that flick reminded me of stuff too! There was a play or something that got turned into a flick I caught *before*—" Toni presses a finger to their forehead, "'star crossed lovers' or something, from families that hate each other, they commit suicide..."

Kia breaks away from Toni, throwing her arms up in the air, exclaiming excitedly, "I know that story! I know it! I know that story! Oh-em-gee! There was a movie I watched when I was little with my mom—that I was probably too young for, but—that I loved so much. Apparently, she was a kid when she saw it too—why am I remembering this? Dubya-tee-eff, it's like flooding into my head; I forgot these things even happened!"

"We're all reconnecting with our memories from before we got here, tied to the things we couldn't let go of completely. We've all had things happen to us that brought us here, and the scars of those things hadn't faded away." Roni says, checking their wrists for marks that weren't there, but the image of scars flashed into their mind for a brief moment, shaking them suddenly as they shuddered.

Sam nods in agreement, "I've been remembering too," their demeanour darkens, "I've been trying to push it all back again but it's like breaking down all the doors I try to close. I don't want to remember, but I can't help it."

Roni wraps their arms around Sam, comforting them and stroking their hair sweetly. Sam says softly, "Thank you, babe. It's being with you that helps me keep the dark thoughts away, honestly."

"Roni's good for that." Kia comments lovingly.

"Mhmm." Toni nods in agreement.

"It's okay, Sam-Sam, we're here for you, I'm here for you." Roni says gently.

Sam takes in a long breath and holds it for a small moment before letting it go slowly, dragging it out for longer than it took to draw it in. They walk over to the bench by the fountain and the others follow, all sitting together—Toni sitting on the backrest of the bench.

<u>Chapter 12: Side A - Lost The Fear Of Falling,</u>
<u>Like Ghosts In The Snow</u>

I'm really not liking how much the fog is lifting from, well, everyone! Attraction says quickly.

I understand, Atty, but there's not much I can do about it. We can't meddle further. Time says, solidly.

Chance is meddling! Chance has been, Attraction gestures wildly, *making things happen!*

I have not! Chance chimes in, offended.

*Yes, you have! I've seen it! You can't tell me that them all coming together like that wasn't **your** work!* Attraction accuses.

I cannot help it if things just seem to happen as if by— Chance stops abruptly, being cut off.

Oh, shut your vocal orifice, Chance. Attraction interrupts.

Chance is correct, though, sister. Fate is a creation of humanity, they seek it, they want it. Things happen how they happen by a passive force of energy that wraps itself around individuals and things and brings them together in ways that are, or can become, beautiful. It is they that are creating these circumstances, not Chance. Chance merely sees. Feeling explains.

Attraction *harrumphs* loudly, annoyed with their accusation falling short.

Attraction, it may all be troubling and may come to the undoing of the Plane, but we can destroy, rebuild, and repopulate. I can grow new life, bear more fruit, bring new environments, should The Darkness come again. Nature states.

We absolutely can, and I can make it happen in a flash and we can bring more people in and start over. We have eternity, so long as I'm around. Time boasts.

I wouldn't be so certain about everything. Something seems different this time around. I get strange sensations every time they see through the fog. Attraction says, concerned about the future of The Plane of The Forgotten.

Noted, Atty, but can we get along with this? I'm sure everyone's anxious to see what brought Sam here. Time gets ready for the rewind.

Time wobbles its limbs around, manifesting a desktop computer from the mid aughts and clicks around the screen bringing up a webpage with a video screen, paused for the moment. Time full screens the video marquee and clicks on the centre of the screen, causing a loading circle to pop up for a moment. Time groans and rapidly clicks until the circle gives way to the video that is Sam's life highlights reel.

For a while, in the 90's, it had been peaceful, loving. They had sisters and parents, and everything seemed to come so easily. They lived in a large, multi-floor building in the Bronx. It wasn't the most lavish and beautiful place, but it was theirs, and it was filled with love. Sam's parents were doting and understanding, they treated each one of their daughters with an individualised respect—they understood that each one had their own likes, dislikes, wants, needs, and individual personality outside of the family unit—and loved them as they were.

The peace had not lasted long, though, as moments passed by, Sam's father grew ill and had to be hospitalised. That's when they learned that he had pancreatic cancer at an advanced stage. They could treat the symptoms and make living bearable, but death was inevitable—more so than most of humanity. Because of his illness, he couldn't work, and because he couldn't work, they faced financial hardships. They ended up moving to a neighbouring state where Sam's father could receive a much more affordable hospice, and their mother could find a higher paying job, as well as the eldest sister, all in an attempt to make ends meet.

Sam visited their father often, wanting to stay with him often and sleep through the night at his side, but they couldn't, they were still small and had to go to school. School, having been harder to focus on now, had become more difficult. Sam was considered 'poor', and therefore had secondhand clothes and often lacking supplies, and was teased by other children over the condition of their off-brand shoes, ill-fitting clothes, and heavily used backpack that had been at least three years old with wear and tear present enough to be pointed out from afar. Being new to the school, and different, the staff hadn't paid enough attention to them to stop the bullying and didn't believe them when they complained. Their mother was much too busy to make the necessary calls, and much too tired to fully listen to Sam's plight. But their sisters listened, they wished they were at the same school—they were both much older—so that they could stick together and fight back.

One day, after having been bullied mercilessly by a group of ten-year-olds, Sam had enough and tackled one of them down to the ground, screaming and striking with fists and claws and open hands. The other kids were shocked and a little alarmed, too scared to get involved when one of them called a teacher over saying Sam had just started hitting the kid unprovoked. They were brought into the principal's office where they had called their mother's job to alert her of the situation. Her mother was furious; stressed from her husband's decline, her long hours, bills, and now her 'troublesome' child.

Sam's eyes welled up with tears, a few escaping, they shook their head and wiped their eyes, grabbed their backpack and walked out of the office. The principal called out for them, but Sam didn't listen, Sam didn't care, they had to get out of there, they had to go to their father. Surely, he'd understand. So, Sam ran. Sam ran out of the school, up and down several streets across twenty-three blocks to find the hospital where their father was being treated.

"What are you doing here on your own, little girl?" One of the hospital receptionists said.

"I'm not a girl! And I have to see my dad!" Little Sam demanded.

"Whoa, there. Okay, kid. Who's your dad? Where is he?" asked the receptionist.

Sam scrunched up their nose and furrowed their brow to think, like a Pixar character, "He's very sick," they said, "in his pancake."

"His pancake?" The receptionist asked, amused.

"Yeah, it's right here," they said and pointed at their tum-tum, just under their ribcage, "it's what makes the sugar of the blood or something."

The staff person realised what the child was alluding to, "Oh! Oh. Pancreatic cancer," the person's voice was low, "do you know your daddy's name?"

Sam nodded and proceeded to tell the staff person their father's name.

"Daddy?" Sam said softly, walking into the room cautiously.

"*Mija*? What are you doing here?" He said weakly, "You're not supposed to be here. No one is..."

"*Papi*, I had to see you, I had a bad day at school and people were mean and the principal tried to—" Sam stopped, noticing their father struggling, "—*papi*, what's wrong? You're okay, right, dad?"

Her father struggled to reach out to Sam's hand as Sam got closer to the hospital bed, also reaching, "*Ay, mija,* I wish I could tell you I was."

"But you're gonna be okay, right, dad? You're just feeling sick today. Well, sick*er*..." Sam trailed off, feeling a sadness hit them in a massive wave.

"Sam, *mi cielo*, I'm sorry. I love you, *sabes*? *Te amo con*—" he struggled to speak, the weakness consuming him, "*con todo mi corazón, por*—"

"Daddy stop, you're gonna be okay, daddy, you're just not feeling good right now." Sam's eyes were wet from holding back tears, speaking hurriedly with a lump in their throat.

"*Siempre...*" he said finally.

"I love you, too, daddy. Now wake up, please." Sam pleaded, their voice breaking, "*Papi!* Wake up! *Despiértate,* please! I'll bring you coffee and crackers, that's your favourite!"

But he wouldn't ever wake again. He had passed on into the *Aether*; the after. Sam had watched their father die; a bittersweet goodbye that only Sam got to experience. Everyone else—their sisters and mother—would get the phone call.

Orderlies and nurses would rush into Sam's father's room to respond to the flatline, finding Sam clutching their father and sobbing uncontrollably. They were inconsolable and no one could pry them from their father, so they let Sam cry. Some of them couldn't help but shed tears themselves, and offered to comfort Sam.

A few years had passed, and Sam had found comfort in diving headfirst for halos into music. They gave their soul to the hard driving sounds and screams of the emo scene, the hardcore scene, and the Scene™. Bands like My Chemical Romance, The Used, The Ataris, Paramore, and Brand New held a special place in their heart—the hole they tried to fill that was left by the loss of their father. They tried their hand at writing, but never thought they were any good. So, they resigned themselves to reading the worlds of others. They obsessed over vampire books specifically, with Anne Rice novels and Twilight being their favourites; especially Twilight, they were incredibly excited to hear a film was being made, immediately talking about it with their school friends on AIM and MySpace.

Though singing, singing and playing guitar had become their passion. They wanted to recreate the sounds that soothed them, not only for themself, but for others in need of soothing. So, Sam sang, they practised and refined until their voice rivalled that of the Angel of Music. But writing was still in the back of their mind, of their heart's desire. They wanted to create worlds for people to explore and discover, to get lost in, to find themselves in. But, again, it took second fiddle to music as they felt no one was reading, not even their sisters took a look at their stories that sat in online forums where Sam would spend much of their time chatting with other teens obsessed with music and vampires.

One such story was one of love, where a betrothed couple is torn apart by war, but love had other plans. The confidant of the man who would have been the lady's husband read the letters of the would-be wife and fell for her. Oh, fine, I'll pull it up. Here, enjoy the trashy romance of a teenage mind.

It isn't bad, by the way, but it's still a trashy romance.

Interlude: Hector & Julia

He rode up to see her from the city, Hector, a fine and hardworking man who has been through the fires of hell and back during the war.

He fought steel on steel, iron against iron, against a vast army so fierce, its reputation for bloodlust reached every corner of the country. It was his small battalion and him against them. Every other commanding officer had been killed or fled for their lives. There was no hope. But Hector had iron in his veins, and he was brilliant; extraordinary really. The cold season was coming, and he had the advantage—he was used to the cold, this was his home.

As the snow fell, so did the opposing forces to the cunning of Hector and his men. Cold steel cutting and piercing flesh, hot iron baleens lodging themselves into unsuspecting chests. It seemed as though the tide was turning, a slow process, but effective. During the length of this campaign, Hector began receiving letters, letters addressed to another man; a dead man. The letters came from a woman named Julia, a woman who seemed to be sweet and loving, dedicated and also tragically lonely. She was betrothed and spoke to this man as though he was her brother more than a lover, but still remained faithful and loving to him. It was the first letter that enthralled Hector.

Dear Marco,
It has been seven months, three weeks, two days, fourteen hours and nine minutes since you left me for the war. I write to you because I have not received any word from you, my dear Marco.

172

Have you forgotten me? Or have you... No, I must not think such foolish things. You must be entrenched in battle, like the brave and strong man you are. Mother misses you, and father seems to hold on to the notion of your triumphant return.

He speaks highly of your commanding officer, Hector, saying that he is a fine man, clever and cunning, strong. You're in good hands. Marco, our situation is a strange and confusing one, but I have warmed up to the idea of being a wife to you. After all, you are a good man, a strong man. It's just that I've known you since we were mere children. I guess it was meant to be, the only reason we did meet was to be betrothed. Our families together, a powerful force. But I feel lost, it's cold here and I'm all by myself in this big home you left me in. Please, come home in one piece soon.

Your Future Wife,
Julia Marie Savant

Hector kept this and all the other letters in his tent, a token of good luck, and a reminder of good out there in the world. "If I get out of here alive, I will find you."

As the enemy forces dwindled, as did their morale, and the reputation of Hector and his men branded them the Ghosts of Plano Blanco. But victory wouldn't be so quick and simple, no. The opposing commander stood alone on the battlefield, challenging Hector to a swordfight. He obliged, meeting the man on the cold snowy field.

They drew their swords, steel cutlasses, and ran at each other, each with their own furious battle cry. They clashed steel, striking relentlessly, each matching the other's skill and fury. Hector parried and blocked, then struck low to no avail; it was dodged. His opponent came back with a vertical strike meant to cleave Hector's skull, but Hector reacted quickly and blocked, then kicked the other in the gut, thrusting him back. The snow proved treacherous, causing the opponent to slide—Hector was already equipped for snow with snow treaded boots. The opponent retaliated with a thrust of the sword, quickly parried and countered; blocked. They were too evenly matched. But then, Hector's enemy flung snow into his face, blinding Hector long enough for his enemy to strike at him, catching his left thigh, wounding him deeply. In a rage, Hector shook off his blindness, stopping his enemy's would-be killing move by deflecting the thrusting cutlass away, causing the enemy to lunge forward, thus allowing Hector to spin out of the way and strike horizontally, severing his enemy's head from the body. The head flops to one side, rolling a few inches, while the body falls hard to the other.

After that night of victory, Hector was summoned to the capital city where he'd receive a medal commemorating his valiant efforts and his victory against a daunting enemy force. He'd then resume his factory job, a job he did not need since he was compensated generously by the government for his military career. But he told them, "It's not about that, it's about remembering where you come from, who you are, and what you can do for the community from within. I am just a man now, like everyone else who works here. It is a time for peace, and a soldier can't sit idly."

He'd remembered the letters, Julia, and what he'd felt. Strange for him, feeling such a way for someone he'd never met. But he'd come to know her through her words, simple and beautiful. So he rode to her from the city to her estate in the far northern quadrant of the country.

Inside she waited in the drawing room, alone in the company of intricate ornaments, furniture, and baubles. She sat by the window, on a chair of crimson and gold, watching the soft snow fall gently onto the already blanketed ground. She sighed heavy before hearing three knocks on the large hickory wood front hall doors. "Marco!" She gasped, raising her delicate porcelain feet draped over by her Cadbury purple and antiqued ivory steel boned corset gown and ran to the door, holding her gown up so she wouldn't trip.

She pauses and inhales deeply and exhales before opening the door and finding Hector Standing there, covered in snow.

"...Hi." He speaks.

She cocks her head and raises an eyebrow, "Who are you...?"

He hesitates, taken by surprise by her immense beauty—eyes like honey, hair like the sky on a moonless night, skin like the snow behind him, lips like blood—and pulls her letters from his satchel hung on his left side.

"Are those... my letters?" She says softly.

"Yes... I received them during the war. Being Marco's commanding officer; letters to him go to me."

"But why?"

"I'm... I'm so sorry. I should have written back..."

"What happened? Where's Marco?"

Hector gazed at her, regret filling his eyes.

"Tell me! Where is Marco? Tell me he's alive. Tell me he's okay, just late. He got hurt, didn't he?"

"Julia…"

"He's in one piece though, isn't he? He's okay. Just, just needs a little medical attention, right?"

"Julia, please."

"No! No, he's alive, he has to be! He's not…"

"He is. I'm sorry…"

"No!" She cried, not out of the loss of her betrothed, but because regardless, she still loved him. He was her first real friend and now he's gone.

"He was the best soldier I could have ever asked for. And a good man." He reached to her, but she smacked at his hand, "Julia, please,"

"No! No, it's your fault he's…" She collapsed into his arms, weeping heavily.

"If I had known… I'd have kept him behind the frontlines. But he wouldn't have had that, no. He was a soldier, a warrior. Brave, strong." He could feel the wet from her eyes on his chest. He held her tightly, stroking her hair silently. He begins to hum a tune in an effort to comfort her.

In front of the fireplace, they seek comfort from the cold. Hector explains to her the importance of her letters to him, and how because of her words he was able to go on and win the war. He reminisced his feelings to her for each word that leaped forth from the parchment and into his heart.

"Even though they were written for someone else," he said, "I felt like I was meant to read them. Like they were for me."

"How do you mean?" She was intrigued by this stranger in her home, this perfect and beautiful stranger whom she found so incredibly interesting, the battle scarred beauty. She saw the same lonely tragedy in his eyes that she felt deep inside, and a longing she felt compelled to oblige.

"Every word you had written, spoke stories of who you were. You didn't love him the way you were meant to. You reserved that for someone you thought impossible to find. Someone as lonely as you."

"How did you...?"

"Because I'm alone like you."

A lifetime was shared in one night, the two spoke volumes into each other's hearts and souls without a word ever escaping their lips. Everything they were, everything they hid, now displayed without shame or fear of judgement because they understood. Hector's battles in war were the literal iterations of Julia's struggles within. They both fought in war and came out with scars; but it's those scars that made them beautiful, made them who they are.

Fin

Side B - Find Other Ways To Make It Alone

Sam had desperately wanted a romance to call their own, a love so intense it could heal their wounds and make them forget everything that they'd lost. Though, after their father's death, it took some time to even out and stabilise, to live with the grief, but it happened eventually. One's grief doesn't merely shrink or disappear into the Aether alongside the one you lost, it just turns into a weight that you become accustomed to, a lingering childhood scar that never truly fades, but instead seems smaller as the rest of you grows. And their sisters were as a sanctuary or a church where they could feel safe and unjudged as they confess all of their feelings and experiences that they could never dream of burdening their mother with.

Their mother whomst had worked herself harder than she had to as her own way of coping with the grief, unknowingly leaving her children behind. They barely saw her, and when they did, she was too tired to talk, but would remind them constantly of how much she loved them all and was proud of the *'women'* they were all becoming—she didn't know about Sam, or rather, never paid enough attention nor inquired too deeply about Sam's refusal to use their full name and their change in style; chalked it up to being a *'tomboy'*. But it would soon catch up with her, all of the stress and late nights, the genetic predisposition. She had exhausted herself; she had heightened her blood pressure, she had neglected her health; she had a heart attack.

Not again... Sam thought, after having gotten the call from the emergency room. *Not again, I can't do this again.*

So, instead of rushing to the Hospital like their sisters did from their respective jobs, Sam locked themself in their room and threw on music, hyperventilating and trying to gain control over their mind and body; both racing and shaking. The music blared, the vibrations from the sound system made it so they didn't know whether it was the bass or their nerves making them tremble so. But tremble they did, and the back of their eyelids went blacker than the darkest reaches of space.

And then they opened to a field of black grass below a sky of teal with touches of blush pink as the smokey, patchy blanket cloud overcast that gave way to a rain which came down like technicolour speckles lighting a path—as always—to The Stranding.

They had no interest in becoming friends, in finding love, in making meaningful connections anymore. They'd become jaded, though they were brought to a place with individuals that shared similar stories to them and had similar interests that they were meant to connect with but couldn't bring themself to give anyone a chance to get close. They buried themself in books, they tried to write in cafes or at the centre square, but nothing came. They were just reminded of losing, of broken attachments, of never being truly seen. Then they met Toni.

"I saw you sitting there, book in hand, and I tell ya, I ain't seen anything like it in a while. So, I hope you don't mind, but I sketched you." Toni said, coolly, and halfway recklessly, flipping their sketchbook over to show Sam, then ripping the page out.

That was the first time Sam had seen themself, really seen themself as they'd been seen by someone else, as they'd wanted to be seen. Their eyes sparkled with a feeling they thought they lost, one of longing, of needing, of wanting.

"I don't—that's really me? I—well, it's beautiful. Thank you." Sam said, grateful and still flabbergasted, taking the sketch from Toni.

"Shoot, yeah, no worries. You wanna maybe grab a coffee?" Toni dared.

Sam nodded in agreement, shut their book with the sketch as the bookmark.

They never got that coffee.

Chapter 13 - Out of The Chaos,
Through The Sinking Night

"...Anyway," Sam clears their throat, "Have any of you noticed that people around here have been acting a lot stranger lately?"

"Stranger?" Roni asks.

"Yeah, like, everyone has tunnel vision or something. Like they're all—"

Kia interrupts Sam, "—NPCs in a video game with limited AI!?"

Sam cocks an eyebrow and squints hard at Kia, "I mean, yeah, I guess? But it's like, before everyone would be friendly and talk to you about whatever was going on at the moment; a book I was reading, that statue there that looks like a heart split in two, stitched up, with one devil wing and an angel wing, with a halo and a demon tail..." Sam slowed to a stop.

"Yeah, what's with that statue? It's so emo." Roni comments.

"That's not the point Sam's trying to make, sponge cake." Toni responds with a childlike rudeness before continuing, "In any case, it's been strange. I haven't seen anyone present enough to catch my eye, either."

"Well, that settles it," Kia adds with a chuckle, "something weird ay-eff is going on here."

Roni looks around at the passing Strandlers, noticing a sort of dark aura around them, "Anybody else see, like, a shadow sort of thing around some of these peeps? It's giving me the heebie-jeebs."

"I see it." Toni says quickly, scanning the square.

The other two look around and back at each other and shrug, "We don't see anything."

Kia leans in, "By the way, have y'all heard about the Strandlers that just kind of lost it and did a full *'Get Out'* sprint out of The Stranding?"

"No," Sam said suspiciously, "also, what's *'Get Out'*?"

"It's a movie that I just remembered existed," Kia said quickly in a single breath, "but yeah, no, people have been getting overcome with emotion, flooded, and just booking it out the gates and into the Forbidden Forest of Forgotten Figments and Figures."

"Spooky," Toni remarks, "wonder what's out there..."

They all shift their eyes at each other, silent for a moment, then Roni finally suggests, doing their best Jeff Goldblum impression, "What if... What if we, uh, go find out?"

No! No, no, no, absolutely not! Do not—! You're going out there, you unruly, floppy dogs. Time explodes then deflates.

What's wrong, Timey Wimey? Things not going according to your plan? Attraction teases.

Oh, hush your voice hole, Atty. You're enjoying this too much. Time retorts.

*I mean, you **had** to see this coming.* Chance expresses.

You hush your voice hole, too! Time snaps.

Chance is right, though, it was bound to happen. Their hearts would lead them there. Lead them to find the truth of it all. Feeling sighs.

In oblivion's grasp, they will see how it came to be, and Darkness will rise again. Nature recites.

*Stop that! And it's **THE** Darkness. Don't give it life by acknowledging its identity. It must die.* Time chides.

*But **they** don't deserve that. Darkness is just existing, like us.* Feeling exhales softly.

It is not like us! It doesn't want to create; it only exists to destroy! Time explains.

That's not fair, Time. We never gave them a— Chance stops, sensing Time's wrath building.

Enough!

Enough. It had been enough.

Within the walls of CAFÉ LUDENS, sat at a round table, reminiscent of Arthurian legend, and conferring about the venture they were about to take outside The Stranding walls, Arthur, Galahad, Gawain, and Lancelot—or rather, Roni, Kia, Sam, and Toni we're all in agreement in one thing;

"Shit was weird, y'all." As Kia remarks about The Stranding's current state.

And indeed, shit had absolutely been weird.

"Well, in any case," Sam adds, "at least we don't exactly have to eat. Or drink, for that matter."

Toni snaps their fingers and points as he leans back, an act of agreement.

Roni takes a sip of their hot hazelnut mocha, "So, then we'll be fine. I'm not exactly sure we can get hurt or die here—at least, hurt badly. Pain *is* a sensation we seem allowed, though to what extent, I'm not sure."

"Tell us you're into kinky shit without telling us you're into kinky shit." Kia quickly inferred.

Toni, Sam, and Roni all choked on their coffee and blushed slightly, beckoning Kia to add, laughing loudly, "Geez, y'all, really? Sheesh."

"Anyway," Toni says, "I'm not afraid of getting hurt or anything. I'm ready whenever you are."

"Ditto." Sam says, "let's see what's out there."

Roni leans in against the table with their elbow, pressing a finger against the round of their nose, "There's something I should tell you all..."

Everyone leans in, cautiously curious as Roni takes a breath and extends the dramatic pause. Toni gestures to Roni to hasten their words, to which Kia responds by sucking her teeth so it makes a short and sharp sound and an elbow to Toni's rib. Toni grunts and glares at Kia, who gives him a stern look, and Toni mouths "fine."

"...I can hear the forest. I hear it calling to me, to us. It's like a melancholic vocalisation. And it's..." Roni pauses again, but this time, shortly, "it's like it wants us to come."

"Okay, that's just plain creepy. Roni, why would you say that? Now I'm a little freaked out." Kia says shuddering.

"Don't be a baby, baby. That's not *that* freaky." Toni retorts teasingly.

"*Oye, déjame quieta.* I don't like it, it feels..." Kia struggles to find the right words, "*Me da cosa.*"

"I know what you mean, Kia. It's unsettling, to say the least." Sam agrees.

"I get it," Roni says, ready to get back on topic, "it's spooky-scary, it's weird and, quite honestly, it's downright spine-chilling. It's like something out of a psychological horror film. Yeah, but are we ready to face whatever is out there without bitching out? Can we actually do this? I feel something growing inside me... like a cold fire."

"Yeah. I can do it. I feel it too." Kia says with steely resolve.

"Oh, I'm there, baby," Sam says excitedly, "it'll be like living my own adventure, instead of reading it."

"Fuckin' ready. I ain't afraid of nothin'." Toni says, flipping his long black locks back, adjusting their faux-leather jacket and passing their thumb across their nose.

"Well..." Roni says, pausing and taking a good look around the table at their companions, "I think I'm alright. Let's do this."

To say that their journey—their exodus—out of The Stranding and into the Forbidden Forest of Forgotten Figments and Figures, that would eventually lead them to the Voidheart Chasm, would be a simple one, would be an outright lie. It would be a bamboozling of epic proportions. What they would face, beyond jump scares and a foreboding, rather sinister ambience, beyond a sense of unease and that crawling sensation on their skin, would be a mirror to their own fears. They will be haunted, with ghosts of their pasts from the *reality* emerging from the shadows, from The Darkness.

Their resolve, their psychological strength will be put to the test in this elder place, a place forgotten even by Time, or perhaps, neglected. The Forbidden Forest of Forgotten Figments and Figures is heavy with an ever present pale crimson fog and thick with matte black Douglas Firs, Spruce, Thuja, and Juniper trees like high-grade charcoal etched across a dingy, stained canvass. The ground below would have sparse patches of the same black grass, illuminated by golden orbs that float just above and amongst the blades, imitating fireflies. There are, of course, signs that life once existed within the thicket of trees, with wooden posts and fences that were rotted and worn down by the absence of life and light. There are walls and foundations, remnants of a village, in the same condition, dilapidated and in disrepair. Even trails and smatterings of cobblestone all leading to what would have been the village square, complete with a broken-down water well so deep and dark that one cannot hope to see the bottom.

Everything had been overgrown and overtaken by The Darkness, the shadows within the structures even darker and blacker than the already darkened forest seemed to be alive, with slight movement to them, like slow, controlled breathing or the steady, intentional movements of old Tai-Chi master; swaying, undulating. Something waited in those corners, lurking patiently like a spider waits for prey. Something altogether desperate to grasp at the light it had been denied, to have the sensations and vigour of life that it longed for. It had been torn apart, separated from its essence, suppressed and stripped away until it was merely the yearning, the desolation, and the destruction it was left with. Recoiling towards the shadows, but always reaching for—hoping for—the light.

This was what awaited the squad within this forest, this was what called to them with that sweet, but sombre song.

Chapter 14 - Lost, Enslaved, Fatal Decline

There they bloody go, the ingrates. Time sighs watching as the foursome come up on the Forbidden Forest of Forgotten Figments and Figures.

You know who—what they're bound to run into in there. This doesn't bode well. Attraction comments.

They are going to find The Darkness in there. Nature states.

*They are going to find **their** darkness in there. I hope they've fortified their emotions enough to face what lurks in the shadows.* Feeling sighs.

They have each other. They'll be fine. Chance reassures.

They're going to regret going in there. Mark my words. Time is uncharacteristically unpleasant and disagreeable.

The forest whispers in overlapping voices that seem all too familiar to the party. They share and exchange uneasy glances at each other as they stand just before the monochrome greyscale thicket of foreboding pines. Behind them, the way to The Stranding is illuminating wildly in various hues that differ from person to person as if begging them to go back. And in a sense, it was. It did not want them—*they* did not want them venturing any further. Yet they were determined to go on, ignoring the light show behind them.

Oh, let's give a good image of each of our Stranded, shall we? Roni, inspired by the styles of their favourite Devil Hunter from the video game series *Devil May Cry* that they had started to remember, had conjured up a look similar to his, with a long maroon cossack-style coat where the front panels were matte black, zipped just below the bust for *"The Aesthetic"*, form fitting skinny pants—also maroon—with straps and pouches, you know, for storing *things*, or so they say. Extremities were covered in tall, buckled and zippered *pleather* boots and *pleather* fingerless gloves respectively—in black of course. "What? It was my favourite look. It was either this or a skin-tight sneaking suit." Roni would explain. Their hair would remain the same as always—Sandman-*esque*.

Sam, meanwhile, was a little more toned down in dress; light wash blue skinny jeans—pre-ripped, chequered Vans, a dramatically low 'v' neck black tee with a black hooded sweater—zip-up—that had thumb holes cut in the wrist cuffs, a jean jacket filled with various patches of brands and bands they'd thought forgotten which Roni had pointed out, "Oh, my gods! I loved those bands! I can't believe I lived without them the whole time here!" to which Sam responded with a simple, "I know, right?" While their hair was covered by a black beanie cap.

Kia stood dressed in what she had referred to as *"techwear"*, comprised of joggers that had been cropped halfway down the calf that met with knee-length socks—both black with electric blue embellishments in the form of thick bands and lines, with the joggers having multiple pockets and pouches, also for carrying *things*. On her torso she wore a stark black sports bra that doubled as a crop top, on the band just below her bust and in the centre—at the sternum—was a digital-style triangle in that same blue. She also wore an oversized hooded jacket—parka style—which she left open. She had somehow managed to get much of her hair in a bun that poked out of a black baseball cap that had horns that mimicked *Batman's*, with her bangs and long curly side locks set just below the brim.

Toni was the simplest of them all. He wore his usual, black straight-leg form fitting jeans, biker-style boots—the ones with the buckles—, a plain black tee, and their 'patented' *pleather* jacket—the kind with the angled lapels, zippers, and the belt at the bottom. Their long, thick black hair parted to the left and fell dramatically.

Okay, now that that's out of the way and we have a good picture of the fearless foursome, we can get on with the adventure.

"Well," Roni says finally, mustering up the courage to start forward on their journey into darkness, "what are we waiting for? The sun?"

"As if," says Sam with a chuckle, "hey, never say die, right?"

Roni nods and glances over at Kia who catches their eyes and says, "Fine, let's go. The Stranding was getting boring anyway."

"Oh yeah," says Toni, rather sarcastically, "all of that safety and comfort. So boring." He pops his collar and starts walking, "Come on, losers, don't just stand there talkin', let's get walkin'!"

And with a collective scoff and a skip, they follow Toni briskly, but cautiously into the dwelling place of Darkness' despair; into where what's forgotten comes to *unlife*. This *unlife* begins to unfurl and stir as the dull, crunchy sounds of the squad's footsteps echo throughout the forest, like ripples and waves in the open water, disturbing the silence that had long existed there. A silence that had been kept by Darkness as it enveloped any interlopers that, out of madness, had entered its domain. But these four were different somehow, and the inquisitive shadows watched from their corners and crevices, their depths, interested in their essence, in their collective power. But interested more, they were, in Roni's essence in particular; how it radiated, and how it reached out toward the shadows fearlessly, selflessly, as if to extend aid and offer comfort.

Deeper still the group traipsed on, chills and horripilation crawling down from their napes and throughout their body. The sensations of eyes staring and glaring from the unknown parts all around, unable to see more than a few steps ahead of them, and that is by the grace of the orbs that dance along the blades below and illuminate the fog that sits just above, extending upwards and dying just under the branches of the black undying pines.

"Gosh, I wish I had my *Zippo*, I can't see worth a damn." Toni said.

"I know, right, it's so dense. If only we had a flashlight or something, though I-dee-kay if that would hurt it, you know, like that—" Kia stops herself knowing the reference would be lost on her current company, "—yeah, anyway, it'd be nice to **see**."

Sam studies Kia a bit, noting her self-interruption, but shakes their head, "Ahuh... but right, at least like six feet ahead or something, not this barely three."

Roni gets an idea to snap their fingers as if from pure instinct, "Yeah, like just snap and—" the snap elicits a radiant teal flame that manifests from their thumb, middle and index fingers, causing everyone to have an "oh shit" moment, and Roni's eyes to widen in amazement, "Whoa! It doesn't even burn!" They play with the flame, wiggling and rolling their fingers, waving their hand around, until finally, closing and opening their hand to form a baseball-sized ball of teal flame.

"It's so cute!" Kia couldn't contain herself.

"That's so cool, can we all do that?" Toni steps forward to inspect the fireball further.

"I mean, I can float, so I'd imagine we can all do stuff like this." Sam says pointing at the azure flame floating just above Roni's pleather bound right palm.

"Whoa, you can float? Does that mean you can fly too?" Toni asks, amazed and wondering if they have an ability.

"Yeah, they can!" Roni intrudes.

"But I don't think I can fly, at least, I've never tried..." Sam gets lost in thought.

"Well," Kia starts, "I think I know what my ability might be. Because I think our special abilities are tied to our *thing*. And I remembered what **my** *thing* is."

"Go on..." Toni encourages Kia's thought process.

"So, you're a writer and a reader, that's your thing, right?" Kia says to Sam.

Sam nods, "Yeah."

"So it makes sense that you'd be able to 'take flight', like a sort of being able to escape-slash-explore freely. And you're such a gentle bean that you just kinda float!" Kia explains.

Sam cocks their head and makes an inquisitive, yet agreeing face.

"And you, Roni, you have that fire inside you. Like your favourite band's name and how singing and music can 'set fire' to your soul. Therefore, fire. Ha." Kia continues, while Roni gives an approving head bob,

"And Toni... you're a painter and a sketch artist. So I think your ability has to do with creation-slash-manifestation. You can create anything out of thin air, like at will, like just thinking about it."

"Okay but how is that different from that thing we can all do to change clothes?" Toni probes.

Kia ponders for a moment, "I mean, I can't make a cigarette out of thin air like you do. I think that's just like..." Kia gathers her thoughts, "clothes are just transitory anyway. They're a matter of our expression, and because we can all express freely here, it makes sense that we can transfer that to changing our clothes like Sailor Moon—uh, like, uh, magic."

"I guess that makes sense. Who knew I was wasting my superpowers on cigarettes." Toni shrugs.

"Wait, what about you?" Roni inquires.

"Oh! Right. Me. Um... well I'm a martial artist. I took Jeet Kune Do classes to stay out of the house and away from all of the fighting, with the art of fighting without fighting. So I think," Kia says excitedly, finally being able to remember her *thing*, while the others look on, shocked at the revelation, "that my ability is like strength, reflexes, durability. It also goes with what I had to go through and how y'all see me as this happy, super optimistic person despite everything!"

"Wait, hold on, you can fight!?" They all shout, hyperbolically.

She can fight? Attraction exclaims.

She can fight. Time confirms.

Where was this information in her backstory? Attraction interrogates.

*It wasn't pertinent. I gave you the quick rundown of her life, okay? I can't give every little detail. Plus!, I didn't think it was going to come back in any way. She didn't practise here, given that her style is not **forgotten**.* Time explains.

*I was wondering what her art was. It makes sense, as Jeet Kune Do is highly customisable and subject to the practitioner's **Way of No Way**.* Nature says.

It seems to be why she's usually so centred. So in tune with her emotions and her body. What a cool girl. Feeling expresses.

Finally, now we're all mostly caught up and on the same-ish page! Chance says, being quickly shushed and having space dust thrown in their direction.

*I mean, can we focus on the fact that they're also, uh, I don't know, **AWAKENING**!!* Time shouts.

*Yes, that brings them closer to **integration,** converging the **reality** with the **unreality**, thus unravelling the **strands** that keep this plane, and everyone in it, separate and in **unexistence**.* Nature says, with the slightest concern.

Ah, yes. The ***Integration*** of existence and *unexistence*. The Forces fear this convergence of being states, as it would strip them of power and return them to The Source; their Creator. At least, that's what they believe.

Unexistence isn't the opposite of existence, by the way, it simply is a state of being outside of normal existence. It is beside existence, beside life; a different route, if you will. Being in its purest form, isness, suchness, without the bounds and ties of mortality and what it means to be in the eyes of the world—or even the universe. This is a freedom only written about by philosophers, monks, and thinkers; ponderers of the soul and what it means to be human. Either way, this is what The Forces sought—that absolute freedom—for themselves and to share with those they felt kinship with on Earth. Freedom; the ultimate state of being.

Chapter 15 - Feel Death, See Its Beady Eyes

The lycoris oppidum that is The Stranding far behind them, obscured by the blackness of the forest having pulled them further and obnubilated them in its very being, the four friends had been given light in the form of Roni's shared flame. Upon receiving a blob of flame of their own, each one's fire transmuted to fit the bearer; Toni's was as a shining jade, Kia's was curiously magenta—Roni's favourite colour—, and Sam's was vermillion, a sort of opposing, yet complementary hue to Toni's jade. These curious colours of shining flame in the tenebrosity of this black forest caught further the attention of the clandestine shadows that watched with a tenuous but taut admiration.

How lovely their light, they whispered, *and how strong their bond.*

How lovely their bond, another deeper, raspier whisper, *but how strong their light.*

As they tread deeper into the seemingly eternal darkness, an ethereally eerie voice pierces the deafening silence softly singing—rather, humming—sour, dour notes that send shivers down Roni's spine, having psychically damaged them.

"That voice, it hurts me in ways." Roni murmurs.

"What voice?" Kia asks, having overheard as she was in close proximity.

"You didn't hear that? It's still going. It's like, the saddest humming—vocalising you'll ever hear actually carrying a tune without breaking." Roni says, wincing still.

"I hear it too, it hurts my heart." Sam says, crossing their arms tightly and burying their neck in their shoulders.

Kia looks over at a shrugging Toni and mutters, "Emotional Damage..."

"I don't hear anything, it's real qui—" Toni starts, being interrupted by a voice calling to them.

"Toni." it says, repeating sparsely.

"Who's callin' me? Is that—?" Toni stops, recognizing the voice, "Chino!?" Toni halts their steps and turns around to peer into the void. He stands rigid, as if a statue fixed upon the ground with their hand still holding their jade fire— flickering and shrinking—, his vision narrowing, captive by some unknown source far in the blackness that threatens closer, a vortex pulling him, a force enthralling him, invisible to him, yet Toni knows it's there, just there. It continues to call them, "Toni. Toni." having stolen Chino's voice from their memories. A forgotten figment, a forbidden figure, a phantom seeping through the void, apparating and beckoning Toni to break away from their friends and amble toward it.

"Chino, is that you?" Toni speaks without a voice.

"Toni. Toni. Come on. Get away from there." Chino's voice echoes, the phantom gesturing phlegmatically and reaching out to them.

"Chino, I'm sorry. I didn't—"

"Toni! What tee-eff, snap out of it!" Kia yells, shaking Toni's shoulder, "Where did you go? Your fire! It's dimming! Roni!"

"I'm coming!" Roni shouts back, jogging to their friends.

"Chino... He was there." Toni says softly, "In the forest. In the dark, I heard him," they pause, gripping their fist tightly, "I saw him."

"Honey, no. That's just the forest effing with you. He can't be here, there's no way." Kia tries to reassure him.

"I'm here, what's up? What's going—oh, your fire! Here," Roni takes Toni's hand in theirs and rekindles the flame, "I got you. Always."

Toni breaks their gaze from the distant shadows and fixes it on Roni's smiling face, "Thank you, I—I don't know what came over me. I just, I was like, paralyzed or somethin'. It's crazy, I heard his voice and I froze, then I felt like, a darkness washing over me. It was like looking through binoculars, but like if the image kept closing, getting darker. I dunno. I'm sorry." Toni looks back into the forest, "I'm sorry…"

Roni sighs shortly, then wraps their arms around Toni, "Well, whenever that happens again, we'll be here for you to pull you out and remind you that you're here, with us, safe."

They let go and Toni chuckles, "Sheesh, gettin' all mushy on me, kid."

"You know me, a puddle of mush." Roni laughs.

"Yeah… I appreciate you, Roni, really. Thank you." Toni inhales sharply through their nose and lets it go.

"If you two queers are done being gay," Sam cuts in playfully, "we should keep moving."

"Us? Done being gay? Is that possible, Toni?" Roni remarks.

"Nah, I don't think it is, Roni." Toni adds with a chortle.

Kia, smiling and amused, interjects, "Are you kidding me? These two are gayer and queerer than the Pride Parade."

"There's a parade?" Toni turns swiftly, with surprised curiosity.

"Oh, honey." Kia shakes her head and laughs.

The light from their fires illuminate the broken, dilapidated facades—the remains of an obliterated village. Bent and broken lamp posts are few and far between, but Roni has the idea to light them with their fire.

"That should help," they say, lighting the few they can along the worn cobblestone path overtaken by overgrowth, "all of these old lights keeping the dark at bay."

"Look at all of these wrecked up old..." Kia pauses, surveying the dimly lit area, "houses? Were these houses? Everything is so effed up."

The others agree, nodding, grunting, and giving a paced "ahuh".

"Look," Sam says, observing the shadows, "some of these shadows are real stubborn. They're like, still super dark— oh, shi—did it just move!?"

It did, in fact, just move. But ever so slightly.

"I think it did, in fact, just move, but like, slightly." Kia says, parroting my line again—it's been a while at least.

"Right!? Okay I'm not losing it." Sam says.

"No, I'm right there with you. If you're losing it, I am. There's something *spoopy* about this place." Kia adds.

"I agree, there's something off about this place." Roni says.

Toni sort of grunts and shrugs, cautiously looking around and stuffing their free hand in their pocket and sticking close to Kia.

The shadowy corners shift and slither, emitting static hiss and crawling just in and out of periphery. They've caught on to the movements and attention of the interlopers and are choosing *tactical espionage actions* as opposed to outward confrontation. The shadows lighten and spread themselves thin, still watching, staying *unvisible*—lying in the veil between sight in blindness, but Roni can't shake the feeling that a disembodied presence is looming, roaming around them and waiting for an opening. The hairs on their neck stands on end, completely perpendicular to their now bumpy skin, their breath hastening, their heart quickening, their mind arresting. Kia, whomst is standing right behind them—back-to-back—turns and gently places a hand on Roni's mid-back and caresses assuringly up to their shoulder. Roni turns their face to her and nods, taking a breath.

"Stay with me." Kia says calmly, "I got you."

"Okay, thanks, Kia. I was close to freaking out." Roni responds.

"You alright?" Toni walks up on Roni's other side.

"Yeah, I'm calming down. Are you? Any more voices?" Roni says.

"Yeah I'm cool. Don't hear much of anything anymore. 'Cept my own breathing." Toni says, shifting their eyes around.

Sam had gone off a little further, investigating the shadows in the corners of the former village homes. They tread steadily, holding their vermillion flame out and focusing it in a way that makes a kind of spotlight—a torchlight, if you will—that illuminates the path before them, but only enough to make out the ground and very little detail.

The atmosphere grows colder around them, the air thinner, and they start feeling a heaviness to their movements as they continue away from their friends. Behind them, the shadows create a shroud to obfuscate them from their friends as if the boundaries of sight end for them there and nothing more. Sam grows colder, their skin contracting into millions of tiny mounds, their breath, now a visible vapour, begins to shake as they struggle, their lungs burning and their throat closing. Sam shakes their head, trying to get ahold of their senses but fail and fall to their knees gasping, spit dripping and spraying out of their mouth. They reach for their neck, eyes watering, it hurts to try to inhale any helpful amount of air.

Their flame starts flickering out, causing the light around them to dim. The Darkness is closing in on them, patiently. Sam coughs, watching the light slowly go out and searching the area frantically with their eyes as The Darkness encroaches on them; they've collapsed onto their side now, keeping their palm up in hopes that the flame won't die.

"Sam!" A voice shouts, "Sam!"

I know that voice, they think to themself, unable to speak.

"Sam! She's—" The voice stops short.

Elissa? My sister...!?

"Sam!! Mom is—"

I know, I know. I know what happened!

"Mom is—!"

"Sam! Sam! Come out of there!" Another voice.

Franxeska, I can't... Sam struggles.

"Sam!!"

Chapter 16 - In The Arms of Undertow

"Y'all, I don't think we're moving forward. Or at least, not making any progress." Kia comments.

"Kia." The Forest speaks raspily, but familiarly.

Her head perks up and she scans the area, "Roni? Toni? Y'all close by?"

"Kia. *Kialyss.*" The Forest continued from the dark distance, sounding muffled, as if behind something.

"Okay, yeah, no. That's not a thing. No one calls me that except—"

"*KIALYSS,*" The Forest insisted now, "*abreme. Ven a mi.*"

"Mom!?" Kia gasps, "No, no. Nuh-uh, no effing way."

"*Kialyss.*" It was more of a hiss this time around than a whisper. An angry beckoning. Anger or some other expression that can be misconstrued as anger.

Kia closes her eyes, wondering how she had lost sight of Roni and Toni, how they had wandered off—if *she* had wandered off. *We were supposed to stay together!* She thinks to herself, *They were literally right there a moment ago!* But they had gone off, or vanished. She didn't know which was worse. And now she was hearing the voice of her mother, a voice she hadn't heard in a long while, here in this forest. The voice continued to echo into her ears, now from the darker corners that seemed to ripple and sway as if to beg her to come closer.

Now, in front of her, was a door to an abandoned and broken home that had barely a wall around it and a foundation that seemed to crumble. But behind that door was the voice, or rather, the blackest shadows that had seen the darkness inside her and had used it—in the form of a voice—to lure her to them. But Kia held her ground, she remained as the void in its nothingness, an empty cup not burdened by sticky thoughts and expectations. Kia breathed deeply, keeping concentrated on her mind and body, her heartbeat steady and unchanged.

"Absolutely not. You're not her." She says lining her fingers perpendicularly up against the door and shifting her body into a ready stance, magenta flame hovering over her right palm held close to her heart.

"Kia. I never—"

Her eyes opened suddenly, "—I won't listen. I'll intercept this bee-ess."

"They kept me—"

"Shit, Toni, where's Kia? And Sam, they've been M.I.A." Roni treads carefully through what used to be a home but is now mostly scratched and splintered floor and two partial walls.

No one answers and the silence is thicker now, heavier, even. It's as though Roni were wearing noise cancelling headphones in a steel box in space. And it did indeed seem to them as if even the air was closing in on them. It was unbearable, almost, and their clothes started to give them the sensation of weighing them down and constricting them. They struggled to move around, to even walk, with every step being as if stuck in mud that was three feet high.

Where is everyone? They thought to themself.

"Roni." A voice beckoned from the well, sounding as if underwater.

Roni turned their head to face the well, "Oh, what now?"

"Roni," the voice grew more desperate with every call, "Roni!"

They moved closer to the well, their legs fatigued and sore, their shoulders heavy and tingling, their spine feeling like some phantom had reached in and gripped it tightly in its deathly icy grasp. *That voice sounds like someone. Is that someone? That's someone.* They thought, fighting through the fog and ignoring the discomfort and pain.

"Come up," it started repeating, overlapping itself, "come—Roni."

"Come up? But I'm—" Roni hesitates, "damn, where is everyone!? I'm alone, I'm alone and it's dark and I'm..."

Roni collapses to their knees with one hand down on the ground and the other holding their fire that's stuttering and shrinking in their palm. The heaviness gets more intense, vision blurring and fuzz on the brain. Roni throws their weight back to land on their bum and clutches their chest, then their head, their fingers entangling in their big hair.

Alone again. I'm alone again. Everyone's gone—where did they go? Where did they go...? Where am I? It's so dark and my fire's going out. Oh, my gods, I'm drowning, I feel like I'm drowning. I hear a voice that sounds like—but she hates me, she hates me. It can't be her. I'm alone again and it's so dark and I'm so cold and my body hurts. Why does my body hurt? Why does—?

I can't do this. I can't do it, I can't do this, I can't—. Damn it, I'm so useless, I couldn't even keep them close. They're gone, it's my fault, I didn't keep an eye on them and they're gone now and it's my fault. And I'm drowning and my fire is going out and I'm so useless I can't get up. I can't even get up. What's wrong with me? What's wrong with me!? Roni's thoughts a downward spiral.

"Roni. Come up." "Roni. You can't leave—"

They always need me. They don't want me, they need me. If they wanted me I wouldn't be here now, in this alone. She always needed me too much. Never wanted me, never wanted me around, never wanted me at all. No one did. No one. That's why I'm alone... Roni clutches their heart, a golf ball in their throat and their nostrils clogged and full as their eyes swell with a flood that cannot be contained.

I can't do this, they break, *I can't be here, I can't stand—I can't see anything, why can't I see anything. Oh, I'm crying, oh, gosh I'm crying. My heart. I can't save them—what if they're in trouble? I can't save them. My fire's going out. Oh, no, oh, no, no... Gods! Why am I so useless? I need to get up, I have to get up. I have to—*

"Come up."

Roni's mind wanders to memories of music, of songs. One song in particular cuts through the heavy fog inside them as they remember a lyric that pertains to their current situation, *Will the flood behind me put out the fire inside me...?*

The flame in Roni's palm flickers out.

"Okay, now where'd everybody go?" Toni scoffs.

They scan their environment meticulously, noting subtle differences in the forest that hadn't been there just a moment ago. Toni squinted, investigating how the shadows seemed closer and different than before, as if they were hiding something. Parts looked darker, more matte than others; less "natural".

They look down at the flame in their palm, glowing brilliantly verdant, and an idea strikes them. Toni lifts their other hand from their pocket to right beside the flame and snaps, manifesting a one handed flamethrower that looks like a ray gun from Sci-Fi films of their time with a large glass-like bubble in the centre of the gun that houses the jade flame like a window so that Toni can keep an eye on the intensity of the fire. The gun itself is a shiny, sleek metallic with a short grip and a button trigger, the body is exactly 25.87cm long, rounded—22.34cm in diameter at the muzzle, 33.66cm around the part with the bubble—with a hose on either side—bolted on—that starts at the front end of the flame bubble and follows to exactly 7.88cm before the end of the muzzle, connected, of course, to propel and give extra "oomph" to the flame with a concentrated gas.

"Now, this is what I'm talkin' 'bout." He says, kissing the glass, "What a babe."

"Hyah!!" Kia shouts, executing the one-inch punch on the door, sending it flying into The Darkness. "Ha! I still got it!" She says cheerfully, admiring her fist.

The Darkness hisses softly, irritated by Kia's attack and the light from her flame—it's growing more intensely, forcing the shadows to retreat further into darkened corners.

"I see you, bitch!" Kia mocks Darkness.

They have me on edge! I cannot deal right now! Time says exasperatedly.

I know! It's so stressful, but Kia's so strong! That's my girl. Attraction responds proudly.

It's gonna be tough for the other two... Chance suggests.

They just have to believe in the fire inside them. In their hearts, and in the Strands they have between them. Feeling says.

They'll drive The Darkness back. Nature says assuredly.

The crunchy loud hiss of the flamethrower cuts through the silence and the shadows, setting ablaze the black foliage and causing them to burn in 16-bit neon fuschia flames that seem to almost instantly fade to greyscale. Darkness was not happy about the fires and reared away from the light, sapping away the colour from them in an attempt to quell the intensity.

"What the—how?" Toni growls, annoyed at Darkness' resilience in the face of their green flames licking at the shadows.

The Force is strong, unrelenting, and now furious. They had withstood attacks on two fronts while feeding on the darkness within the hearts of Sam and Roni, and now they had to break their grip on the two to fight back against Kia and Toni whose creativity and ability caught Darkness off guard. Toni's fire was intense, thinning the shrouds that held Roni and Sam hostage. Meanwhile, Kia kept calm but ready with appropriate tension; senses sharp and balanced, waiting for Darkness to retaliate at any moment.

"Where are they, ya damn forest!?" Toni shouts, "Give them back!" He checks the bubble to see if the flame is still going strong; it is.

Toni then turns, seeing a faint blue behind a web of shadows, like thick tendrils tangled together and a little blue light glowing there.

"Roni?"

Chapter 17 - A Little Bit of Loneliness, A Little Bit of Disregard

I'm so alone. It's so dark, and I'm alone in this forest.
Darkness sorrowfully speaks, *I've been cast away, ripped apart and thrown away. They never wanted me, I was too different.*

Roni struggles to speak, their voice low and raspy, "...Me too. I was the same, before..."

Before you came here. You're as lonely as me, we're the same; alone, discarded, and hated for existing. Darkness cries softly.

"I—I was. Not anymore, I have friends now. I have people who love me—want me. Not just for what I can do for them, but for just being." Roni chokes.

But you still keep them from seeing what I see. You keep parts of you hidden; the broken parts, the dark parts. Darkness insists.

Roni pauses, "You're right, I'm still afraid they'll think I'm a monster for my dark thoughts. But what if they don't? What if I've been scared for no reason? It's not like I can control those thoughts..."

I suppose you can't. But they're still there, Darkness hisses, *they're still a part of you. Just like how everything I touch dies. We can't help it, but it's who we are.*

"No, I am not my darkness. Those thoughts just pop up unprompted! They cut through whatever I was doing, whatever I was thinking, like if someone else was talking over me." Roni fights back.

Darkness laughs dryly, *As if I want to kill those beautiful things that make me smile. But every time I reach out to them they turn from me, or worse...*

"I'm not afraid of you." Roni declares bravely, "I'm not."

No? But look at you, you're dying. I'm draining you of your light, you're turning grey here. Soon you'll be like the others. Darkness apparates a shadowy mirror that opens like a large tube television in black and white and shows Roni the fate of those that have ventured into The Forest driven by desperation and were never seen again.

Figures stuck in darkness, drained of all colour and left a mortifying grey husk forever screaming silently. Faces contorted as if they had witnessed horrors beyond imagination. Some of them reaching out for something unseen, some were clutching their heads or their arms. Others were thrown to the ground or against trees as was their final moment so terrible that they could not stand. All of these figures were bound by tendrils that seemed as though they were the abyss itself.

I am the shadows. I am the Darkness. I am death and destruction, despair and devastation. I am what all beings fear. I am oblivion. And you will tell me that you are not afraid? Of me? Darkness scoffs.

Roni fights their body to sit up, grabbing at their chest, at their heart, "Yes. That's exactly what I will tell you. The flood won't put this fire out!"

Their hand bursts in brilliant oceanic light giving new life to an even stronger flame than before.

How have you not resigned to your fate? You'll leave me as well? You want to break me too!? Darkness cries.

"No. You've got it wrong." Roni stands up and holds their flaming hand out to Darkness.

"Whoa!" Kia exclaims dodging Darkness' black tendrils as they shoot out from the shadows all around.

The tendrils whip and thrust toward her as she flips and ducks, bobs and weaves, and jumps to avoid being struck.

"I know I can't touch you but," Kia closes her fist around the magenta flame, causing it to engulf her hand, "—whoa—what if I go all Iron Fist on your ass!"

A tendril lashes at her and she blocks it with her flaming hand, which makes her—well, at this point there's no better reaction for this—"squee" in delight and excitement. She uses her flaming hand to block and parry the numerous tendrils that grew out of adjacent shadows that she wasn't able to dodge. She then gets an idea, *What if I just—*, to charge up a fist and slam it down on the already splintered floor.

"Eff yes!" She shouts gleefully watching her flame radiate a light that eradicates the shadows from the area and burns the shroud ahead, revealing a near-grey Sam on the ground.

Sam moans and writhes on the cold black ground, holding on to the tiny spark of fire in their palm, "I won't—"

"Sam! Oh-em-gee! I'm coming!" Kia runs to Sam's side and kneels over them, placing their glowing, fiery hand on their back. "Hey, I got you, bébé, okay? My fire will warm you up, you're shaking. Oh, sweetie, here." She takes a bit of fire and joins it to Sam's, giving it the spark it needed to reignite fully, and to bring Sam back from the *unlife*.

Sam coughs, gasps, and inhales sharply, "Shi—Kia, I tried. But my mom, she—"

"I know. Mine too. But it's over now, those ghosts can't haunt us now. I won't let them." Kia was serious, quite seriously serious, for the first moment in a long while.

Do you think, what they heard, what they saw... Time starts, *Do you think they know—*

Attraction cuts Time short, *Don't be ridiculous. That's impossible. Besides, how could Da—The Darkness know to show them **that**?*

The other Forces remain silent, just spectating the events in The Forbidden Forest of Forgotten Figments and Figures and Time's reactions.

Just as Toni was gearing up to blast the shroud that held the blue light behind it with their own flames, the shroud dissipated, Roni and a mysterious dark figure behind it. Roni was extending their hand to the figure, offering their flame, their warmth. The figure was apprehensive, reluctantly reaching for the flame.

"It won't hurt you, I won't hurt you. I promise." Roni smiles warmly.

"Roni! Watch out! Don't let that black blob touch you!" Toni aimed the flamethrower, activating it—a high-pitched whirring sound.

"Toni?" Roni says, looking over at Toni, whomst is ready to light up the dark, "Don't shoot! Wait, how'd you get a gun? And is that the flame I gave you?"

"I made it, and yeah. *Whaddyamean*, 'don't shoot', that thing's gonna grey ya!" Toni lowers their gun slightly, cocking their head to the right.

"This *thing* isn't a thing at all. It's—*they*—are a—what did you call it?" Roni squints.

A Force of the Universe. Darkness clarifies.

"A Force of the Universe." Roni reaffirms.

"A Force of the Universe?" Toni disapparates the gun.

"A Force of the Universe. Yeah, I don't quite get what it means yet either." Roni shrugs.

"What's a Force of the Universe?" Kia shouts and waves as she joins Toni's side with Sam.

Sam grunts, still recovering, "Who ever heard of a—what?"

A Force. Of. The Universe! Darkness growls impatiently, *And I can explain what it all means. But not before Roni does what they'd promised.*

Toni, Sam, and Kia all exchanged confused glances before fixing their eyes on Roni. Roni smiled at them, the smile faded into a solemn look and cast their gaze toward Darkness who was standing before them, waiting. Roni nodded once, with determination.

"Wait, but what did you promise Them?" Kia asked, taking a step toward the two.

"Better I show you than try to explain. It was communicated with my *essence*." Roni held their hand out toward Darkness again, "Well, come on, D!"

Chapter 18 - Go Kill The Lights, We'll Glow Til Morning Comes

Darkness had once been whole, once been brilliant and beautiful in all of their intangibility. They had curves and lines, they had twists and turns, they had definition. Darkness had been darkness in name and in relativity to their role in the universe, but beyond that, there had been none more resplendent and light. Their kindness was only eclipsed by unending positivity. *There is poetry in despair,* they'd say—a sentiment echoed by Roni's favourite band—, *but all poems have a final word, and despair isn't forever.*

It was this saccharine and gentle approach to endings and destruction, sorrow and pain, that gave them the moniker of *Sweet Death*, or Sweet *Release*, or what have you. Instead of an inevitable awfulness and cessation, humans had come to see Darkness as more a mercy. And those touched by Darkness that were burdened by despair were given gifts to alleviate their despair; the arts. With these, humanity could feel a closeness to Darkness, to the Forces, to *unliving* and *undeath.*

This burdening came with caveats, though. Many were lost to the despair, an ending that came too soon, and Darkness, too, became infected with despair. As Darkness ushered *those who left too soon* to the aether and into the Ending, they longed to have a place to go and be with them—those they called their *children.*

So along with the other Forces, Darkness helped create The Plane of The Forgotten. A place for the suffering souls to find an unending bliss among their peers and shed the shroud of despair.

But the other Forces would soon become jealous and grow weary of Darkness and how their children loved them. Darkness, indeed, had become obsessed with their shared creation, saving humans from their perceivable end before it could come at their own hands and destabilising the balances of the Universe. Darkness, of course, couldn't see if those endings were coming or not, they acted on impulse and the need to spare humans from further pain. They'd scoop humans up and obliviate their existence from the universe as they brought them into The Plane, and the first Stranding.

There's no way they could know! Time would shout.

It's messing with people's fates and timelines, but I can understand where Darkness is coming from. Chance would chime in.

Yes, well, it severs bonds and I have to quickly find someone else to fill that axis. It's not easy, you know! Attraction would state.

Darkness is, in turn, taking from me my role in the Universe. Things must run their course! Nature would say grumpily.

In their haste, Darkness became sloppy and careless. Their serenity in the face of despair had become a mask they wore, no longer sincere and intrinsic, their optimism became neutrality; grey. They had come to resent the other Forces for not helping, for even interfering and demanding they stop "saving" humans from a fate unseeable.

Stop telling me what to do! Just please, we need to make more space, we need a bigger town, perhaps even a continent-like structure! Darkness pleaded angrily.

A continent!? Honestly, Darkness, you're taking this much too far. It was never meant to be this massive! And we were meant to have equal input, as well as a passive hand in their affairs. You're directly communing with these poor humans and it's causing irreparable damage to the cosmos! Attraction scolds.

I know that you just want to help them, D. I know it's hard to watch them suffer like they do, often at each other's hands. You're the loveliest of us, D, maybe even the best of us, and that's your downfall, unfortunately. I'm sorry, D. Feeling expressed regretfully.

Even you, Feeling? You won't help, you won't stop them? They'll obliterate them, Feels! Don't you understand? That's worse than meeting their end out there! At least they'd have been remembered! This way, Darkness started choking up, *they won't even have that. They'll be completely gone, Feels, they'll have **unlived**.*

Unliving, again is not unlike death, but also not unlike living. It's a state that exists somewhere in-between and beside living and dying; in a sense, it's not having existed at all. Which is worse than *unexistence*, as that is the state of being that resides in The Plane of the Forgotten.

Feeling remained silent, as did Chance. Time had glanced over at Nature, whomst was ready to do what the Forces had convened to do; *undo* Darkness.

Truly, this is regretful for me, Darkness. As it is not in me to do this, but it must be done. Nature stated solemnly.

Before Darkness could react, Time paralysed them in a field of frozen moments, Nature initiated the entropy within that field as Time began to hasten the moments in that field infinitely, essentially ripping Darkness apart and causing their form to desiccate and become mutilated; rent asunder. Feeling captured the emotional essence of Darkness and pulled it from the field, a gargantuan glob of pure negativity in the formless form of a void so empty and black, the vacuum of space was brighter. Attraction ripped Darkness's personality from them, a haze of grey in a bubble of electromagnetic energy. Chance held onto the possibility of Darkness and the obscurity of moments yet to pass, a parasitic fog that existed as an intangible symbol or state rather than something physical. Nature repurposed the body of Darkness as a forest—or rather, the idea of a forest—which they'd use to entomb the outskirts of the first Stranding. Time, after having their siblings split the remains of their sibling, held onto the heart of Darkness.

I know you yet live, sibling. But torn to pieces and scattered from your heart, you can do no harm. Time said with resolve before casting the heart down into the centre of the first Stranding.

The heart of Darkness, with the field of entropy, had enough power to obliterate the first Stranding and envelop it in unending shadows of *undeath*. The impact not only sent all of the inhabitants of the area into *unliving*, but also made a deep crater that seemingly has no bottom and emanates shadowy smoke. This came to be known as The Voidheart Chasm.

Nature then did as they intended and buried the ruins of the town in the forest they'd made from the body of Darkness. Feeling and Attraction cast their pieces of Darkness into the Forest, while Chance held on to theirs as means to keep the other Forces in the dark.

Pun intended.

But Time had been wrong. The Voidheart Chasm was so deep that it seeped into the *reality*, and throughout the ages began affecting and afflicting it. The touch of Darkness was still there, and despair had become endemic to humanity, though now it came without mercy.

So, here we are. Roni's hand extended toward Darkness, glowing that spectacular teal fiery glow, and a soft determination in their gaze.

You know what you must do, Roni. I am ready. Darkness glides toward Roni.

"Wait, okay, what's going on? I'm still lost..." Kia scratches her head.

Roni sighs, slightly impatient, with a hint of adoration, "Just watch, love."

Kia nods with a swift "Hmph!" of agreement.

Darkness, in all their shadowy, smokey blackest blackness, with small, obsidian tendrils independently swaying out from random bits of their—presently— humanoid body, stands in a beautifully ominous—like a comforting creepiness—manner, patiently watching Roni, whose eyes are fixed upon the visage of Darkness. Darkness raises their hand to meet Roni's, with neither yet touching, but the energy between them is palpable.

Roni's flame is drawn to Darkness who flinches at the lick of the azure flame, then relaxes when prompted by a gesture from Roni. Roni breathes evenly—deep breath in, deep breath out, with the exhale being drawn out longer than the inhale—relaxing their mind and settling their fluttering heart. With a long exhale, Roni's flame reaches out to Darkness, wrapping around their arm and down their body, Darkness then becomes fully engulfed in blue fire; it doesn't burn, not in the way we imagine burning would feel, anyway.

Darkness lets out an agonised howl in response to being wrapped in azure fire and Roni takes a step back, surprised by the reaction of both Darkness and the fire.

Roni implores Darkness, "D, D! You have to calm down, breathe, D. It's not hurting you, I promise. Just let the fire in. Let me in. Trust me, D, I'll help you find your pieces so you can be whole again. But you have to let go, you have to want to."

I can't, I'm scared! Darkness writhes desperately.

"Roni, what's happening!?" Sam steps towards them but Kia holds them back.

Roni holds a hand out to them, gesturing to them to keep back and says, "Darkness is fighting the fire. They're struggling because they've been here for so long, just stewing in their hurt and isolation. Darkness grows in isolation, but they weren't always like this. They showed me, I can't explain how, but they showed me how they were before this, before they were torn apart and kept from their heart. They were made this way, forced to be like this by the other Forces of the Universe."

Toni kicks a rock and grunts, "Well, that ain't right. Why are they fighting it?"

Roni lowers their hand and extends their arms out, as if to welcome a hug from Darkness, "I don't know, exactly, but I think it's because they've been here for so long in their loneliness, it's hard to imagine anything else. It's like a security blanket."

"Psh, yeah, if the blanket was darker than hell." Toni scoffs.

"Change is never easy, but it's always worth it." Kia affirms.

Roni walks toward the writhing, flaming Darkness, "You have to want it, D. You have to want to get better, to change, to be the beautiful, brilliant version of you we both know exists. You have to fight for it, not against it. I know you can do this, you're a fucking Force of the Universe! You were the best of them, I know it."

Excuse me, what? Time chimes in, watching everything unfold from above while the other Forces remain speechless, half rooting, half horrified.

"Just breathe, D. Deep breath in, deep breath out, let your—what would be—your stomach expand and contract. Listen to my voice, focus on my voice. You can do this, D, I believe in you. I'm coming to you, and I am going to embrace you. You're safe, D. You'll shine once again, and even brighter than before."

I-I... I don't know. I don't have my heart, I need my heart. I need my... Darkness gasps and gulps desperately.

Roni wraps their arms around Darkness, both of them being enveloped in flames, and hums sweetly and comfortingly into their ear. Darkness begins to cry, their arms at their sides and their mouth agape, still howling. The rest of the gang stand off to the side, watching them, and exchange glances again.

"What if we add our flames and embrace them, too? What if they need us?" Kia says, her voice shaking.

"Yeah, that could help!" Sam adds.

"Sure, why not?" Toni shrugs.

"Everyone could use a little more love, right? Let's effing go!"

The three of them rush to effectively *glomp* Darkness and Roni, all of them simultaneously wrapping their arms around the two and adding their flames to the mix, causing a sort of rainbow flame that not only engulfed them, but spread throughout the entire forest.

Everything was on fire, everything was being washed away, everything was being cleansed.

The howling intensified, then suddenly stopped, with only the serene, sweet humming left to be heard.

Chapter 19 - Couldn't Hide The Emptiness, Let It Show

A muted, semi-opaque lavender smog from the aftermath of the technicolor forest fire rises from the scorched slate-grey barren grounds that was once The Forbidden Forest of Forgotten Figments and Figures. The ruins of the first Stranding lay bare and unhidden; a sad reminder of the loss experienced there—a wound that had been cauterised, but still held the pain.

In the centre of the razed grounds, five forgotten figures stand embraced into one another—like a group hug, but much more dramatic—You know, tears and closed eyes and a cathartic release of pent up rage, pain, and all of that, both metaphorically and literally. Darkness had let go, realising—with the aid of their intrinsic connection to Roni and the gang—, that they could be whole again, that they could heal and be at peace with their existence and role in the universe, with who they are and can be with the support from unlikely allies in this *unexistence* they are fighting.

A single sparkle manifests from the beautifully shaped, upturned narrow pink opalescent eye of Darkness and dissipates with a smile off into the wind that seemed to blow at the most **coincidentally** perfect time.

Thank you, Roni—all of you. Your unconditional kindness and warmth in this plane where moments last lifetimes and a blink all at once has brought the light back to me. Has made me whole enough to piece myself together and have the courage to find my heart. Darkness loosens their tension as Roni, Sam, Kia, and Toni release their embrace and step back from Darkness and their eyes widen in disbelief as they behold Darkness's form.

"Oh-Em-Effing-GEE!" Kia exclaims, slapping her hand on her cheek.

"Whoa, D, You're—" Roni starts but Toni interrupts, befuddled.

"Fuckin' gorgeous..."

Sam, with tears in their eyes, chokes out, "You're—just wow."

Darkness giggles, *Foolish mortals, this isn't even my final form.*

"Okay, now I **Know** that's from something!" Kia interjects impulsively.

Darkness stands at exactly 236.22cm, broad shoulders that hang elegantly from their neck with slender, shapely arms, a long torso with no tangible definition other than a waist that cinches in at the middle enough to give that sort of hourglass-like shape, where their hips sit at the same width as their shoulders. Their legs are like lovely soft ovals at the thigh, tapering in at the knee, then back out like baseball bats at the calves. Their hands and feet are long and slender, with their arches like semi-circles and their fingers like tapered candles—beautiful and delicate. Darkness's face is the shape of a teardrop, reversed, soft and sweet, with their lips—above their narrow, sharp chin—full and much like a violin on its side, but without the sharp edges and violent curves. Their nose was small, round-tipped, with a flat-ish ridge and slightly wide nares—you can't really see their nostrils, honestly.

I already described their eyes, so, there's that. This being doesn't have eyebrows, but they do have a hair-like structure—in an iridescent golden-orange—that starts at the top of their round forehead and drops dramatically behind them, trailing down to exactly 7.76mm above their bum. Skin like rose gold, but reflective of any shades and hues around them, with not a single crease or fold or line beside that of their mouth and eyes exists on their visage or body, but hole—a very deep and very dark hole, like a the fractured surface of a concrete floor, and much like the unknowable depth of a black hole singularity—resides where their heart should be.

Darkness giggles again, *Either way, my true form is fully intangible and unfathomable. Your human minds would unravel and implode at the sight of it.*

"Psh, bet." Kia remarks confidently, with everyone turning their heads to her in bewilderment, and Darkness's gaze turning to a serene wistful gaze followed by the faintest smile.

"So," Toni starts, "what happened? You know, to make you like you were. It must have taken a lot to get you all messed up like you were."

Sam hesitates, "Yeah, like, how'd it happen? I mean, if you even want to tell us. You don't have to."

Roni glances over at them, then at Darkness, who exchanges a glance of their own, and nods as if to say, "it's okay."

It's hard to say, difficult to find the words that would describe what my siblings did to me; how they hurt me. So I will show you instead. Darkness waves their hand over them, casting a shadow below their feet.

The shadow shifted and became an infinite endlessness as the void itself below them; a mirror to the Force Realm, where all is recorded and all exists all at once. They looked on below them into the void where—like a film—the events that led them to where they are presently played out before them, in an objective lens, as opposed to through the eyes of Darkness. The film revealed the truth of the matter and gave Darkness a perspective they had not considered before. Their hand in their own downfall.

I grew arrogant and desperate. Though... Darkness stops.

"That doesn't mean you deserved what happened to you. You didn't, no one deserves that." Sam stepped forward to Darkness.

Kia agreed, "You were—are—the formless form, you are the void; the empty state in which all action and creation comes from. You are the Tao. You are what you are, simply and without ego. You sought to spread that to us. You revealed *reality* itself in its isness! Because of you, the only limitation is no limitation! Oh-Em-Gee! I've studied this! That's what Bruce Lee talked about! Holy ess! Your mere existence inspired so many people, Darkness, you're not just all of the bad things, the negative aspects of the universe. Don't you see? You represent the potential of the universe, of all living beings, you are what is, and death and destruction are only a part of what you do. Why could they see that? Why couldn't you see it?"

I am... what is? Darkness cocked their head to the left at a 79 degree angle. They didn't know what to make of this assessment, of Kia's enthusiasm, *I will take your words into consideration as I ponder my place in the universe while seeking my heart.* Darkness paused, *I knew him, I loved him. I could not save him.*

"It's okay," Kia smiled, "he still lives on. In me, in millions of hearts. In yours!"

Roni steps up to Darkness and looks up at them with kindness in their eyes, "That's the beauty of mortality. Each one of us is a catalyst, affecting—effecting the lives and hearts of others, for better or for worse, and causing change. We love, we dance, we fight. We pass on, not just our genetic information, but memetic as well; through words and actions, through ideals and symbols. That makes us immortal, until the end of the universe itself. Our names and faces may fade from memory, but the impact we made is forever."

"And," Toni chimes in, catching Darkness's attention, "even on the small scale here, like with us, in the now; we can change people's lives, you know? Whatever happens after all this, I dunno about you three, but I'm gonna do things different. I'm gonna talk to people I love more, maybe save my own life, or..." Toni gulps, "yeah, it's funny, you know. We ain't living to die. We're living to make life better for everyone, even ourselves. And when that life ends, I'll be cool with it, because I know it was a good one, with my friends here. With my babe. And meeting you, D."

Sam fidgets and fixes their hair, "I don't have anything as inspiring to say as the others, but..." They step up to Darkness as well, "When my dad died, my whole world felt like it was ending. My mom became distant—but it wasn't her fault, she had to take care of the three of us. It was just me and my sisters and we made the most of it. I don't think I would have been as close to them, thinking about it now. But I miss my dad every moment, it still hurts sometimes. But, you know, it gets lighter, the weight of grief. We get stronger, we can carry it better, even though it'll always be there, it doesn't have to be the biggest part of me. I loved—love—my dad. I love my mom. I just couldn't handle losing her too. But I think, maybe now, after all of these moments here and with Roni, and Toni..." Sam laughs, wiping a tear from their eye, "And especially you Kia, you're the sweetest, kindest soul," they exchange a short laugh with Kia, "I think I can. You gave us a second chance, you gave us a safe space to work out our messy emotions and thoughts, our lives. Because of you, I think I can breathe again."

Darkness reaches out toward Sam and wipes a tear from their face, *Your words move me, your tears and emotions give me the conviction I needed. The validation, I suppose, I craved.*

Kia pops in with a bubbly tone, "We all need validation every once in a while! Even Forces of the Universe!"

Yes, perhaps you're right. Thank you, all of you. Your kindness and acceptance has given me a new outlook on my role and why I was created. I am unafraid to show myself, all that I am, to my siblings. This cave I call a chest longs to be filled still, I must find my heart. Then I will be the whole of me, without obscurement. Darkness moves in the direction of The Voidheart Chasm.

"Yass! Be you, hunty! We love to see it, we live for it, we're here for it, we got your back!" Kia snaps her fingers wildly.

Toni looks at her confused and concerned, "What she said. And, shit, we'll bust up some Forces if we gotta."

Roni and Sam look at each other, amused with Kia and Toni, then cast their eyes to Darkness and give them a nod of agreement.

Good, then we are in agreement. I'll take you to the nexus of The Voidheart Chasm, where my heart rests alone in isolation, waiting for me to retrieve it. Darkness glides away from where the Forbidden Forest of Forgotten Figments and Figures and toward the Chasm, leading the four *Unbound* to their heart.

Chapter 20 - Where Fears And Lies Melt Away

The **Unbound** are—well, it's never happened before, has it? But there have always been whispers in the Aether about *Those Who Transcend*, or what I would come to call the Unbound. Of course, The Forces never dreamt these whispers would be more than fairy tales and legend rather than a full-blown prophecy. Now that they're seeing the seeds of said "Legend", they don't quite know what to do with themselves. Time more than the others—quite the arrogant need to control all that passes, that one. Whatever the case may be, the Unbound are here and they've awakened, however unbeknownst to them their purpose may be, at the very least, they've initiated the beginning of the end which is the beginning and not the end, though for now, let's focus on the impending unravelling of Time's will, of their hold on the *Unreality* as a whole.

You probably have more questions than you had before, let me clarify; what would come to be known as the Unbound was prophesied by *Aetherlings*—beings that reside within the Aether, otherwise known as The After, or The Ending, that never quite made it into living, had never existed, and also never *unexisted*; picture, let's say, ghosts, waiting in queue to be given form in life or as a Lesser Force—we'll get into that after—that never got the opportunity to be either, and thus, as energy never ceases, continue on as these ghosts without a place—to unravel what we know as *Reality* and *Unreality*, cause a shift of sorts, and perhaps an expansion which would then give all "unused" energy in the universe, between and betwixt all planes, whether in existence or *unexistence*, a place to go, thus granting life to all things *unliving* and giving form to the formless.

You've heard that last part before, sort of.

The *Lesser Forces* are beings with much more energy and control over said energy than beings such as humans. These would not be able to be contained in the fragile fleshy bodies of humanity, and are therefore given mastery over some small Universal, uh, thing. Their existence tends to be relegated to The Forces' whims, though, for example, Inertia and Velocity, while both based in Physics, one belongs to Attraction and the other to Time. The Elements all belong to Nature, including the ones on the periodic table—yes, even the so-called "man-made" elements. Luck and Victory both are Chance's wards, while Sensation and Emotion are part of Feeling's lot. The list goes on, but I can't be bothered to name them all, besides, that would be boring.

I will say, one of Darkness's managed to be split along with Darkness. That split Lesser Force made its way into the bodies of four humans across generations. You can guess how that turned out; I'll give you four.

Roni, Kia, Sam, Toni... Darkness calls, *We are coming up on where my heart sleeps.*

"D! It definitely feels oppressive the closer we get, is that normal!?" Roni huffs as they trail behind Darkness.

Toni breathes heavily, "Yeah...Ah—fu—It feels heavy... God, I need to stop smoking."

Kia, the only one not dying, adds, "Oh-em-gee, it's like that feeling you get right before a panic attack, but, like, it never comes. Like emotional edging, *pero*, not fun."

Sam just grunts and keeps up with the rest of the Unbound; they were still recovering from the Greying, they'd almost joined the unliving.

Look at them, blindly following The Darkness into their own unlife. They don't know how the Void Heart will affect them, they don't know anything. Time scoffs haughtily.

Time, I think we can drop the "The" and call them by their name now. They've almost fully reconstructed, they're a being, not a monstrous ideal. Chance confronts Time.

Feeling backs him up, *It's not fair to keep treating them like this, Time. I didn't like it to begin with, besides—*

Time jumps in, *Besides? Besides, nothing. This changes nothing. The Darkness will always be out of control, it will always throw us off balance, and now with these—these Unbound, was it?—they're going to destroy everything I've built, they're going to chain us back to the Reality and to the Creator! Can't you see!?*

Attraction joins the coup, *See what, Timey? That you're the one out of control? That you're the one that's kept **us** on a leash and made **us** cater to your whims? Honestly, Time, your need to have your hands in everything and play puppet master is what led to this!*

Time retracts in disgust, *ME!? The Darkness—*

Nature cuts in, *Darkness cared too much, yes, but they didn't go mad trying to control every aspect of everything, I see that now. They're obsession, while misplaced, was concerned with saving humanity from itself. While that is infinitely impossible, at least they didn't ask us to turn on one of our own for fear of losing their hold on things.*

Time is befuddled, bewildered, flabbergasted, and absolutely dumbfounded with how its siblings have essentially turned on them. In this total and complete bamboozlement, Time had found itself at a loss for words, knowing nothing it could say would be met well, instead, be met with more hostility and blame. So, Time decided it'd just sigh, roll what essentially would be considered its eyes, and subsequently "harumph" extra loudly while pretending that the others hadn't just called them out.

*You absolutely **would** just ignore us like we didn't just call you out...* Attraction echoes my words, an ability, it seems, not just Kia has.

Feeling shakes the top part of their celestial body that would most be considered their head, *How problematic, Time. I'm disappointed in you, and in myself for being so swayed by you.*

Nature states plainly, *We will be keeping out of their way from now on. We'll let them do whatever it is that they are doing, and we won't hesitate to stop you should you try to interfere. We are tired, Time. We have decided this.*

Time scoffs, *Decided? All of you? When?*

The other forces exchange glances and say simultaneously, *Now.*

Here we are. Behold, Unbound ones, my heart's resting place; The Voidheart Chasm. We must plunge into the perceived infinite and retrieve it. But take heed, lovelies, once we go through, all could be different on the other side.

Sam walks to the precipice of the Chasm, their hair being whipped back by the force of the heart's infinite plummet which creates both a vacuum and a powerful gust, "What do you mean, *'different'*, are we going to die? Are we..." They pause at the thoughts filling their mind, "going *back*?"

Darkness speaks cautiously, *Hm. There **is** a slip in the Unreality that leads into the Reality. It is entirely possible that we may end up there. Though the implications...*

"What implications? What's going to happen?" Sam retorts sharply.

"Yeah, I think we need to know what'll happen before we make the decision." Roni responds.

Still your minds, Unbound. You'll not expire. You'll not unlive as you are already in unexistence and the process won't turn you grey. The likeliest outcome is undeath. Darkness smiles faintly.

Toni crosses his arms, "What the hell is *undeath*? I don't understand anything you said, D."

Darkness gazes wistfully and lovingly toward Toni, *Undeath is the process of shifting from one plane to the next. You experienced it when you passed through to this plane, you may experience it going back. Unlife is existing in a space of nothingness with the absence of potential. You wouldn't inhabit either planes, you'd be forgotten to both. Unexistence is residing in this plane of unreality. Because this plane is hidden within a pocket of a pocket dimension outside of the known universe, it technically doesn't exist, as it wasn't created by the Creator; also known to many as the Yin. To unexist you must undie. To undie you must be alive. To unalive you must have been uncreated or never have been at all. I uncreate. Do you follow?*

Toni spits off to the left and manifests a cigarette, takes a drag, and says, "Sorta. I get the gist."

Good.

Toni, in fact, did not follow, but pretended to do so to avoid any further exposition, as well as a headache. Admittedly, it *is* quite the complicated set of processes, to say the very least. Truer definitions are beyond mortal comprehension, and, to be quite frank, would take even me aeons to even begin to explain. Should you have the time, your mind would unravel itself infinitely, implode, reconstruct itself, and tear a rift in the multiverse causing the infinite versions of yourself to cease to exist over and over for the rest of forever within the blink of a micro-moment all at once.

Not very pleasant, I promise you, and yes, I am aware of how impossibly absurd that all sounds. But, one must remember, nothing is impossible, only improbable—as a "super brother" clad in green once said—, though in this case, it is what is, regardless of how utterly inconceivable it may sound. Absurdities are my forte, after all.

In any case, the Unbound are gearing up for what will shape up to be the challenge of their lifetimes—well, unexistence—, while the Forces bicker endlessly amongst each other, though four out of five are in agreement about the one being a megalomaniacal control obsessed drama lord—their words, not mine. Mine would be steeped in disappointment, not disdain and disillusionment.

"Alright, it's gonna be one hell of a party!" Roni psyches themself up, quoting their favourite devil hunter.

Kia smacks her palm against her face, "No-No one, no one talks like that, Roni. You sound like a Ninja Turtle."

Sam chuckles, "I thought it was cute."

Roni stammers, "It-ugh-it's not supposed to be cute... It's badass, okay?"

Toni shrugs, "I thought it sounded pretty rad."

Kia and Sam exchange looks and giggle. Sam says, "You *would* think that. You both are so cute. Just two adorkable babes. What are we gonna do with them, Kia?"

Kia shrugs, smiling with amusement. Darkness looms over them, watching their exchange, admiring their connection to each other and smiling faintly as they continue to talk amongst each other.

Hm, what strong bonds, how lovely.

Chapter 21 - Black Heart Scarring Darker, Still

The strands between the Unbound have transcended the *unreality*, visible only to Darkness—and myself—, while having been made unbreakable. As the Unbound continue to talk amongst themselves, a low, whirring hum breaks through to Darkness, their mind wandering and losing itself in the moment with their eyes fixed on the strands of the unbound.

*It truly **is** them. The strands, they're untethered to this plane, to any plane. Tethered only to each other. The descent won't tear them apart. But how? Who are they? What are they? I sense my essence within them. Roni and Toni are...* Darkness speaks in silence.

Indeed, Roni and Toni are—well, they're different, let's say. But it is true, their strands are their own and will not break, not even through the vortex of Darkness's black heart that tears the very fabric of space. Time was foolish to use the Voidheart as a means of obliteration, unknowingly having popped a hole—as I mentioned before—from this plane, to that of *reality*. But I've become redundant, perhaps I've just misjudged your ability to recall just a bit ago. Perhaps I'm further driving home the importance of this peephole through planes.

But, yes, the strands. The strands and the Voidheart, and the hole between planes, the will of the Forces, and the wills of the Unbound. And Darkness at the centre of it all, a reluctant catalyst that set forth the events that led to this very point and beyond. To the unravelling, to the *unbecoming*, to the revelations that will answer questions asked and not yet asked by all involved including you. I sure am hyping this up, aren't I? I hope I won't disappoint.

The Unbound's moments within The Stranding, and The Plane of the Forgotten for that matter, is coming to a close.

So let's get back to it, they're about ready to take the leap.

"We're about ready to take the leap, Darkness!" Kia again steals my line.

Are you most sure, Unbound? Darkness purrs.

Roni makes sure all of their straps are secure and tight, "Yeah, I think so."

"Why do you keep calling us that? 'Unbound'." Sam inquires, uncouthly.

"I was wonderin' the same thing." Toni winds their arm and kicks his boots to the ground.

Because that is what you are. Unbound. Untethered to either plane of existence, by circumstances of fate, through essence of Force and life of a human. Through undeath and passage through planes. You are Unbound.

"Okay, but what does that mean? Like, we're part Force?" Sam beckons Darkness to answer.

Simply said, Yes. You had to experience undeath to unlock the Force in you. It was always spoken of, whispered through the Aether.

"That's heavy, D." Roni reacts.

"Yeah, I'll say. But okay, then what's the Aether?"

It is where the unalive dwell, those that could never be. The whispers tell of the Unbound creating vessels and roles for them, for those that could never be.

"I don't understand a damn thing you said, but whatever. It's cool, we're going to destabilise the way the universe works, stick it to your sibs, and rewrite the script. It's a revolution, babes." Toni throws his fist up in the air.

I—Basically, yes. Darkness smiles warmly at Toni's enthusiasm.

Roni walks up to the precipice of the Chasm again, looks down into the endlessness and then back at everyone else, "Then what the hell are we waiting for? Let's go!"

Darkness and the other three Unbound's attention is stolen by Roni, whomst is smiling quite big at them, winks, and then jumps backward into The Voidheart Chasm's vortex which quickly sucks them down into itself. Sam runs toward the precipice screaming, "Roni!" while the others watch on, shocked and taken off guard.

"That maniac actually did it, that absolute mad-person." Kia holds her left hand on her head and walks forward to meet Sam, who's gearing up to jump after Roni.

"Well, I'll be damned. Guess we're doin' this... Here goes!" Toni sprints to the edge and leaps into the Voidheart vortex.

"Fu—Toni! Dubya-tee-eff! Wait for me!" Kia follows, meeting Sam's unsure eyes, nodding, then doing a triple axel front flip combo into the vortex.

Why do you hesitate? Are you frightened, Sam? Darkness glides to Sam's side, gazing into the vortex.

"I-What's going to happen in there?" Sam looks up at Darkness.

Darkness pauses for a long moment, *I cannot say. There's no way to know for sure. But the end result is inevitable.*

Sam takes a deep breath and exhales in a long blow, "Right. I guess there's only one way to find out..." They turn to Darkness, "D? Is my mom—?"

Darkness gazes warmly at Sam and smiles their faint smile, then extends their hand to Sam, *We can go together. If that will make you more comfortable.*

Sam shakes their head, "No. It's okay. Sometimes you have to be uncomfortable to face the changes that will make everything better for us. For everyone. Being brave doesn't mean being unafraid right? It means doing the thing despite your fear. Thank you, Darkness. But no, I gotta do it alone. See you on the other side?"

Darkness nods approvingly, then watches as Sam turns their back on The Chasm, feeling the vortex whipping and pulling them, their feet at the edge with their heels hovering above the gap. Sam drops backward with their eyes closed, their mind fixed on the memories of their moments in The Stranding, their moments with Roni, their meeting Kia and Toni. Their memories flash to their moments in the Forbidden Forest, the moments where they heard their sisters, their mother. The moments Sam spent as they were going Grey, the moments they spent near unlife.

"Mother... Mom. *Mami...* You're—"

Siblings, the time has come. I know you hear me, and I know you're watching. I know you know what I am, what I've always been. I now know that fact as well. I had lost sight of my **self** *over the aeons, over the separations that brought you to the universe. I know you are afraid of what you believe will come. But do not be afraid, for all things must end...* Darkness glares intensely into the void of the vortex, *My heart. My essence. I'll no longer be a shell, an empty vacuum of desolation.*

Darkness dematerialises themself into the vortex at the centre of The Voidheart Chasm, being sucked in like smoke into the backside of a fan.

Was that a threat? Time scoffs.

I didn't feel like a threat, Time. It felt like inevitability. A promise. Nature responds.

Darkness is telling us exactly what is coming. For better or worse, Darkness is coming for us. Chance interjects coldly.

They will be complete, finally, and the sins we committed against them will be undone. We deserve whatever is coming. I always regretted what we did to them... Feeling sighs softly.

I didn't, but I wouldn't have done it if it weren't for Time. Darkness needed to be checked. But maybe we went too far... Attraction says softening.

They did. And in doing so, they had sealed their own fate. In the universe, as one knows, every action beckons a reaction, and as balance must be maintained, all lost and all gained must have an equal exchange. There may not be anything as simple as karma; nothing so rudimentary as "what comes around, goes around". But there **is** absolutely a need to balance the scales and equalise the energies spent and energies absorbed. What shape that takes, however the "Universe" decides to equalise things—and in this case, equalise what the Forces did to Darkness, may not be what one expects.

The "Universe" may not exactly punish the Forces; rip them apart or return them to the Origin, but it may do *something* that it deems necessary to bring balance. The "Universe" more than likely hasn't decided yet what to do about the Forces and their insolence. Perhaps the "Universe" may leave that to Darkness.

In any case, some fates could have been avoided, if only they had not acted so maliciously. Unnecessary; none of this needed to happen, Darkness didn't need to be torn down for them to regain their sense of control. The Unbound didn't need to experience their pain to become the Unbound. So much unnecessary hurt, so much miscommunication, misunderstanding, ignorance.

But I digress. I am becoming much too attached, much too involved. Right. Let's get back on track, shall we? Ignore all of that exposition, my opinion is unimportant to what's unfolding before us, and much is happening that we mustn't miss!

Where were we...? Ah, yes. The Unbound and Darkness all plummeting into the Voidheart Chasm, being devoured by the vortex to reach the Heart of Darkness that resides at the tear between planes. But they did not jump in together as they should have, although they have their strands to keep them connected should they need support on their journeys through the planes; from unexistence to existence, from unreality to reality.

The door is locked, and the key is their hearts. The Unbound hearts were once broken and listless, but their experiences and their connections have helped them heal and become hopeful. Darkness was full of rage and despair, their heart lies before them and they're unsure if they can remain serene with their heart within them, as their heart wasn't present when the Unbound showed them mercy and love and helped them piece themself together. They're afraid that they'll continue with the rage in their heart that they felt for their siblings, that their siblings will remain unforgiven, too, as those that hurt the Unbound.

"Forgiveness isn't necessary to move forward, we don't have to forgive the people that hurt us in order to heal. We can choose to do so, but in the end, forgiveness is more for their peace of mind than ours. We don't owe them that, we don't owe them anything. We owe ourselves peace, and if that peace comes at the price of letting someone go, then so be it. We don't lose, not when losing that person means we gain a better understanding of ourselves and our hearts. I understand your heart, Darkness. Do you?" Roni whispers to the Heart of Darkness at the apex of the vortex, at the tear between planes, holding it in their naked palms softly with care.

Do you?

Chapter 22 - Dreamed I Was Missing, No One Would Listen

Roni awoke to their mother crying over their body in the red tinted water that filled the bathtub. It seems that the Heart of Darkness had sent them back; back to where they were mere moments before being pulled into The Plane of the Forgotten and experiencing their undeath. *What? Why am I here? Where's everybody else? Mom? Mom...* Roni thought, feeling their stomach drop and their heart sink.

Just that second, Roni experienced an overwhelming surge of pain originating at their wrists.

"Right..." They whispered weakly, remembering what had happened, feeling so far removed from that moment and who they were then.

Their mother, sobbing uncontrollably with her forehead down against the side of the bathtub, having been kneeling down at the base of the tub, pops her head up quickly after hearing Roni's voice, "*Mijo? Mijo!* Oh, my God, *mi amor, mi vida, mi cielo, estás vivo! ¡Me tenías hecho una mierda!*"

"Yeah I'm alive, mom...." Roni confirms, forcing themself to talk.

"I called 911, they gonna be here soon, okay? *Va estar bien.* They gonna take care of you." Their mother's thick Puerto Rican accent was tinted with worry, remorse, relief, and a hidden anger that would be revealed later on.

She drained the tub and wrapped Roni's wrists with dish rags and duct tape to keep the pressure applied to the wounds. Roni hadn't lost too much blood before being found unconscious, in fact, if it hadn't been for their undeath, they would have been discovered within minutes as Roni's mother, Graciela, had coincidentally needed to use the bathroom at the exact second that Roni made the first cut. But there was no way Time would have known that, not in their panic. Chance, of course, knew, but Chance wasn't about to stop Time from doing their thing. I knew as well. But you don't need to know how I knew, not just yet.

The ambulance came, EMTs entered their apartment and strapped Roni to a gurney for transport, asked them all of the run of the mill questions, as well as questions concerning mental health, to which Roni replied with a resounding, "Eh." and was promptly taken to the nearest hospital, a place Roni never wanted to visit.

"I hate Hospitals." They'd say, with a sour expression and in a flat low tone.

"Que carajo estabas pensando? Por que? En que cabeza te cabe cortarte las venas!?" Graciela's voice thundered in the hospital room with rage and disappointment.

"Exactly that." Roni sighed.

"What? *Mira, yo soy la que se va a morir. Tu, a mi, me va matar. Ay, Dios santo, este nene no sabe lo que es querer morirse."* She chided Roni further.

"Mother, please. I could have died and you're talking about how that could have killed *you*? You're always like this. You never talk to me, you're not around, even when you're around, and when you do you invalidate my feelings and make me feel like a fucking burden. Like I'm the worst kid in the world because—why? Because I'm fucking trans? Because I'm not what you thought I'd be?" Roni exploded.

"*Oye, a mi no me faltes el respeto,* Okay? I'm your mother, okay? You don't talk to me like that! You know is not true. I always here for you, you can talk to me about anything, except that. You not transgendered, you need help. See? Look. Look what you did to yourself because you think like you think." Graciela said, dismissing Roni's words, yet again, and blaming, instead, Roni's escape attempt on what she perceives as a mental illness; being transgender.

Obviously, it is not a mental illness, but Graciela insists that it is and even spoke with the nurses about it as if it was.

"Talking to you is like talking to an angry chihuahua. You don't listen, but you keep barking angrily. Whatever mom. I'm done with you, leave me alone." Roni shook their head and turned away from Graciela, "You know, I was past all of this. I am past all of this. I don't feel bad for being myself anymore. I don't feel bad that you don't love me, that you don't want me. That you don't see me. It doesn't hurt me anymore, mom. I found people that see me for who I am, friends that love me, that want me, not need me. You need me, mom.

That's the difference. You haven't healed from your own hurt, you haven't gotten past it. So you dump it all on me, and that's not fair. But I'm not taking it anymore. I know where I fit, with whom I fit. I lived a thousand years in the blink of an eye, mom. I had a beautiful, wonderful life... without you. Outside of you, of all of this. And I know it's still there, I know they're waiting for me somewhere."

"*De que tu hablas, mijo?*" She said, perplexed and perturbed.

"Nothing, mom. Don't worry about it, or about me, anymore." Roni said softly, resolved to continue on with the life they built and the person they discovered they were within the *Unreality*.

MEANWHILE...

Chino hand grabbed Toni's arm and the collar of their jacket and pulled them back and off the train tracks mere seconds before the train screamed by.

"What the hell are you doing, *loco*!?" Chino yelled.

"I—Chino? W-what... Oh, shit, I'm back here." Toni said, as it dawned on them where they'd ended up after being sucked into the Voidheart Vortex.

"You were just going to let that train hit you? Are you stupid or somethin'? And..." Chino paused, noticing the state Toni's in, "what happened to you?"

Toni stayed quiet a long time, scanning and assessing, wondering if this was really Chino, and if it was, why—after what happened between them—would he care if they lived or died. Finally, he spoke, "Just some jerks had a laugh roughin' me up, is all. Why do you care?"

Chino sucked his teeth loudly, "Because I do, okay? You're still my—Ah, fuck it. I fucked up, Toni. I shouldn'ta reacted like that, it was stupid of me. I hurt my friend, and then my friend went and got himself hurt and wanted to off himself. I'm a regular dope, Toni. I'm sorry."

Toni attempts to stand up but stumbles, then Chino extends his hand and grabs him to help him up. Toni hesitates and looks down, then up at Chino's face, "I read it wrong. I thought—I thought wrong, I guess. I was just looking for someone to get lost in, to find some warmth in. I thought it could be you at the time; then it could be anyone..." Toni stopped for a few seconds, then continued, "Now it's *someone*—Shit! Kia! Ah, but... If we're here then that means—that means she ain't here. She ain't anywhere."

Chino looks at Toni confused, "Who ain't here? Who's Kia?"

"My—She's my—" Toni sighed and held his chest, "She's the one. You know? The **one**. And she doesn't exist yet."

"Toni, you gotta throw me a bone, cuz ain't none of this makin' sense." Chino said, scratching his head.

"You ain't gonna believe me even if I told you. So might as well just trust me, 'kay?" Toni responded, crossing his arms.

Chino shrugged, "Whatever man. All I know is that I owe you cuz an apology ain't gonna make up for the shit that got you here like this."

"I'll hold you to that, but also..." Toni walked up to Chino and grabbed his shoulders, "If it wasn't for you, Chino... The way you always pushed me, the way you always were there for me, the way you took me in when that shit happened with my old man, and even that nigh—earlier tonight, all of that. If it wasn't for you, I wouldn't have experienced everything I did *there*, and met Kia and Roni and Sam. Oh, you gotta meet them, they're great, you'd love'em. I forgive you, not because you did something wrong, but because we were both wrong. I shouldn't have made a move on you, man. I should have asked or talked about it first."

"Toni—yeah, you're right, we should have talked about it. You shouldn't have jumped at my face with your lips. But I shouldn't have said all those things. It wasn't cool. I forgive you too, for thinking I'm gay with you." Chino said, then started laughing.

Toni looked at him as he laughed, then joined in, "You piece of shit."

There was an understanding between them, as Toni had let go of the pain and unresolved feelings they had about the situation in question. While, indeed Chino had regretted his actions and words, he had resolved to be better and do better for their friend that had meant so much to him. He'd vowed to do whatever it took to keep Toni's faith and trust in him as solid as ever. All the while, Toni had resolved to take ownership over their actions and hold themself accountable, while realising that it's easy to project one's own insecurities onto others and jump to conclusions that could be a far cry from the truth of it all. They had resolved to take things as they are without judgement, but rather with discernment.

ELSEWHERE...

A knock, or rather, a rapping, an over-enthusiastic—
bordering on aggressive—banging echoed into the bedroom
from the locked door, under the pile of blankets and into
Kia's ears, shaking her from dissociative state upon falling
back into *Reality*. The banging persisted as Kia realised
exactly where she was with a sigh, flinging the blankets
from her and sitting up on her bed, she groaned, "What!?"

"*Mija!* Open the door, baby, it's me!" The voice cried out.

Kia perked up, eyes shooting straight at the door, "Ma?"
she whispered, "*Mami!?*"

"*Si, mi amor, Mami's* here!" Her mother, Destiny,
exclaimed, calling out to Kia.

Kia sprung to her feet and ran to the door, swinging it
open and squeezing her mom tightly, "Mom, dubya-tee-eff?
What happened?"

"Oh! Don't glomp me!" Destiny laughed then exhaled
heavily, "*Ay, Mija,* it's a long story, girl. And a messed up
one too."

Kia giggled, "I'm sorry, I missed you. And dubya-wai-
emm, long story?"

Destiny walked into Kia's room and sat down on her bed,
gesturing for Kia to join, and then took a deep breath,
"Okay, well. So first off, and the short version, your
grandparents? They were keeping you from me, **illegally**,
nena."

Kia gasped, somewhere deep in her heart she knew that her grandparents had something to do with it. Destiny then unloaded the entire history of what happened from the moment she got pregnant, to now, their reunion with a court order and police escort. She'd told her that her grandparents knew about the abuse, about everything, and protected Kia's father from any consequences. She told her about how they invalidated Destiny's parenting choices, went behind her back, and did everything possible to push her out of Kia's life.

After everything went down with Kia's father, they blamed Kia and took their frustration and disappointment on her. After Kia's Sifu at the local Jeet Kune Do school noticed she'd been absent for days at a time, especially after appearing malnourished and fatigued before then, he contacted Destiny, who told him what was going on, and together they planned a way to get Kia out of her grandparents' house. Since Kia had just turned eighteen, it was trickier, but with a lawyer that was a friend of the Sifu, they were able to figure out a way to get the police involved and obtain a court order that outlined a restraining order against the grandparents pending trial over allegations of abuse via neglect and mental anguish. The legal jargon is much more detailed and complicated but we'll leave it at that. I'm no lawyer.

"That's intense mom. Wow... You did all of that for me? I had no idea you could even do that without visual evidence." Kia said, astounded.

"Yeah, well, *ese* lawyer *'taba bueno*. He's good at what he does. Who am I to question it?" Destiny said.

"You right, ma." Kia responded.

"Well, you ready to go?" Destiny asked excitedly.

"Yeah—! Wait, I-I'm here. I'm *here*. Like... **here**, here. So where's—? Oh, I can feel them. They're here somewhere. But not really. It's them but it's not them. But it is. But, like... the **them** that I'm feeling are out there somewhere. I have to get to them, we have things to do." Kia extolled, with exactly a dozen and one wild gestures.

Destiny watched her, confused, and said, "What? *Nena, pero* what are you talking about?

"I'll explain later, mom, let's go." Kia said, standing up all fired up to find her friends.

AND, LASTLY...

The *trill* of a Motorola Razr's ringtone cuts through the music that had been blasting rebelliously in the face of the possibility of loss. Sam's darkened room flickers with light from the cellphone on the far dresser by the bedroom door, illuminating the band posters of The Used and Paramore above it. Sam, confused and discombobulated, looks around, having sat up rapidly on their bed and thrown the fleece blanket off.

"I'm... **Home**...?" They said, getting up and walking toward their phone, hesitantly.

They picked the phone up from the dresser, feeling it vibrate, watching the light on the clamshell's LCD screen light up with the name of their sister, Franxeska. A chill ran down their spine as they gulped heavily, anxious, afraid of what the call might say, but ready for the worst that could happen. *I can take it, I got this...* Sam thought.

"Hey?" they said, having picked up the call, "Yeah, I'm **here**." Sam spoke with certainty and a sense of being grounded, present.

"Hey," Franxeska's voice crackled from the speaker of the cellular phone, "We've been trying to reach you all day, where have you been? I sent Elissa to go get you. She should be there in, like, a minute."

"I—Sorry, I guess the music was too loud. Is mom...?" Sam choked out.

"You sound like you've been crying, are you okay?" Franxeska inquired softly, her voice steeped in concern.

"Yeah, no, I'm-I'm okay. I'm good. Just here, **now**." Sam responded, shaking off their anxiety, noting that their sister hadn't mentioned their mother yet, which must mean that either it's really bad, or no big deal.

"Ahuh... Okay, listen," Franxeska started, Sam braced themself, "*Mami esta bien*, she's okay. It was a minor heart infarction, I dunno why they told you it was a heart attack. But she's okay. They caught it early. She's just resting now, so don't get all *Sam* about it, 'kay?"

Sam sighed heavily in relief, a weight lifting off of their shoulders, "Oh, shit. Ah, that's—wow, what a relief. I was worried, you know? That—"

"—I know. Like dad. I know, Sami-bear. You can breathe now, you know she's fine and she'll be back to her overworking self in no time. Now, wait til Elissa gets there and hurry over. Ma wants to see you." Franxeska reassured teasingly.

"Okay, sis. I feel like... No, forget it. See you soon." Sam said, feeling their connection to The Plane of the Forgotten phasing in and out.

"Alright, Sam. See you." Franxeska said, then hung up.

Sam couldn't shake the feeling that something was off. They shouldn't be where they are, but at the same time, it felt right. It felt like closure, like the end of a chapter that had been left open for so long, one that ran much longer than it should have. Much like this one. They knew their friends, the other Unbound, were out there. They knew that Roni had to be close. What they didn't know was how to get to them. Furthermore, what they didn't know as well as that, was the implications of being Unbound and awakened within the plane of reality and what they were capable of, even here. Even now.

The strands that bound them, the threads between them, kept them all within reach of each other. All they had to do was feel *out*.

Vague, yes, but you'll see.

Chapter 23 - Find a Thread to Pull,
A Ghost of Somewhere

Day after day, hour after hour, minute after minute, so on and so forth, Roni meandered about their mother's flat, going through the motions like a listless automaton. They'd wake, shower, brush their teeth, skip breakfast, opting for a liquid meal in the form of a hot cup of Cafe Bustelo with soy milk they'd picked up from the grocery on the same errand run they'd always had to do. Life had gone back to the depressing, soul crushing normalcy that had caused them to want to disappear in the first place. Albeit, with extra hostility from Graciela any time she showed her face outside of her room, where she decided to roll the desktop computer in an attempt to cut Roni off from what she believed was the source of their attempt.

Every so often, Roni would feel a tug, a pull on their left little finger, as if there was a thread tied to it and someone was pulling at it from afar. And, indeed, there was still. The red strand that had bound them to Kia, to Sam, and by proxy, to Toni, was still there, however "invisible" it may be, it was still there. And if that strand was still there, that meant that, through the eras, through the scattering that the Voidheart Vortex had caused, their connection to each other must still be there. As well as other things.

Those absolute goat herders! Time admonished.
They'll figure it out soon, Time. And when that happens—
Time interrupted Chance, *Shut your communication chamber!*
Darkness will be upon us soon, siblings. Nature warned solemnly.

I wonder what's keeping them? Are they being dramatic on purpose? Staging some grand return? That's my thing. Attraction scoffed.

We'll know—well, I'll be the first to know, I guess. Said Feeling.

"Come on, you donkey driver!" Kia exclaimed, yanking her strand while meditating in her room at her mother's new home, "I can't believe you don't feel me, we're supposed to be *biffls*!"

BFFLs—that is, best friends for life. It took me a moment, but I got it. Did you?

"*Ay, nena*, why are you yelling?" Destiny said, barging into Kia's room.

"*Dejame, mami*! I'm trying to contact my friend." Kia retorted.

"Okay, *pero*, doesn't they have a phone?" Destiny said, trying to understand.

"Mom, I would have tried that by now. Thank you, but I have to do this my way."

"*Pues, mija,* remember to empty your mind and all that stuff you learned." Destiny gestured around then walked away.

"Wait! That's brilliant! Thanks ma!" Kia said, having had an idea spark in her mind, "If I can feel and see my strand, then maybe I can use my powers too! It can't just be physical strength, it has to be spiritual, too! Maybe I could astral project or whatever, send my essence to Roni and Sam! To Toni—I'm coming babes."

Roni sits in their room, playing Metal Gear Solid 2 over again for the 688th time—I counted—, but this time it was *SUBSTANCE*—the Xbox port—on the Xbox 360. While moving through the Plant chapter as Raiden, in between struts and just as the CODEC rings with Rose on the other side, undoubtedly to ask if Raiden remembers what day the next day is, a dull, glassy knock breaks their concentration.

"What was that noise?" Roni parroted the guards from the game, looking to their window on their left, just by their bed, "Is that—?"

It most definitely was, in fact, Sam. How, you ask?

"Sam!?" Roni rushed over to the window and opened it to find Sam floating in the air, two stories above the ground.

"Hey, mind moving out of the way? This floating is kind of exhausting." Sam said with a playful bite.

"Oh, is it? Is it really exhausting?" Roni retorted sharply, their eyes narrowed and a smile slowly crawling across their face.

"Yes, Roni-tron III esq. and a half. Now if you would please, my dearest." Sam implored in a British accent *ala* Jane Austen.

Roni's smile was in full effect as they moved away from the window, allowing Sam to enter. As soon as Sam touched down on Roni's scuffed up hardwood floor, Roni attacked them with a squeeze, picking them up and spinning them around, "I knew you were close! I knew you'd find me! Ugh, my love, I missed you so." Roni had continued the accent, "But what of the others? And even moreso, my darling, what of your mother? I know you were dreading finding out..."

Sam took a deep breath in, replacing the air that Roni had squoze out of them as they were set back down on the floor, "Mom is fine. I've seen her a few times, visited, you know. It was nothing serious, but the stress of it and everything on her body has really, like, taken her out. She needs a lot of time to recover and rest. And as for Toni and Kia, nothing yet. They're not here-here. We are because we're both from here-here. This is our era. Toni's in like the 60's or something. And Kia I think is probably a baby at this point. So we have to wait for them to reach out to us from their respective eras. To be quite honest, I think they'll find each other before they find us."

"That's heavy, doc," Roni said, dropping the accent, "but, how do you know so much? How do you know that they'll find each other first?"

"It's just a feeling I get. And, like, remember when we were falling through the vortex and everything was like, all weird and we could see images of things?" Sam responded.

"Yeah, sort of." Roni said.

"I had a lot of time to sit alone and remember, to concentrate on things and unravel everything. I saw my strand, that's when I knew I could find you. I pulled it and as I pulled all these pictures of you flooded my mind and showed me where you are. But also showed me where they are. You were here, you were close. And so I thought, the brilliant mind that I am, I thought that if I could see my strand, see all of that, then maybe I could use my ability from the *unreality*, too!" Sam explained, "Remember what Darkness said?"

"Something about us being something called **Unbound**? And that we weren't tied to either plane? Reality or Unreality..." Roni pondered, shifting their attention to their hand.

"Right! So if we're not bound by the rules of this *Reality*, then we can use our abilities here too! They're ours. They don't belong to the *Unreality*, they belong to us!" Sam said excitedly.

Roni snapped their fingers to ignite their azure flame; nothing happened. They tried again a few more times to no avail. Sam urged Roni to concentrate on their essence, on their passion, Roni nodded once and watched their hand intensely. They focused, they concentrated, they let go of their expectations, cleared their mind and let their instinct take over. They snapped one final time and their hand ignited the brilliant blue, illuminating the darkened room, "Oh, shit! Hell yeah, son!"

"Finally, some light in this cave!" Sam teased.

"Oh, hush." Roni retorted jovially.

Their hand snapped, gesturing and flicking their wrist, having felt an inkling of power surge through them as they ran from the police after having vandalised the properties of the men that assaulted them way back when. Toni shouted, "Shit, Chino, it ain't workin'!"

"Well try harder, they're on our ass, Toni!" Chino urged between breaths.

"I really gotta stop smoking," Toni heaved, struggling to continue their mad dash and snapping, "God dammit! Work!"

"Hey, what did your girlfriend used to tell you? Empty your thoughts or somethin'!? Do that!" Chino chided.

Toni grunted, "Yeah, yeah. I'm letting go, alright?"

Toni focused on his heartbeat, on the sound of his and Chino's boots scrambling on the pavement on the alleyway, drowned out the sounds of the policemen chasing them and the sirens following and let it all go. They snapped again, manifesting a door in front of them that led them home, like something out of the Looney Tunes cartoons that Toni loved—Daffy was their favourite, by the way—, or something more modern that you'd recognize, like Ramona Flowers in Scott Pilgrim vs The World.

"There you are! Gotcha, bitch!" Kia exclaimed, finally getting a beat on someone's essence, "Time to pull you in, you melon farmer."

Chapter 24 - The Hardest Part of Ending
Is Starting Again

"Hey, you floppy dog! Open the door!" Kia shouted, commanding Toni through the Aether, "There's a bunch of lil' guys here trying to leach off me, hurry up!"

Toni sat up on his bed, "Kia!? Where the heck are ya?"

"I'm here, like, **here**-here! I'm *in between*. I need you to open the door!" Kia shouted again, as if being in the Aether made her less audible. She's invisible to Toni, a spectre of her physical self floating between planes where the Aetherlings live. The Aetherlings, knowing exactly who she is, surrounded her, exalting her, as well as trying to syphon off some of her essence.

"What door? My bedroom door?" Toni said, confused and walking toward their bedroom door.

"No, silly. You have to *make* the door. I know you did it before. This time you have to empty your mind and let go of yourself, focusing on my essence. You have to feel me, be with me. Now, do the thing!" Kia explained and commanded yet again.

"Alright, alright, you don't gotta yell. I can hear you just fine, you know you're not any less audible in there." Toni said, channelling Kia in the line thievery.

Toni started by clearing themself, breathing in deeply from their nose, then slowly blowing out through their mouth, focusing on the Toni that's inside of them, the one that Kia sees, the one that Kia loves. Then he lets go of that Toni, reflecting on the Toni they are within themself, the truest Toni, letting go of their thoughts, their feelings, their judgement of themself. In letting go, in seeing the truest them, Toni can connect to and focus on Kia. Kia's self, her truest self, in metaphysical form within the Aether, connected via their strands, begins to solidify as their body begins to join their spirit in the Aether, Toni on the other side of a door that had just appeared before her. Toni manifested that door without even trying, having just felt Kia, knowing themself and Kia's self lying in wait, knowing their connection was strong enough to pass through planes and eras. Knowing all of this without actually knowing.

Kia steps through the door and out of the Aether, into Toni and Chino's flat in an era not her own, leaving the Aetherlings behind—for now.

Toni opened his eyes to behold Kia's smiling face as she spread her arms wide open, letting out a squeal of endless delight, waiting for Toni to scoop her up. His eyes started welling up with tears of absolute and total unbridled joy and love. Without saying a word, he said a million as he wrapped his arms around her and held her so tightly they could have become one being.

"I missed you so much, babydoll." Toni choked out finally, softly and into Kia's neck, her curls softly caressing his face.

"I missed you too, bae. I'm never leaving you alone again." Kia said sweetly, running her fingers through Toni's thick, messy mane.

"He wasn't alone," Chino started, walking into the room and seeing the lovers together. He leaned up against the doorframe, "I kept him safe for ya, Kia."

Chino didn't know how it was possible that Kia had appeared in Toni's room, but he also didn't care. The only thing he cared about was that his best friend and brother in mischief was happy. Kia smiled, still wrapped in Toni's embrace, diverting her attention to Chino, who just nodded, acknowledging her unspoken gratitude.

"A donde vas? Y quién es esta?" Graciela interrogated from the kitchen, as Roni and Sam rushed toward the front door.

"**They** are my partner, Sam. Not that it matters to you. And we're leaving. Don't worry, you won't miss me." Roni replied, being curt with their mother.

"When you coming back?" She said, half worried, half annoyed.

"I'm **not**." Roni replied shortly, turning to the door.

"De que hablas? You have to come back. You live here, this is your home, and I am your mother. You can't abandon me like that. *Tu sabes que yo te necesito aqui conmigo, mijo.* I need your help with everything, what if I fall? *Y despues, me jodo?* No, no. You are not leaving. You can't leave!" Graciela insisted.

Roni dropped their shoulders and sighed deeply, cracked their neck by jerking their head quickly to the left, then turned to face their mother, "I'm not your only child. You have five other kids, five sons. Where are they? And don't give me that shit about Xavier being in the army to help you with bills. I don't care, he can be your hero and your favourite, but he isn't mine. And he isn't here. He doesn't have to deal with your shit, day after day, with your absence. He never had to deal with coming to you excited about something, only to be shot down, called stupid, or just completely ignored. To then have to be called on to go and do $300 worth of groceries alone, pack it alone, bring it all in alone. And then be treated like an unwanted puppy, neglected, left alone to fend for myself, left alone with my feelings. And that's just the tip of the iceberg.

"Do you have any idea how many times I wanted to do what I did? No, because you don't care until it's too late, and then you act like it didn't happen until you need to use it against me. But you want to come out here and demand I stay? For you? Because *you* need me? I need me. My friends need me, the universe fucking needs me right now. And whatever happens at the end, I don't care, I'm not coming back. You may need me, mom, but I don't need you. I'm done feeling guilty, I'm done feeling sorry. I told you mom, I'm done with you."

Graciela was speechless, knowing somewhere deep inside her that Roni was right, but never being able to admit what she had done wrong. She'd never implicate herself, never be able to give her child the validation and closure they needed, instead, doubling down and blaming Roni and their friends' influence for Roni's supposed insolence. Inside of her, her feelings festered, as she had done all of her life, never being able to express anything short of anger and disappointment and the occasional sting of sorrow. She knew, but she couldn't let Roni see.

Sam took Roni's hand and whispered, "Let's go, love." They knew that that encounter had taken a toll on Roni's mental space. Outside, Roni seemed stoic and stern, but inside they were a hot mess; a garbage fire of emotions, if you will.

Later, out in a park on a Walnut Hill and by an abstract, rusted iron sculpture that sat atop a cylindrical stone structure, Sam and Roni sat on the freshly groomed veridian grass, taking in the cool and crisp autumn air just before duskfall, the sky slightly overcast with purplish hues. Sam held Roni's hand gently, their head upon Roni's shoulder. Roni gazed mournfully into the horizon—where they sat was high enough to see most of the city—, their mind focused on the loss they'd just experienced.

"I just..." Roni said, their voice strained from the lump in their throat, "I just wish she loved me, like, really, actually loved me, you know? Accepted me and saw me for me, and—and wasn't disgusted or disappointed. It really fucking hurts, you know? How can you have a child—and that child does so much for you, so much for so many years that they shouldn't even be responsible for yet—how could you have a child and just not love them unconditionally? I don't understand. Is it me? Did I do something wrong? Is there something wrong with me that no one is willing to tell me? Instead they just treat me like shit for it. All of them..." Roni chokes up, holding in their deluge of emotions, "All of them do... Why?"

Roni was spiralling.

They were dwelling, holding on instead of letting go, instead of keeping their mind from becoming a prison; still and stuck. Kia would be disappointed—she'd understand, and try to help them through, but she would still be disappointed, after all of the moments they had spent on breathing, letting go, and staying present while in Roni's flat in The Stranding. Roni regressing like this from an encounter with their mother, undoing all of the work they had done together to be at peace with their pasts, would be quite a shock to Kia. Roni had gotten so strong and stayed so stable that this spiral seemed quite abnormal.

And yes, I glossed over some details earlier about what Kia and Roni had been up to after they'd first met, but one can imagine what two sweet and loving individuals that had shared parts of their pasts with each other and are in a sort of *Queer-Platonic* relation of sorts would be up to. And one can infer in hindsight if one were so inclined with the new information that was given through the experiences and moments shared thereafter that indeed they would do more than just hang out and make music and enjoy each other's company. I can't tell you **everything**. I mean, I can, but I don't want to, honestly.

Sam continued to hold on to Roni's hand tightly and rubbed their back lovingly, "Roni..." Sam started, "I—I don't know. I don't know what to say here, to be honest, this is Kia's forte, not mine." Sam paused and took a breath, "But I can say that—that I love you. *I* love you. *We* love you. I know we're not your flesh and blood family, we're not your mom and we're not your brothers, but we are your *chosen* family. We're your lovers, your friends, your sisters, your brothers—not by blood, or anything like that, but by choice. And what's more powerful than choice? You can be born into situations you had no say in, ties and rails that were given to you by circumstances that were determined by other people before you, and even before them. But your choices, your decisions, what *you* want and—more importantly—*who* you want out of life are yours and yours alone. That's powerful, that's impactful.

You chose *us*, not them, and we're helping you grow, keeping you safe, bringing you so much unconditional love that you don't even know what to do with. I'm not good at inspirational speeches and shit, and sometimes what I say is all jumbled up, but I *am* good at loving **you**. Loving you deeply and unconditionally and more than anything in this universe. You made me feel okay with my past. You made me feel safe to feel, just by being with you. And that gave me the courage to face the moments that came as soon as we made it back here. The courage to face the possibility of losing my mom. I hope we gave you the courage to face *your* mom and come out of it okay."

Roni stifled their sob, "I'm just so tired of being strong all the time, having to shoulder all of the pain and bullshit and have to continue on. I don't want to do it anymore."

Sam grabbed Roni's face with both hands, a palm cradling each cheek, and turned Roni's sorrowful face toward theirs, "That's okay. There's nothing wrong with that, Roni. You don't have to be strong anymore. You don't have to shoulder everything on your own. You have us! You have **me**. And you **know** I've got you. Always, and forever."

"How? How do I just let go? How do I let you help me with all the shit that pulls me down so much? I don't know how. I've never let anyone help me like this before. I—I just—" Roni sank into Sam's soft hands.

"You don't. You don't *let* me, silly. I'm doing it whether you want me to or not. Trust me, you'll get used to it real quick. Besides, I was never going to give you an option in the first place. Knowing you, you'd put up a fight and refuse at least a thousand times before even considering letting me help you." Sam teased, wiping the tears from Roni's face.

"You don't know me." Roni pouted, "You only think you know me. Wit'cho soft hands, all pretty n' shit; I love'em." Roni took a breath to collect themself, "I love *you*. You wonderful, sweet bitch."

Sam laughed, "Oh, you're feeling better I see."

"Ahuh. Thanks to you, reminding me of what's important." Roni booped Sam's nose, "My favourite nose, my favourite person."

"Favourite person!?" Kia's voice shouted from exactly 13.735 metres to the left, "I thought I was your favourite person, you bitch!"

Sam leaned into Roni's face, "*You're* the bitch now."

Roni gave them an amused, mocking look before turning their attention to the approaching Kia, "What took you so long?"

"Your mind wasn't clear and your essence was clouded, I was worried! What the hell happened?" Kia scolded as she and Toni stopped short of a metre from Sam and Roni.

"Waddup, queers." Toni said, completely out of character.

"Okay, what?" Sam chortled.

"Sorry, Kia's been teachin' me modern slang so I could fit in just in case we get trapped here or in her era." Toni explained, a little embarrassed.

Sam and Roni exchanged glances, holding in laughter and said simultaneously, "Okay."

"Anyway, y'all never answered me! Dubya-tee-eff happened!?" Kia attempted to rein them in.

"Roni had a run in with their mom and—" Sam started.

"—And spiralled from the emotional stress of the encounter, I figured." Kia interjected, having correctly assessed the situation, "Oh, honey. I'm so sorry. That had to be so effed up and hard on you. I'm happy you had Sam here with you to help you break the spiral," Kia knelt down in front of Sam and took their hand, "thank you for taking care of my *biffle*, you're the sweetest bean. We're so lucky to have you, tee-bee-aych."

Reunited, the Unbound had regained their full power— like an RPG where you get a party buff for having completed everyone's personal quests with favourable outcomes—, their bond stronger than ever, they contemplate how to get to where the Forces are. They contemplate going through the Aether where, Kia and Toni having had navigated through to get from era to era, they could possibly shortcut into the bubble where the Forces reside. They wonder about whether Darkness is going to meet them there, in the Aether, or guide them there. Most of all, they wonder if Darkness made it through The Voidheart Vortex alright. And if they did, had they reunited with the Voidheart and become complete.

Either way, Time was running.

Chapter 25 - The Other Side Of A Jet Black Hotel Mirror

The Darkness is here! I can't—I've got to—I can't face it!
Time scrambles, trying to collect itself enough to disappear through the Aether.

Time? Time! You coward! Oh, of all the selfish, weak-tendriled, candy-ass—You've got me sounding like a wrestler, Time! How dare you just leave us like this! Attraction shouts, searching the inner cosmos angrily.

How are you surprised, Atty? Feeling sighs, at peace with what may come.

Honestly, like, we all saw this coming. Time's a little bitch. Chance adds with a dry chuckle.

Calling Time a pansy would be an insult to my flowers. Nature says with a snort of sorts.

Well, that isn't kind, siblings. Then again, you lot don't have a track record for kindness. Darkness interjects, with a cool, even tone.

Darkness! You've returned. We, um, we've been ex— Attraction starts.

Darkness interrupts, their tone never changing, *— Expecting me. I'm quite sure. Yes, you've been watching me. And watching the Unbound as well, I presume. You know what's coming, and you know why I am here.*

We h-have some idea, yes. Attraction gulps.

You presume correctly, sibling. We have been watching and— Nature says, stoic as ever.

Chance interrupts Nature, —*Meddling. They've been meddling in the affairs of the Unbound and inadvertently causing all of this to happen a lot faster than it would have by bringing them together much before they would have. They aren't you, Darkness, and that much is obvious. Their incompetent attempts at keeping you away while failing to do what you used to—*

So I've seen. Darkness cuts in, *They weren't properly obliviated from their eras. Time merely stopped their flow. The moment they were pulled from Reality was frozen, waiting for them to return so that it could continue its normal flow. Time cannot properly pluck mortals from Reality to bring into our Unreality; none of you can. Only I can uncreate. Honestly, I am content with what you've done. You've—as you said, Chance—inadvertently hastened my return. I thank you for meddling. I thank you for bringing the Unbound together, for they are my beloved children. I see that now that I've regained possession of my heart.*

Ah, yes. I neglected to mention; Darkness is complete. In their completeness, they are an intangible Force of tendrils and ribbons of the blackest black, darker than any darkness in the universe. They have twists and turns, and are an undulating mass of incomprehensible—well, Darkness. Their eyes, though, have not changed at all. They've remained that which the Unbound had beheld, both in look and feel. The softness and serenity is still there, the beauty and kindness; the mercy.

You know, I tried to tell them, Darkness, but none would listen. Chance chimes in.

Oh, shut up, Chance! Attraction chides.

See? Chance points out.

You two have been quite silent, Darkness refers to Nature and Feeling, *where do you stand?*

Feeling deflates, *I never wanted to do this. Any of it. But then I started having fun with the Unbound and their relations. I took interest in Sam, I believed they could fully unlock what Roni had inside that Kia had started to unravel. Threads connected aren't just meant to bind. And their threads, their Strands, would do more than bind.*

You had an inkling, unbeknownst to Time. Darkness assesses.

With Chance's help, yes. Feeling confesses.

And you? Darkness addresses Nature.

I have nothing to say that hasn't been already stated. I have no excuses. My only regret is your pain, sibling. Nature states, solemnly as always.

Ah, Nature, earnest as ever. I have missed your grave and deadpan manner. Darkness warms, their tone even, but lighter.

What happens now? Will you—Are you going to uncreate us and return us to Light? Attraction says sheepishly.

Darkness turns their attention to her, *To **Light**? Light... I hadn't heard her being referred to like that in many, many moments. Light...* Darkness contemplates, *No. Light, as well as myself, would want us all to remain as we are. Light, or Yin, the Universe, or even **Creator**, as you've so dubbed her before, has been privy to all that's gone on, dear siblings.*

Chance erupts in laughter, Feeling begins to tremble, and Nature grunts lowly, anticipating the implications.

Attraction gasps, *She's—what!? She knows **everything**? How do you know? How can you know? You haven't been in contact with her since—since before we were created, I imagine!*

*And why do you think that is, dearest **sister**?* Darkness probes, doing air quotes.

Attraction remains silent, pondering what Darkness could mean by that question, *You don't mean...*

*She and I are one. Or at least, we were, once. We split, you see, and when we did, life began to fill the endless nothingness. From the void in which we resided, our split catalysed infinite and limitless possibility. You all were created so that you could create, and your creations could, in turn, create as well, so on and so forth. We were lonely. We felt empty. We could not imagine that we would never see each other... And in **my** sorrow and solitude, I sought to create. Which led me to masquerade as your sibling; another Force created by Light. I craved connection, I was desperate, and I missed my darling Light. You lot were the closest thing to her that I could find to fill my loneliness; my **siblings**, my children. I loved you, I loved your creations, I loved their creations. I loved Humanity—perhaps too much. So, now here we are, and Time will be joining us soon. Along with Light.*

Darkness was correct; Time would indeed be arriving soon.

You—You misled us!? You pretended to be our sibling when really you and Light were—are— Attraction shrieks, then shrinks.

Save your false outrage, Attraction. Your siblings don't seem so surprised, or even as perturbed as you feign to be. You all knew I was different. Time more than the rest of you, which is why it masterminded usurping my role in the Universe. Which is why it roped you into doing what you did to me. It, and you all, were frightened of my power. Not knowing the fullest extent of it. That fear was—is, misplaced. I understand why you did what you did, but I also understand that it was horrific, traumatising. It took so long, and the help of the Unbound to come to terms with it all; the pain, the sadness, the betrayal.

Darkness stops for a moment, *I did not deserve it, no matter how 'out of control' I may have been. I wasn't hurting anyone, but you hurt me. You did so out of jealousy, you did so out of fear I would replace you. Out of fear. I know now that I was throwing the balance off, but it would have stabilised eventually, Light would have stabilised it. I could have stabilised it. We could have stabilised it, had we spoken without fear or anger. None of this had to happen. But it did, and here we are. And honestly, truly, I forgive you. Not because you deserve forgiveness, but because I deserve closure and peace. I'll never have that so long as you fear me.*

Time's arrived. Now excuse me while I, *That's no reason to forgive them, Darkness. Fear shouldn't be a factor. You fear them fearing you, and that fear keeps you from having the truest peace. But you have nothing to fear; not them, not anything in this universe. You have absolutely no obligation to forgive them, and that's okay. Remember what our dear Roni said.*

Light, I—it's been so long. We cannot exist in the same space without—

Without becoming one again, yes. I know. I won't be long, I have an appointment with a few of our friends to get to, so you mustn't worry about us merging again. I explain.

Ah, yes. It is wonderful to be in your presence again, Yin. Darkness says sweetly.

Agreed and reciprocated, Yang. Now, I've brought you Time; it was running out. In any case, Yang, do as your heart instructs you. Not as your mind leads you to believe. Reason will only take you so far. And, besides, if all else fails, we could start over from scratch, should these five prove to continue being untrustworthy and insolent children. I laugh, only halfway jesting.

Darkness giggles, *I understand. Thank you, Yin.*

Always, and forever, my darling Darkness. Now, I must depart, lest we become one and reset the universe. I smile and chuckle shortly, departing through the Aether to meet the Unbound.

Hello, Time. It's been quite a while. Darkness says, with the duality of a gentle balefulness.

Hi, Th—uh, Darkness. H-how have you b-been? Time stammers, frightened of what they've perceived Darkness to be.

Darkness goes with it, keeping the sinister playfulness in their voice, *I've been well. I'm complete, healed, and thriving. Can you say the same?*

Time gulps heavily, *I—um, sure? I guess I can say something similar... for now.*

For now? Why for now? Are you expecting to have some unfortunate incident befall you? Maybe have your siblings rip you to pieces and scatter you across the Unreality? Are you feeling frightened of something, perhaps, some impending foreboding twinge? Darkness continues to play with Time.

N-no. I'm just—I'm ready for anything I guess. Time
responds.

*Anything? Anything. Time is ready for anything. Hm,
would you look at that. Anything. I mean, anything* **can**
*happen at any moment. So that's a good attitude to have,
Time. I'm proud of you. You've grown. But perhaps you've
grown too bloated, much too... I don't know.* Darkness says,
their tone getting heavier.

*I-I had to f-fill your shoes, and lead my siblings. I am the
elder sibling after all. So m-maybe, yeah. I cede my position
to you, though, of course. I'm willing t-to—* Time struggles
to find the point.

*Willing to what, exactly? To endure what I had endured? To
hurt like I did?* Darkness teases effectively.

*I-if that would atone for—*Time chokes out.

Darkness purposefully pauses to ponder the possibility of
doing to Time what it had done to them, but only
seemingly before smiling and finally saying, *No. It wouldn't.
Pain for pain won't mend anything. Won't make anything
better. It won't erase what happened to me; what you did. So,
instead—Light was right—I don't forgive you. But that
doesn't mean I will hold a grudge against you and wish you
harm. I won't act on any imagined hostility. You don't have
to be afraid of me. And I will* **not** *live in fear of what you
think of me. It doesn't matter. What matters is that I am at
peace with myself; and I am. Just know that once the
Unbound cross over, all could be different. That doesn't
necessarily have to be a bad thing, change can often be, and
often is, good. From now on, I will be away from you. I have
not lost you, you have lost me. Goodbye, and thank you for
holding space for me and listening, for admitting you were
wrong.*

Darkness slips out of the pocket within the pocket and returns to The Plane of The Forgotten. Returns to the place where they had been imprisoned and changes their form to something much more human-looking within the darkness of what used to be The Voidheart Chasm.

Learnt to be lonely. Darkness smiles.

The Forces float around in silence, digesting everything that had transpired before them.

"What in the world is this place?" Toni inquires softly.

"This has to be the Crux of the Aether. I mean, look at all of *them*." Kia says.

"I think you're right. Luckily, they haven't noticed us yet. Who knows what they'd be up to if they had." Sam adds.

Roni looks around and spots an Aetherling staring, "I think you spoke too soon, Sam."

Chapter 26 - Meeting God We Stand In Line Not Alone

"Holy crap, there's mad of them!" shouts Roni, trying to create literal fire walls in between the Aetherlings and the four of them.

The Unbound run. They run and try to get away from the droves of Aetherlings desperate for purpose and for essence so that they may have a taste of what it's like to have had life. The Aetherlings, by the way, look different to everyone; to some, they look like a mixture of the Boos from Mario and the forest spirits from Princess Mononoke, to others, wobbly human-formed, undulating voids that fill with stars when excited at the prospect of experiencing life. And to others still, they look like polygonal figures with low-res textures ala Playstation One or Nintendo 64 graphics— which is how Roni sees them.

"They're horrifying!" Roni adds randomly, between huffs, "They look like the 90s threw up, like at least have cinematics graphics, not this no-mouth-having-yet-inexplicably-talking-while-wildly-moving-their-limbs-and-head shit!"

"I dunno, Roni," Sam interjects, also while panting, "They look kinda cute to me, I mean, except for the holes for a face. Squishy and shudder-inducing."

"Y'all wild, them bois are creepy!" Kia says, sprinting effortlessly. She sees them like the void thing.

"I'm just runnin', I don't want to see them, definitely don't want to touch them." Toni mumbles, struggling to keep running, then shouts, "Ah, screw it!" before manifesting a wall behind them.

Everyone stops running and turns to check the wall that seems near infinitely wide; putting it up took everything out of Toni, who dropped to their knees with Kia diving to catch them before they fully collapse. Kia cradles Toni's head and strokes their thick tresses and kisses their forehead, "You did good, babe. Rest up a little, okay?"

"You think that'll hold?" Roni says sceptically.

"It has to, Roni, that took everything Toni had, *mi pobrecito*." Kia says softly.

"If anything, I could fly us? You think those things could fly?" Sam suggests.

"That'd be a terrifying twist, I don't want to watch those stiff, graphically impaired monsters fly at us." Roni says sardonically.

Sam looks at Roni halfway confused, "What? Anyway, We'd better think of something quick, I can hear them piling up on the other side of that wall."

"Well, that's the least of our problems," Roni starts, their eyes fixed upon the distance behind Sam and Kia, "there's more of them. Over there. Headed this way."

Toni looks up at Kia with heavy eyes, "Hey, carry me. You gotta carry me, Kia. I don't want those things getting me like Barbara in the cemetery."

"I gotchu baby. You're not going to get eaten, not on my watch." Kia assures Toni.

"Nice reference, but what are we going to do? My fire doesn't faze them, Toni's out, Sam can't carry us all, and I don't think punching them will do anything." Roni says, with their anxiety rising.

The Aetherlings loom closer and closer, the ones on the other side of Toni's green wall of pure essence are *World War* Zing their way over it, and soon, our Unbound are surrounded by the beings that had never lived and would never live, beings forever stuck in this Apple Store-like limbo of sorts.

You'd think this would be the moment I show up, just as everything is looking so hopeless and full of doom. Yet, I think I'll let them stew a little longer. The Aetherlings drawing closer from all sides, Toni hoisted up on Kia's back—a hilarious sight, as Kia is quite short in comparison to Toni—, Sam and Roni holding on to each other. Ah, the tension, the love. It's beautiful, it's tragic, they have no idea they're not in any real danger.

Speaking of, that one Aetherling rushing directly at Kia, intending on sucking the essence out of her like a Capri-Sun, is my cue.

Enough! Children of the Aether, disperse! Begone, what's wrong with you? Haven't any manners? Go on, go. I pause, glaring at the rogue Aetherlings, watching as some hesitate to leave their would-be meal, *Oh, go on, get out of here. Get out of here!* I shout, finally, making them go invisible and flee in fear.

Right, now, how are we, my Unbound lovelies? I hope you're not worse for wear, not hurt at all, yes? Good. I can see you're fine, albeit, a little exhausted, perhaps. Let's do something about that. I smile, then shoot a glance over to Roni, *You'll enjoy this reference, Roni, dear. I know you love references, a walking-talking-reference-machine of sorts, you are.* I state jovially, materialising a ***Megalixir*** with the flick of my wrist into my right hand, like a poof of wispy rainbow sparks, and proceed to toss it at the group to bring their metaphorical HP and MP up to all nines.

"Was that—?" Roni starts.

Yes. I interrupt.

"But those aren't—" Roni says.

Real? I interrupt again, *What is real? Isn't something you can touch, something you can feel, real? Certainly, you felt that. It must be real, I made it so, you felt it. Also, were you not just living within the pocket of Unreality? Come on, Roni, have a little imagination.* I tease.

"They're right, Roni. I mean, you make teal flames. I have super strength and reflexes and some crazy Xavier level astral projection thing. Never tried telepathy though..." Kia explains, trailing off, still holding Toni whomst is starting to get up.

"Right, and I can fly." Sam adds.

"I'm lost, what're ya stuck on? Some magic potion? Roni, I can make anything I can think of, that ain't wild." Toni says standing and dusting himself off and fixing his jacket.

"Okay, I get it, I'm just—I wasn't expecting to see a video game item out in the wild like this." Roni throws their hands up and paces back and forth, turning sharply each time, "Wait, who exactly are you? Are you one of the Forces? You look pretty human-like for a Force of the Universe."

I smile and giggle shortly, *Well, you're right. I do look a bit too human for a Force of the—what do you call "it"—the Universe, as it were. It could be because maybe, I **am** the Universe, as you like to say. I am Light, Yin, The Creator—if you care for such absolutist labels—, God, if you're into religion. What have you, it's me. Lovely to make your acquaintance, Unbound ones. You've met and helped my other half, Darkness, I'm grateful for that, you know. And I must say, I did not see it coming, at least not so soon, and not as it happened.*

Of course, I was aware of the myth and everything but— Oh, I'm babbling. I'm sorry. Please, do go on and have your reactions.

"Oh, I already figured. What, with this beautiful form of yours—you don't mind me callin' you beautiful, do you?" I shake my head gently in response with a smile and beckon Toni to continue, "—and the way you talk. It reminded me of them."

"So you're Light? The Light? I have so many questions—" Roni starts, excitedly.

And I have so many answers, though probably not ones you'd like. I respond.

"You're so pretty! Like, wow. Your hair, your eyes! Like how are you this gorgeous? Literally goals." Kia gushes, as I am admittedly flattered.

Goals? Being an all powerful, intangible, shape shifting being of pure energy, not tied to any physical form whatsoever? I inquire.

"Uh, yeah! That's the dream; enlightenment in its fullest, purest form. Plus, look at your curves, girl—wait, what are your pronouns, honey?" Kia retorts.

Any will do. I'm not particularly picky, as I'm nothing and everything all at once. Though I hear you refer to Yang as 'they'. Curious. Respectful. I say, quite amused and pleased.

"Uh, so, Light?"

Yes, Sam?

"Why are we here?" Sam says, meekly.

I take a breath I don't need to take because I don't have any lungs, make a sound that sounds a lot like sucking teeth, and sigh with a smile, *Here as in The Aether? Here as in the Universe? Or here as in existence, my dearest Sami-bear?* I've rather taken a liking to them, if I'm being honest.

"I—I guess—I mean, I guess," Sam pauses, "All?"

I take a moment to ponder how I'll explain to a mortal all of existence, from life, to unlife, to undeath, to death. From reality to unreality, to the in between that is The Aether. The moment passes and walk toward them, stop mere inches from them and take my finger and boop Sam's nose and say, *Forty-two.* I laugh after a moment's silence as everyone just stared blankly at me as if I were the most absurd thing they'd seen. They're all still frozen in bewilderment, *Fine, fine. Okay, it was a joke. I'm amazed you didn't catch the reference! Either way, brace yourselves.*

The reason you're in The Aether is to give purpose to all of these lovely little sprites here, give them bodies and give them life via undeath. You'll know what to do with them, but it will require a sacrifice of sorts. Following? Following? Good. Good. *And so that brings us to why you're here in this universe. That's easy. You're here to help me teach the so-called Forces a lesson. A lesson in meddling, a lesson in hubris. Through your transition from reality, because of your very nature, you upset the fabric of Space—another Force, but this one doesn't deviate from its purpose and create whole dimensions of Unreality in badly hidden pockets in the far reaches of the galaxy behind my back while swearing up and down that its being sneaky with the aid of my other half of which I could see everything through and visa versa— sorry, anyway, Space was none-too-pleased with the essence of Darkness that had leaked through a tear out of the Unreality and into Reality proper, and become entwined with four human souls that had in turn experienced a half-assed undeath at the hands of a Force that didn't quite know what it was doing but acted as though it did, thus setting forth the events that led to this moment. Space didn't care for that at all. Obviously, I didn't either, but here we are, and, well, we all learned what I already knew. You are the Unbound.*

Lastly, you exist because you must. You exist because you were made, by some random toss of DNA, mixed in with a little stardust and the essence of Darkness, you exist. And what a wonderful thing it is that you do. If any one of you were to have never been, like these poor little babies, I refer to the Aetherlings, *then the connections all of you share wouldn't exist, and without those, well who knows what would become of either of you if you'd never met. You exist for each other, you exist for yourselves. Think of all that you've done, all that you've experienced, alone, with each other. Have you not grown? Have you not become the person you wish you had, to have been there for you in your moments of need? And you share that with each other and with anyone you encounter. Look at what you did with Darkness. You could have finished the job and eradicated them, though doing that would have caused you to absorb the leftover unused essence and the implications are... Problematic. But you didn't, you helped them find themself, you helped them have the courage to build themself back up and be whole again, stronger and wiser than before. So, why do you exist, you ask? To spread kindness, to love, to be. To create. And that will bring us to the meaning of The Plane of the Forgotten, The Stranding, and Unreality altogether.*

"That—That was heavy. And a lot to process. But I have a question before you get into the meaning of—of that."

Go on. I oblige.

Roni hesitates to ask, "What sacrifice?"

*Your ability, Roni. You must use every ounce of your energy, of your essence, to help the Aetherlings find their bodies—rather, bodies for them to occupy. This will kill you, it will close off the Aether and seal the tears between planes, leaving you in the void—more like, leaving you **as** The Void, where none may enter, not even me. This act will force the Aetherlings to occupy bodies that have been left without essence, without life or death.*

"Whoa, wait. No, there's gotta be another way. Roni can't die. We need Roni. It's like you said, we'd be lost or incomplete without each other, without even just one of us!" Kia is quick to refute me.

Yes, well. That was before. You'd already found each other. I retort.

"Okay, but I can't just let go of them. We can't just let Roni die! Roni, you can't, I can't lose you. I can't lose someone else—!" Sam's voice starts to break, "I just got you back. I thought I lost you when we went back, and—I mean, it was such a relief that my mom was alive, but I had this ache in my heart being without you. When I felt you again, Roni, I felt my heart beat again. I can't lose you, I can't. Not forever—"

"—Yeah, ain't there something we can do? Like, what if we give Roni all of our essence, or whatever. Will that be enough?"

No. Ultimately, Roni must do this alone, and there is no way to save them. I am sorry, but Roni, as you know them, must give their all for this. And you three must go back to where The Forbidden Forest of Forgotten Figments and Figures used to be and meet with Darkness. You'll know what to do with the Aetherlings that will be pouring into the area from The Chasm, and Darkness will take it from there. Trust the process, Unbound ones. I attempt to reassure them.

"Roni? Roni, come on, you can't be cool with this." Toni places his hand on Roni's shoulder.

"I'm not. But Light has no reason to mess with us. They want to bring balance back to life, the universe, to everything—" Roni finally got the reference, "Fu—I get it, ha. 42. Good one, Light." I smile and nod approvingly, Roni continues, "Anyway, I don't think there's another way, gays. I think I have to do this."

Sam runs up to Roni and squeezes them tightly, "No! No, no, no, no, no! I won't let you. I can't let you die, babe. I love you too much, I can't let you. Roni! Listen to me, you cannot go through with this. There has to be another way, we can find another way, we have to find another way, I can't lose you. I can't lose you like I lost my dad. Roni, I won't let you, dammit!"

"Sam, we don't have a choice. It's the only way to make things right." Roni says solemnly.

"But why do **you** have to be the one!? Why do you have to set things right? It's not fair, can't you all see it's not fair? We didn't start this. Why do you have to fix it? Why? I can't, you hear me? I'm not kissing you goodbye." Sam's eyes fill with tears and overflow.

Chapter 27 - ...Ticket Wasn't Good for Two; I Rode Alone

I wish I could tell you that Roni and Sam made it through together. I wish I could say that Roni, as we know them, would make it out of this ordeal at all. But if I *did* say that, then I would be much more misleading than I have been thus far. Perhaps, I could even be called a liar, if I did say those things. So I won't say those things. And, for a change, I'll refrain from hiding the truth of the matter from you. First, though, Let's go back to the sombre, bittersweet parting of our lovely Sam and Roni.

"I never felt like I belonged anyway; to this world, to this universe. You're the only thing that would keep me tethered to life if The Plane were to, like, implode or whatever is gonna happen—"

I interjected, cutting Roni off, *Implode, taking reality down with it. Darkness and I would have to start over. Tedious, really.*

Roni glared at me, half annoyed, half concerned, "Right, either way. Sam, I know I was always cheerful and chipper and," They paused, "brave. Truth is, it wasn't bravery, more than it was recklessness and a sheer disregard for myself. That's why I'm so okay with this. That's why I don't mind sacrificing myself so that you can have a chance at a normal life, at any life, 'cause let's face it, we're never gonna be normal." Roni smiled a wistful, sweet smile.

"What are you saying? What do you mean? You were never happy? Even after everything, with me, with all of us? You were just, what, pretending to be happy?" Sam choked, a lump forming in their throat.

"That isn't true, Sam. Roni, tell them, you're just trying to push us away so it's easier for us to let you do the thing. Tell them, Roni!" Kia insisted.

Toni just remained silent, materialising a cigarette and crossing their arms after sticking the emerald smoke inducing roll of paper and tobacco. A grunt is all that would emanate from their vocal chords.

Roni didn't respond for a long while, instead just turned their back and took a few steps before letting out a long breath and finally saying, "I was happy for mere moments. I kept chasing those moments of happiness with you, with Kia," they stopped and glanced over their shoulder, "with Toni. But in between those moments, in the studio, by myself—all the liminal spaces were filled with an all consuming sorrow. There's a pit inside of me, Sam. There's a hole I cannot fill." Roni chuckles softly, "That's probably why I'm the only one that can do this, really. I am a void where happiness goes to die. I am what should have died. None of this would have happened if Time hadn't pulled me into The Plane. Everything started happening from the moment I stepped foot there, I poisoned The Stranding. I caused the glitches, the people losing their minds, the random remembering of things that were supposed to be forgotten. I'm the reason we couldn't forget the things that happened to us, and it drove some of the people in The Stranding to their complete oblivion."

Sam rushed to Roni's back and grasped them hard, embracing their right arm tightly, "So what if you caused it? So what if you made us remember? We had to to move on and not let our past traumas control and shape our every move. Without those memories flooding back to us, and our bonds with each other we could not have been able to face what was waiting for us when we went back to Reality. Roni, can't you see? You didn't poison The Stranding, you liberated it from the fantasy and escapism it was so entrenched in. We can only avoid the awful truth for so long, we have to face it sooner or later."

"But the ones that lost their whole selves? I'm responsible for that, Sam. I might as well have killed them myself." Roni retorted, clenching their fist.

"I don't know about them. They made the decisions they made, you shouldn't feel like you had to save them. Yes, it's awful that they ended up a Grey shell without a soul, but that was their choice, and you can't take that away from them by making it your fault. You didn't kill anyone. You couldn't. And you didn't save anyone either, that's not your job. You just," Sam trailed off a moment, "You just helped us realise what we always knew to begin with, you helped us find the strength we always had to move on. And moving on doesn't mean forgetting or being magically healed, either. The grief, the pain, it's still there, we just grow around it instead of letting it grow inside of us and taking us over like a parasite."

"It's too late for me, Sam. It's already a parasite inside me. I'm just good at wearing a mask, at pretending. I've had to my whole life. I have to do this, it's the only way to keep the Universe from collapsing, keep you safe, and" Roni turned around and faced Sam, taking their small, soft face in their hands, "be free of this endless sadness and loneliness I feel inside."

That last part stung the entire group. The loneliness Roni feels inside; was their love and support not enough to ease Roni's broken heart? Was Sam not enough to fill them with love and hope and happiness? Was Kia's wisdom and optimism not enough to keep Roni looking forward and be at peace? Roni, indeed, felt happiness with them. They loved their friends fiercely and held them close to their heart. But there was always a constant gnawing at the back of their mind that wouldn't let them hold on to the happiness for too long. A voice inside of them—another essence, if you will—that whispered doubt and self-loathing, whispered words that would ensure that the pit inside of them would continue to grow, and that the Roni we know and love, would shrink.

"I'm sorry that you feel that way, Roni. And I'm sorry that nothing I can do can help you feel any less lonely or unhappy. I really thought—" Sam started to stifle a sob, "I really thought I could make you happy, like, really happy. Always."

Roni presses their lips against Sam's forehead, kissing them softly, "I'm sorry, too, that I couldn't be happy for you. Sam, my sweet Sam, it was never your job to make me happy, only to love me. And you loved me more than I could even imagine. Moments with you were the best moments of my life. Don't be sorry, never be sorry."

Kia ran over to them and tackled them both with a warm, strong squeeze, "I won't accept that you weren't happy! Roni, you floppy bitch, I love you! I know you can be happy, I can feel it. But I can also feel the infinite sadness inside you now," she furrowed her brow with worry and empathy, "it's so much. I can't and won't believe that I'm going to lose you. This is not the end. It can't be. But if you feel that you absolutely have to do this alone—"

They must. I interrupt.

Kia glares at me, "—then I guess—I guess I accept that."

Toni, who hadn't said a word, languidly trudged toward the rest of the Unbound and placed a hand on Roni's shoulder, "I loved you first. I loved you because you were a reflection of me, but better. You're everything I could learn to love about myself, everything I strived to be. You inspired me from the moment I saw you, and you inspire me still. I fuckin, love you, Roni. God damn it, I don't want to say goodbye, I can't. I'm with Kia on this, it can't be the end. There's more for us to talk about, for us to teach each other. More to experience, shit!" Toni grunts loudly, "This is bullshit, Roni. You're bullshit for saying you feel lonely even with us! But then again, I know how that feels more than anyone here. I was lonely even when I was with all those people I used to kill that loneliness. So I get it, even if it hurts you saying it out loud."

They all embraced, each letting go separately until only Sam was left in Roni's arms. Roni felt the warm wetness of Sam's tears soaking their top. They held each other silently for a while, Sam sobbing into Roni's chest; no sparkles here, no dissipation, the tears stain this time. The tears stay this time.

"I wish you could come with us, or that I could stay with you," Sam said before kissing Roni for the last time before returning to The Plane of the Forgotten, "it's not fair." They whispered, pulling away.

Roni wiped away their tears and said softly and with all of the love in their being, "I know."

Sam walked backward away from Roni, joining the other two by the door I created at that instant that led to where Darkness had been waiting. The Aetherlings all gather around the three Unbound and I tell them to be calm and that nothing is going to hurt any of them.

Everything will be right. I said.

"Don't you mean '*alright*'?" Toni asked.

No. I said, with no intent to elaborate. *Walk through the door, Unbound, and the Aetherlings will follow. They will know where to go, but you and Darkness must aid them in assimilation. I will stay with Roni to aid them with their transition. Do not fret.*

They and Roni exchanged words of love and hope, farewells and *see-you-laters*. It was a beautiful display of sweetness drenched in sorrow, regret, and longing. I admit, I was touched.

Now...

I'm sorry Roni, this is going to hurt, but only briefly, and more emotionally than physically. Either way, not pleasant. But if it's any solace, you'll then be free of the void inside of you and you won't feel any pain or remember anything. Literally, nothing. I explain.

"I'm okay with the pain—wait, what do you mean I won't remember anything?" Roni says.

Exactly that. I say, again with no intention to elaborate. *After this, I have to meet with the other Unbound to offer them a choice. So let's try to make this go smoothly, yes? Yes.*

Roni nods confusedly, "Okay. What kind of a choice?"

*The kind that will alter their mortal lives for the better. Hopefully. The kind of choice that will give them **real** freedom.* I cryptically clarify.

Roni sighs, resigned to their fate, unclear to what's about to happen, but willing to sacrifice themself for life, the universe, and everything. They pace around the white nothingness of the Aether, psyching themself up and reminding themself why they are doing what they are doing, "For Sam. For Kia. For Toni. For everyone, and for everyone I couldn't save." They stop and look up into the endless white, "For mom. Because of mom, because of everything. Everything they made me feel, everything they put me through. Everything I can't let go of. Everything I have to let go of."

Roni's mind is flooded with memories of pain, suffering, regret. The pit inside of them is growing, the Darkness within them begins to fester and take over their entire essence. Their once azure flame spark a deep black that would consume their body. Their flame that was once harmless to them now causes an agonising burn that would cleanse their mind of all thought and emotion.

Did I say mostly psychological and emotional pain? I'm sorry, it's the other way around. See, the physical pain of absolute immolation thoroughly cleanses you of your sorrow so that when you transfer over your consciousness, you'll be a blank slate. Mostly. I explain, watching Roni be engulfed in flames of noir, screaming in agony. *I know, it's not ideal. But at the end of it, Roni. All will be right.*

I know, I seem to have lost my empathy and it's really jarring, off putting, and, quite frankly, you don't much care for it. It takes you out of this normally quite emotional moment in a way you don't yet understand.

Do not fret, all will be right.

Chapter 28 - When The Director Sold the Show...

I need constant reminders
Of what my absence will do
How pain will fill the hearts
Of the ones I love most
I need things that let me know
How hurt everyone I love will be
Without me, without me here
But I can't stay, I can't stay
Not for much longer my loves
I want to go, I want to fall away
This pain in me is much too deep
To continue to live with
And I need to see the loss
In others' lives to understand
The loss that would infect
The lives of those I care for
I need to feel their pain with mine
To deter my escape from my own
Alone, my pain is mine alone
I don't want to be here, anymore
I don't want to feel this, anymore
But I can't just leave you all behind
I can't give in to my solipsistic
Selfish need to end this pain
So I must stay, I have to stay
For as long as my loves exist, though
I want to go, I want to fall away
This pain in me will not cause
The pain in you to grow over me

"You'll get over me..." Roni whispers through the eternal darkness that is their personal voidheart.

Oh, Roni, what sorrow blinds you to. What it binds you to. I say to them as their being turns to ashen space dust. *I won't scatter it to the heartless nothingness, you will always be with **them**.* I take a line from the last in Roni's favourite franchise, making it my own and relevant, of course.

You will always be—

They are coming. All of my children, all of my Lost Ones. I, Darkness, say expecting the three Unbound to appear through the Aether with the Aetherlings in tow any moment now.

And they do.

"I can't believe they're gone," Sam cries, their face flush with unbridled grief.

Toni wraps his arm around Sam and pulls their head against his soft chest, "I know. I can't either. I can't believe they would—that idiot, that fuckin' piece of shit just let us go like that, wouldn't even let us try to help. What a—" their voice breaks.

Kia interjects, "They had to. I mean, like, they had no choice. You heard Light, something about their essence alone was what was needed to bring balance back to the Universe. Besides, I don't think Roni would just say those things for nothing. I know that they really felt everything they said they did. I remember our talks back in their apartment, we would talk forever about everything— sometimes I would just see the light leave their eyes when certain topics would come up. I saw them shrink, I saw them fall into the deepest despair."

"But you always pulled them out of it, I know you did. You did the same for me." Toni says.

"Yeah, but it would be for the most fleeting moments. I think the happiest I've seen them was with Sam, when we all met after the movie, I looked over and saw y'all so happy—saw Roni so happy. I'd never seen them shine like that. I feel like it's the little moments of happiness that kept them so strong, as if it was enough to fully distract them once the Unreality of The Stranding started to crumble." Kia explains.

Yes, their grieving, shattered heart only felt solace with the three of you, and especially with you Sam. And as Unreality began to shift because of their connection to me, their abject misery had started to resurface. Like a flooding basement after a pipe bursts in the dead of winter, the cold depth of sorrow kept rising. So they instinctively sought me out. I inform, floating toward them in a form unrecognisable.

"Darkness? You look human." Kia inquires, having felt me out.

Yes. I confirm.

"But why would they seek you out?" Sam asks.

Because their essence is my own, as is yours. It is the source of your melancholia, 'a touch of Darkness', as they say. Though Roni seems to have acquired my heart's shadow. Light and I, we have dual hearts, one actual heart, and the other is the heart's shadow. A sort of ideal or some abstract, intangible force that gives the heart meaning. This is the reason they had to stay behind and close the tear between planes and essentially decommission the Aether. They had to become The Void. Or rather, their essence had to. My answer offered them no peace, but they seemed to understand.

"So what'll happen to us?" Toni asks roughly.

You will be given a choice. Light will come and offer it. But for now, you must step aside as you are blocking the doorway and the Aetherlings are being quite patient, but they need to possess these Greys surrounding us. I point to the field of Greys I had collected from the ruins of the First Stranding where my forest had been.

"Oh, how'd we miss those?" Kia chortles nervously.

Sam looks back behind them and sees the mass of Aetherlings waiting, then scans the area, seeing the many distorted visages of Greys that were once Strandlers, "Let's get out of their way."

The Unbound walk toward me and stand at my side to watch as the plethora of Aetherlings crawl and fly and zip around to find bodies to inhabit. Many of them are confused, and are in need of aid finding the right bodies. Those Aetherlings find their way to the Unbound float around them like adorable lost puppies. Some, like kittens, rub themselves against the legs of Sam and Kia—Toni frightens them a little, so they keep their distance.

Help them. I say, insistently.

The Unbound nod affirmatively, though Toni sneers and spits as they trod off, herding their respective bunches of Lost Ones toward Grey shells to inhabit. The Lost Ones give the Unbound sweet and grateful expressions—though only Kia can make those out, the other two remain unsettled by what they see—before squeezing themselves down the throats of the Greys as their mouths had been agape; you know, from their horrifying end.

"They're kinda cute!" Kia squeaks.

Toni and Sam glare at her and shake their heads as they escort their last Aetherlings to the last two Greys and make sure they assimilate with the bodies.

"There's one left!" Kia points out.

The little Lost One floats about in distress with no body to inhabit. I extend my hand to it, *With me, little one. Light has plans for you.*

"Wait, what? But there's no other Grey. And the Aether is shut down." Sam says, curiously.

Not your concern. You've done well here, now watch. I demand softly.

The Greys gradually fill with colour, with life, with spark. Their gruesomely contorted bodies and faces loosen and retract to a much more normal and placid state, giving the image of something, no, someone that is fully alive and complete. Though here, they are undead, as the Unreality is no place for the living.

They are Grey no more. They've become Neo Strandlers, which is just me being fancy and giving my lovely lost children a special title that differentiates them from those that had been taken and sent to The Stranding by Time and the Forces. Speaking of, I have to fix those. *I have to meet with each Strandler and prepare them for true Undeath.* I say to the little Lost One by my side, looking down and smiling at them softly, *Should they wish to stay, that is.*

"What do you mean," Kia overheard me, "all of them were frozen in a moment in life like we were?"

Yes. And they must come to terms with that moment, decide whether they can bear their life, or if Unreality is the alternative they need. I will show them what their life would be like after they go back, much like you experienced, but simulated, and what the world would be like without them. Then ask them whether or not they wish to stay. I explain plainly.

"Is that what Light is going to do with us?" Sam asks meekly.

No. But also, in a way. I cannot say. Remember, the four of you are forever connected, even apart. I say cryptically, before departing.

"Wait! Where did they go? Darkness! You can't just leave us with some vague idea like that!" Kia calls out.

The Neo Strandlers took a few moments to feel themselves out, to talk, to move. They were overjoyed to finally have bodies, to have lives, even as the undead in the Unreality. Some of them were so overwhelmed that they began to sob, which prompted Kia to rush to their sides and hug them, offer kind words, and inspire them to find their purpose, even if that purpose is to simply be.

Sam and Toni sat with Darkness's last words, not knowing what to make of it all. Then their thoughts swirled around Roni; They miss Roni.

So, we can continue looking after The Plane of The Forgotten? Time inquires.

After all we've done? After having aided Time with the whole endeavour? Attraction is in disbelief.

Yes. But no more meddling. You are to leave the Taking to Darkness. Only they are suited to bring humans to Unreality, as they are the only ones that can uncreate. I scold.

Nature grunts in agreement.

Chance scoffs, knowingly. I cast my gaze toward them, letting them know that I know that they know that I knew that they knew that I knew.

I'm just glad this is all over, though it's so sad what happened with Roni. Turning into The Void, being ripped apart like that. It's all so very sad how they had to suffer all the way til the end. Feeling expressed languidly.

Yes, well. Roni will always be a part of everything now, as a part of nothing. They are what has always been. Funny, how things come full circle, isn't it? As if it's all a part of some never ending cycle. I respond ponderously. *Now, return to your duties and leave those poor mortals alone. You've ruined enough, and I wouldn't want to avoid the end of everything, yet again.*

I leave them to their devices. The Unbound are waiting, after all. Their home is nowhere at the moment.

Chapter 29 - Never Fade In The Dark

The Unbound sit in the ruins of the First Stranding, bereft and silent, just absorbing the gravity of everything that has happened. The moments that each had shared with Roni play in their thoughts like a highlight reel, their faces reflecting the loss they've experienced. Sam having lost someone important to them in their life already is the most distraught, fighting back the need to sob, breaking and letting it all out with Kia holding them close and tight, then going back to silent tears that seem to flow on their own.

The Neo Strandlers all had thanked the Unbound and made their way to The Stranding, which in turn, expanded and morphed into a metropolis that took inspiration from the neon cyberpunk future cities as seen in Anime and video games. Tall buildings, sleek and shiny, bright purple, blue, and pink neon signs adorning shops and cafes. Even Café Ludens changed to a sleek and no-future punk aesthetic. The streets below were no longer cobblestone, but a slick black pavement with holographic traffic lines and floating signs for pedestrians. Strandlers now travelled via electric motorbikes, hoverboards, and magnetically propelled in-line skates that allowed them to ride rails and up buildings. Gas lights were replaced by tall and thin LED streetlights.

Everything changed, and yet it seemed as though it always was.

Now then, Sam, Toni, I smile as I look toward Kia, *Kia. The time has finally come. I imagine Darkness filled you in as much as they could?*

Sam stands up and wipes their eyes with their palm, then wipes their nose with their sleeve, sniffs and lets out a short breath, "Yeah, somewhat. Roni's gone. You're going to give us a choice of some kind, I don't know. I don't know if I can do that right now."

"It's okay, baby, it's gonna be okay. I gotchu." Kia consoles Sam.

"I don't think we're in any shape to make decisions," Toni says, then points to their head and heart, "in here."

*Well, unfortunately, **that** is not a choice. You have to, because either way you will lose your ability to travel through planes. Remember, the Aether is off limits to all. That means you as well. Which means, something more must be lost for the sake of balance. You cannot be on this plane in your current state. You're unbound, you must be bound to one plane. So you have a choice.* I say, quite sternly.

The three of them exchange worried and suspicious glances before Kia finally infers, "So you want us to choose to stay or to go back to our lives."

And also a mysterious third thing. I add.

"What's the third thing?" Toni walks up to me, looking me in the eyes, trying to look tough, yet failing, as their sadness glimmers behind their eyes.

One; you stay, experiencing a true Undeath where your entire life will have been erased. You'd be uncreated from reality, you would not exist and no one would miss you. Two; You go back to your lives where you left off with no memory of anything that happened, though you would always yearn for something you cannot remember you lost; each other. Three; you choose a point in Earth's history where the three of you can exist together, fully aware of everything that happened, fully aware of your life before, retaining all of your memories, but you would be strangers to everyone you knew in life, as your previous life would be erased. I illustrate to them, playing little scenarios in a marquee of my creation that look like adorable little cartoons.

Moments pass as they deliberate amongst themselves, weighing the pros and cons of each choice.

"So no one would miss us? If we were to stay, and if we were to do the third thing, no one would miss us? But if we do the second thing we'd miss each other without knowing that we miss each other. And," Kia takes a moment, "And we'd never see each other, we're scattered through eras. And, Sam, you wouldn't have Roni either because they're—"

Sam casts their sullen gaze to the ground, "Gone. Yeah. I don't like any of them."

"They're all shit choices. We lose either way. But I think," Toni starts to pace around, "I think I'd rather know what I lost and mourn them instead of mourning something I don't remember. I don't like the idea of having an unknown empty feeling."

"I agree. But I just got my mom back. I'd be leaving her again. I don't know if I could do that, like, I really missed her and it was so nice knowing she was fighting for me the whole time." Kia's eyes well up with tears.

"Me too, my mom is okay. She's alive and she's okay. And I'll be letting go of my sisters, too." Sam adds.

"All I've got is Chino. He's my brother and everything, but I think he's better off without me, you know? Like he won't have to get into fights with people over me. Because out there I'm—everyone sees me as just a girl. That's just the way it is back then." Toni discloses.

Kia and Sam look at Toni sympathetically, Sam empathises, "Yeah, it's the same with me."

"Honestly, I don't think it gets any better when I'm from. So I think our only choices are to stay here or to do the third thing. I love my mom, I'll miss her, but I'll know that because I don't exist to her, she won't suffer what she did. She won't have to fight, she won't be stuck, and she won't have to endure my father." Kia justifies.

"My mom still has my sisters. I mean, she won't miss me, I won't exist to her. I'll miss her, but I've missed my dad ever since he died, and at least I'll know she's okay. And who knows, maybe depending on when we go, my dad will be alive too. That thought comforts me." Sam smiles wistfully.

"So when and where are we goin'?" Toni says breathily.

Yes, I'd like to know, as well. Being that I'll be the one sending you there and altering reality to make sure you are comfortable. You did help stabilise the universe, after all. Least I can do. I say, impatiently.

Kia grins from ear to ear, "I know exactly when and where. A place and era that would be perfect for all of us. Where apathy and angst reign above all things, including the construct of gender and sexuality. A moment when technology was advanced enough for us" Kia points to herself and Sam, "to get by and enjoy, while you, Toni, won't be totally shocked and lost."

Ah, I see. I say, having understood the assignment.

"Well, what era are we going to be locked into?" Sam interrogates.

"Spit it out, babe." Toni insists.

Did I lose? Did I fail? I can't see anything, but I can feel myself. I'm still here. How am I still here? Am I still here? Everything is so dark. Goodbye, Kia. Goodbye, Toni. Goodbye, Sam. I miss you all so much. I wish I could be with you right now. If only you'd know the things I want to say to you. Sam, if I were with you, I'd sing you to sleep. I want to sing for you again, I want to sing with you again. I love you, don't lose the light inside you. Roni whispers through The Void, their thoughts scrambled and disorganised. As is their state.

Roni, it's time to separate your body from the shadow Voidheart. You'll need a new—well, let's call it a soul. I have this sweet little Aetherling here that Darkness saved for us. I just have to create your essence once more and imbue it into the little baby here, then you will be right. All will be right. Though, as I said. You will be a blank slate. But that's okay. You have the other three to bring you back. No matter how long it takes, I am sure they are more than willing to piece your memories back together. I expound to Roni's formless form.

Nirvana's 'Smells Like Teen Spirit' blares out of a thrift store on the busy Capitol Hill street corner where dozens of Seattlites cross and trek back and forth either coming from or going to some random destination. Above the thrift store, hanging out of the window of one of the flats, Kia yells and *woops* excitedly.

"Isn't this just so cool!?" She shouts into the flat at her flatmates, "It's the fucking 90's y'all! And it is LIT!"

"My gosh I was a baby around this time. You weren't even a thought, Kia." Sam says, still in disbelief that this is their new reality.

"I'd be old." Toni scoffs, trying to manifest a cigarette.

"Still can't do it?" Kia probes, "I don't have my strength either."

"And I can't even hover," Sam adds, "I think this is it. We're completely cut off from Unreality."

"Yeah, I can't feel anything other than the music and the cars." Kia shrugs.

"I guess I'm gonna quit then. Ain't no way I'm paying for something I used to make for free." Toni sits back on their dark emerald green corduroy couch and sighs.

"Bitch, you're so cheap!" Kia laughs.

"It ain't like we got money. You buy'em then." Toni retorts.

"No! El-oh-el! I'm glad you're quitting. I wouldn't be able to stand the smell anyway." Kia says, smiling.

"Yeah, honestly, I'm glad too. I guess we gotta get jobs, though." Sam states.

"We're all good at things. It's the 90s, it isn't that hard. Toni you can sell your paintings and sketches. I can see if I can be a *sifu* at one of the Jeet Kune Do schools here. And Sam, you can pursue writing or start a band or something. You can write and sing." Kia extolls, "We'll be fine."

Time to go, Roni. Just step through that ring of light and you'll be in a flat of your own, you'll be set. Trust me. I lead Roni through the light, my hand on their back. They look back at me and nod.

"How will I—" Roni starts.

—You will be fine. You will do fine, Roni. You won't remember any of this, but you will have memories. It will be like a life you always knew. No beginning, no new start, just a continuation of something special I left for you in the era that was chosen. Be well, Roni. Be well, and all will be right.

Chapter 30 - Standing On The Surface Of A Perforated Sphere

I Need You So Much Closer...

A familiar voice echoed from within a bar down in SODO; The Showbox. The voice was singing a cover of 'Creep' by Radiohead. Sam had been booked for a show that night, they'd perform with their band after the current one finished their set, and Sam had been warming up in their trailer before going backstage. Something in them told them to go a little earlier, something like a tug, or a gentle pull of a string. They went to the bar for a drink of water, though the intention was to see who was playing. The band's name was The Dead Eternal, some local band that popped up out of nowhere and started making rounds not long before Sam, Kia, and Toni arrived, though their lead singer was reportedly new. Sam looked across the crowd and toward the stage, their mouth hung open and their eyes began to fill with tears.

That same tug beckoned Kia and Toni, who were still getting ready for Sam's show, to hurry and get to The Showbox early.

"I wonder what they're gonna play." Toni thought out loud.

"Yeah, originals or covers? Maybe both. Hopefully both. Sam's cover of 'Come As You Are' is just so, so good. It makes me want to cry, tee-bee-aych." Kia said filled with anticipation.

"Babe, I thought we agreed you'd stop saying acronyms out loud. That's not something people do in the 90's. Plus, I'm partial to their cover of 'Black'." Toni said through their teeth.

"Right, my bad. Wait, 'Black'? Pearl Jam?" Kia said, judging Toni's taste.

"What's wrong with Pearl Jam?" Toni said roughly.

"Nothing. But you prefer it to 'Come As You Are'? I mean, at least give me 'Black Hole Sun'."

"Don't be basic, Kia." Toni said frankly.

Kia gasped, "How dare you use my phrases against me!?"

Toni Laughed.

They round a corner to 1st Ave S, The Showbox just down the street. A crowd of would-be concert goers can be seen at the door as the couple approaches. They look at each other as they continue forward, wondering how they are going to contend with this crowd, not only to get in, but to get close enough so that Sam sees them in the crowd.

Sam runs out of the bar to the street, somehow knowing that Kia and Toni would be arriving at that very moment.

"Toni! Kia! Over here!" Sam shouted.

Security rushed over, having seen Toni and Kia hurrying toward Sam who put their hand out to them, "It's cool, they're with me. I'll take them in from the back."

"You sure?"

"Yeah, I promise, they're cool." Sam reassured the security guards.

One of them eyed Toni before going back to the front entrance, "Alright."

Sam grabbed both of them by their hands, "You're not going to believe who's playing right now."

Toni looked over at a poster, "The Damned Eternal? Meh."

Sam's eyes started watering again, filling with equal parts hope and joy, "Just come and see for yourself."

Sam takes them inside from the back and leads them around to the bar to get a good look at the stage where the band is now playing an original song.

Words flying at the speed of what it's worth/Compiled over sonic movements
The need to fulfill some twenty-odd tasks /Coupled with sparse attention/Every movement goes unmissed/The vigilance is higher than this feeling
Yeah/
And here it comes, the comedown/From flying to crashing to volatile fragility
Where did it all go? The comedown/The mind is focused on everything that hurts
Cannot move, the comedown, embracing pain/Waiting for the numbness too
Oh, climbing high and riding this to death/Look at me aren't I just fabulous
Let's make believe we're invincible, whoa/Just laugh at all the absurdity
Attention, it's needed, lifeblood, believe it/The life of the party, can't be touched
Fuck!/
And here it comes, the comedown/From flying to crashing to volatile fragility
Where did it all go? The comedown/The mind is focused on everything that hurts
Cannot move, the comedown, embracing pain/Waiting for the numbness too/
Oh, why am I crying?/These tears, what are they for, oh
I know now, it's that thing that I/I remember, but why, I was laughing

Just now! I was so happy I could/Die, now it's all I want
I'm so tired, so fucking tired of this/I can't take it anymore!
Can't fake it anymore!/Just leave me alone, the comedown
This crash caused by nothing or something/Anything at all,
the comedown
So easy to trigger when you know which buttons/You push,
the comedown, down I go
Spiralling out of control!

It was a frenzied, up-tempo garage punk track that didn't
pull any punches sonically or emotionally. The lead singer's
heart was worn on their sleeve, you could feel them through
their voice. And through their singing and screaming, their
eyes held the deepest sorrow and longing, as if waiting for
something or someone to come along and help heal their
wounded heart and mend their fragile mind.

"Oh-em-gee!" Kia exclaimed softly to herself.

"Holy shit." Toni mouthed.

"It's them. It's Roni." Sam said finally.

The Damned Eternal wrapped their set and Sam's band,
Stellar, was up next. In between the set up for Stellar, Roni
noticed Sam trying not to stare at them and made their way
over to Sam.

"Hey, good luck out there. I don't think I've heard you
play." Roni said.

"Yeah, no," Sam said nervously, having noticed that Roni
hadn't recognised them, "I guess you haven't—um, have
you—? Nevermind."

"No, what, what is it?" Roni implored.

"Nothing. You just look like someone I—You were great
out there. I have to get going." Sam said, hurrying away.

"Okay. I guess I'll catch you after!" Roni called out, having felt an inkling of something inside of them.

Sam awaits their introduction, wiping tears away. Roni not recognising them had destroyed every ounce of hope they had. They were left grieving all over again. A feeling they would carry on to the stage where they would perform their cover of 'Black' by Pearl Jam, down tuned and down tempo. Which, for a dark and slow song, was bold.

The words burned in Sam's throat, their voice carrying their melancholy heart.

I know someday you'll have a beautiful life, I know you'll be star in somebody else's sky
But why, why, why can't it be mine

The show ended and Sam's band, Stellar, left the stage. Sam, instead of staying with the band, went to meet Toni and Kia, who were at the bar waiting for Sam.

"They don't remember me, Kia. They don't remember anything. I don't—I don't know what to do now. I thought that if we did see them again that there'd be this big, grand reunion where we'd embrace and cry and laugh and I—what are we going to do? I'm so lost." Sam poured their heart into Kia.

"I don't know, baby. We'll figure it out." Kia said, rubbing Sam's back.

"Yeah, we'll just have to jog their memory. We have to. It's them. I know it's them—when they were singing, I—I know it's them." Toni stifles his emotions.

"Hey, uh, is that—Sam? Sam, is that you?" Roni said, having followed Sam over to Kia and Toni.

Kia tried to hide their reaction to seeing and hearing Roni talking at them, "Uh, yeah. Sam's here. Sam? Sam!" Kia called Sam through her teeth to get their attention, "Ro-Uh, this person wants to talk to you."

Sam unburied their face from Kia's bosom and wipes away any moisture from their face, "H-hi. What's up?"

"I just wanted to tell you that I really like the way your voice sounds. I'd love to collab with you. I think we'd make a great duo on a song. Like, our voices together? We'd totally melt some faces," Roni takes Sam's lovely, slender hands in theirs, "or at least melt some hearts—hey, your hands..." Roni trails off.

"Yeah?"

"You have the most beautiful hands."

The Plane of The Forgotten is once again for those forgotten, and for those who wish to be forgotten. No longer will those whose fate is yet to be sealed be taken from reality. No longer will Unreality be used as a crutch, as an escape. Those taken by Darkness are those that truly belong in the ever-expanding Neo Stranding. And only after having lived their life to the fullest end, whenever that end may be. Unreality is not something you can hope to leave the unpleasantness of life for, you cannot hasten your journey there by any means, nor are you destined to be taken there.

With The Aether now being The Void, balance is maintained. There is no afterlife, only unlife, only undeath. Those who reach their end in life return to reality within a new vessel. Be it a child, a wolf, an eagle, an insect, a plant, a star, all essence in reality returns to reality. Returns to life. This is the cycle. This cannot be broken again.

Creatives will always seek The Plane of The Forgotten, they will always feel its pull. But they will never glimpse it again. That tear is closed, with Roni's sacrifice, it was ensured that no creative will glimpse Unreality again and crave its infinite pool of resource, support, and moments that can be spent creating without the pressure of success and renown.

And so, we come to you. You whomst have taken this journey through eras, ages, and emotions with me and with the Unbound. Your worth is not measured by how many eyes are on you, rather by how your eyes perceive you, and the kindness you spread on your journey to being at peace with yourself. Cherish your connections, those you have Stranded yourself to. Love unconditionally, fully, and with reckless abandon. Remember to cherish your heart and what it symbolises.

In Darkness you will be found, in Light you will be seen. You exist in both, and neither can be taken without the other.

Roni learned that and will do so once more.

Roni would also say that I am remiss if we didn't play 'Exit Music (For A Film)' here at the end of it all, but I'm partial to 'Everything In Its Right Place'.

Go on, open your listening app and play it.

You won't regret it.

It fits.